THE BOYS OF ALPHA BLOCK

IT'S TIME TO BREAK OUT...

NANCY NAU SULLIVAN

Relax. Read. Repeat.

THE BOYS OF ALPHA BLOCK
By Nancy Nau Sullivan
Published by TouchPoint Press
Brookland, AR 72417
www.touchpointpress.com

Copyright © 2021 Nancy Nau Sullivan
All rights reserved.

ISBN-13: 978-1-952816-43-7

This is a work of fiction. Names, places, characters, and events are fictitious. Any similarities to actual events and persons, living or dead, are purely coincidental. Any trademarks, service marks, product names, or named features are assumed to be the property of their respective owners and are used only for reference. If any of these terms are used, no endorsement is implied. Except for review purposes, the reproduction of this book, in whole or part, electronically or mechanically, constitutes a copyright violation. Address permissions and review inquiries to media@touchpointpress.com.

Editor: Jenn Haskin
Cover Design: Colbie Myles
Cover image: Adobe Stock, silhouette three birds on barbed wire by Sergey YAkovlev

Visit the author's website at www.nancynausullivan.com/

lastcadiauthor NauSullivan nancynausullivan

First Edition

Printed in the United States of America.

To the boys.

*I'm made of sand, jagged edges or smooth,
I bet you didn't know I can walk on water.*

~Reginald H., Manatee County (Florida)
Juvenile Justice System, Spring, 2000

PREFACE

I TAUGHT AT A BOYS' PRISON IN FLORIDA for five years, five days a week, until 2005. Some of these students were with me the whole time, and when they left, they were well versed in commas, diagramming, Ernest Hemingway, and Richard Wright. And, I always hoped, the will to make a new start.

A couple of years into my teaching career, one of the inmates who "graduated," wrote me a letter. (They often wrote me letters, requests, poems, essays, the outlines for books, resumes, paeans, and complaints.) But this letter was unusual; I received it after he left, and a drastic outcome soon followed.

He was nearing twenty, extraordinarily bright. He'd served more than three years for drug pedaling, with weapons. At the facility, he was popular with the other youth, and he'd made friends with a number of the deputies. When he completed the "exit," the teachers and staff had high hopes for him. He had family behind him and job prospects. He'd whizzed through the requirements for the Graduate Equivalency Degree (GED). He was talking about college.

His letter was addressed to me but it was written to include staff and the boys he left behind:

> *August 22, 2001, Oldsmar, Florida.*
>
> *Dear Teachers and Youth:*
>
> *It's becoming more difficult to reach all of you one at a time, but I don't want you to think that I forgot about you. I want to let you know that I'm working hard and starting school, so I've been very busy. You wouldn't believe the things I do and the people I meet, fellas. Being a new person is very fun and brings many opportunities.*
>
> *On three different occasions I've been offered (I said offered) management*

i

positions from people who didn't even know me. When I go to job interviews, I tell the employer, "I'll contact you!" How does that happen guys?! I'm no different than any of you; these opportunities belong to all of us. This may sound great, but I've had corporations find my record and terminate me on the spot. These are setbacks, but they mean nothing because I know from the start my chances of getting hired or terminated in the places I go; ex-criminals shouldn't be there anyways! Haha.

For those mature enough to understand, I spent three and a half years in there making a big deal about playing the game. Each day that I'm out I realize that the program was teaching me to play the game because out here in the business world you need to know how to adapt to your environment so you don't get fired or arrested; very important!!

I wish the best to all of you!

Sincerely,
Ronald C.

Not long after I received the letter, Ronald C. was dead following a run-in with cocaine and the police. We all talked about what happened to him. One deputy said, "I expected it. Kid couldn't see further than his nose."

I've never forgotten Ronald. Prison was not a new beginning for him; it was the end. What could we have done differently to change that ending? We gave him the tools, but he didn't use them. He took it as a game, and he lost. We did, too, because Ronald lost.

Ronald was one of many, sixty at a time, going through the drill of rehabilitation at the juvenile prison. They were all different, some so down they'd never find their way up and out. Others had promise, but I treated all of them like they had that in their favor. To view my students any other way than on the mend was to give in to defeat from the beginning.

This story is fiction. Ronald's name is changed here. The characters are made up, but experience feeds the imagination. This novel comes from more than ten thousand hours of experience—teaching, counseling, "living" my version of prison life. I was part of a team that tried to make some good changes.

The work we did, by turns, was sad and gritty, happy and hopeful, and sometimes just plain miserable. It's the "miserable," I faced each day and hoped to hell I could mitigate some of it.

Now we've all moved on. The prison is closed, the boys are back out in the world, and wherever they are today, I wish them well. They treated me with deference, respect—and appreciation. Most of our time together we were all on a learning curve, and I thank them for that, for all that I learned. I hope they have library cards and jobs, love and family, and have made good changes to start new and better lives—and that they never see the likes of jail again.

CHAPTER ONE

Intake Blues

TARVIS PHILIP JAMES STRAINED AGAINST the seat belt, balling himself into a tight human fist. Making himself invisible. Well, it was too late for that. The deputies up front could see him, and worse, they could smell him and the vomit and stench he carried with him from the Bradley Detention Center.

He sat up, careful not to make a sound, and peered out the side of the van as it rumbled down the drive. A grey concrete block building squatted among the palm trees. An ugly place. Only one way in, he could see, and certainly no way out.

The van screeched to a halt. Tarvis's knees shook. His insides were screaming. The back window was open an inch, and the quiet—except for the crackle of palms in a light wind—was unnerving.

What if I just bust out of here and make a run for it? What would they do? Shoot me?

The metal double doors on the side of the building blasted open. Two, maybe three, deputies in green tumbled out of the darkness, shiny metal objects jangling at their waists. To Tarvis, it seemed like some damn alien movie.

One deputy sauntered toward the van. A pair of handcuffs spun round and round on an index finger. He yanked the door open. The damp, swampy air of a Florida morning rushed at Tarvis. The yellow bile pooled at his feet. He folded his arms tightly against his chest, cringing against the back of the seat. He hated to stay, he hated to go, but he didn't have much choice. He didn't have *any* choice.

"Well, what do we have here," said Deputy Martin Haver. He clipped the handcuffs onto his belt. "It ain't smellin' like a rose."

1

Tarvis did not look up. He drew down further.

He couldn't go back to where it all started. That would be unthinkable. A bitter taste hit the back of his throat; his thighs ached though he couldn't remember why. His only feeling was panic, like a cornered wild thing.

In one swift move, Haver's beefy hand clenched Tarvis's arm. He stumbled out of the van and stood on the asphalt. His knees shook so badly, he thought he'd collapse. The deputy's fingers gripped him in a vice and squeezed. There wasn't a chance of moving an inch, up or down.

"Welcome home." The leering expression on Deputy Haver's face said otherwise. He dragged Tarvis across the short stretch of scalding parking lot toward the building. The brown rubber sandals—a gift of the detention center—were too big. He couldn't negotiate the steps in time with the deputy, and he nearly fell, stubbing his toe and drawing blood against the burning asphalt.

Birds twittered and the trees whispered in the hot sun, but Tarvis hardly noticed the soft sounds. To him, it was all harsh and dry. He was going to prison for three years, which seemed like a lifetime, and the fear of not knowing what would happen next doubled down on his anxiety every time he thought of it.

Tarvis found himself in a long hallway, the vague shape of a metal door at the dark end. Deputies walked around him, slamming doors as they went. Tarvis was scared, and other feelings were exploding so fast and gone again that he couldn't quite sort himself out. He could smell the vomit streaking his jeans and the front of his t-shirt that read: "Rock and Soul. Get loaded." It was a message to consider with deep regret, since that's what had gotten him into real trouble: He'd been drunk as hell. Waved a loaded pistol in a convenience store. Several times in the past few nights, he'd woken up sharply and replayed the events, thinking about how very stupid he'd been. So smart and smooth at first, so stupid in the end.

He nearly sweated to death remembering it all. His friend Randall had said it would be an easy gig, and who was Tarvis to question that? Randall had been around the block a time or two. He was one smart honky with a steady job as a "stocking engineer" at the busy crossroads of the Quick-All convenience store in Palm-ghetto. Sometimes he was "management," but mostly Randall stocked

THE BOYS OF ALPHA BLOCK

cans of Vienna sausage and Dinty Moore stew in neat rows on the shelves behind the donut display. He'd told Tarvis it would be an easy inside job.

"*Sweet as cream in yo banana pie...*"

"*What's that supposed to mean, Randall? I ain't no pie eater.*"

"*But yo is sweet, T.*"

The plan: Randall would set up the time for the robbery, pick up the guns from that flea brain, Ash Kepple. Tarvis, packing, would act as a screen and distraction when it all went down.

Randall went down, hard. He never knew, or forgot, that Nidal, the clerk, had a pistol of his own under the counter, and when things got hot, he didn't hesitate to use it on both boys. Tarvis had managed to stay out of the line of fire, but Randall had not.

Tarvis had the fleeting thought, as he considered his prison sentence, that Randall was much better off than Tarvis, planted as he was six feet under a soft green carpet at Miller Field Cemetery in Pokatoy, Florida.

It was all Tarvis could do to stay on his feet in that hallway. He tried to straighten up. Lifted his chin. Haver was back. "What's this shit," growled the deputy in a gust of fetid breath. He stood inches from Tarvis's ear, jabbing his finger in the back of Tarvis's shirt that read, "The Blues When You Need it: Mercenary Blues Band."

"My band."

"Oh, yeah?" Haver planted his feet farther apart and crossed his arms. His biceps bulged like small melons, and Haver, with a nervous tic, or just because, made the melons jump up and down. Tarvis was mesmerized, and to his horror, tried not to laugh.

"Yeah." It was the wrong thing to say. Tarvis found himself face down on the concrete floor, a large hand on the back of his neck, fighting to keep his teeth and lips intact. Then just as fast as he was down, he was up again and facing Haver.

"You'll start right now. Didn't you read the handbook, boy? *Cain't* you read?"

Tarvis tasted blood. "Yes. I *can* read." He didn't move.

Haver was lathered up. "It's 'sir, deputy, sir' when you address me or any other staff around here, and don't you forget it," he said. "And the ladies is 'ma'am,' but you ain't gonna see much of the ladies, my man."

Tarvis tucked his chin in; stared straight ahead at nothing but the pock marks on the concrete block wall.

"Mr. Band Man," Haver said, still poking the back of Tarvis's shirt. "What is it you do for The Mercenary Blues Band? I can't imagine, but what the hell."

Tarvis was surprised the deputy was asking him about music. "Lead guitar and singer," he said. "Old school blues, mostly." Out of the corner of his eye, Tarvis caught Haver's sneer, but his hands stayed clenched at his sides, his chin pinned to his chest.

"No shit," said Haver. "Well. Welcome to your new band. By the way, I thought you assholes only liked that punk ass god awful rap shit."

Tarvis felt his scalp bristle, a terrible knot forming in his chest.

So this is how it is going to be. More shit from the man.

Haver stuck his face, red and rock hard, close to Tarvis. He wanted to bite off the deputy's nose, but he still possessed a shred of common sense—and an instinct for survival.

The deputy shook his head, picked up a clipboard off the wall, and began scribbling on the pad. "Just shit," he mumbled.

Tarvis had trouble keeping it in. Especially where music was concerned. "It's a free country," he whispered. "I like all kinds of music. Blues, Stones, Tupac, Beatles, all of it." He wanted to add, but didn't, that the best white music came from Black music. Tarvis had been playing Robert Johnson and Blind Willie and Honeyboy and Lead Belly and the roots of great rock from the time he could get a decent reach on the strings of the beat-up Martin his Uncle Tendris had given to him. The guitar had come to Tarvis with hours of stories about the musicians who traveled with Tendris throughout the south. Tarvis had wanted to get on that circuit one day. He wanted to go on the road with his uncle and play until the air all around him was charged with music and nothing else and all the other sounds of any misery in his life were drowned out. But Uncle Tendris died, the needle still stuck in his arm, a bottle of muscatel soaking the bed clothes. He took most of Tarvis's dreams with him, except for the buds of hope he left in his nephew's soul. Tarvis often got that guitar out, stroked its smooth sides, his fingers sliding past the ragged hole dug out with pick and passion under the strings.

As soon as Tarvis opened his mouth and said it was a "free country," he regretted it. Held his breath. The remark finally registered with Haver, and his volume shot up to ear-splitting. He shoved Tarvis against the wall inside the receiving den.

"Did you say free country, asshole? Free country? We'll see how free you are," screamed Haver. "And I just told you, and I ain't gonna tell you again, you address me as 'sir,' faggot. And don't you forget it."

Yes, I will address you as Sir Faggot. And then I will be dead.

He had an unquenchable urge to laugh. Again. But the thought of doing such a thing sobered him up. "Sir, yes, sir," said Tarvis. It would be hard to address the deputies with respect, he knew, but he had to try if he were to survive.

They would all be "sir" or "ma'am," and Tarvis would be Youth James. He would precede and conclude all comments and responses to men with "sir" and to females with "ma'am." To do otherwise would warrant a stroke on his chart. A good dose of those would only make his life more miserable. It was one of the many initiation rules in a book full of them he'd been given at the detention center. But it was all a blur.

He still stood in the receiving den. It was freezing cold and the vomit had congealed on his clothing. Deputies milled about, mostly ignoring him. Another metal door opened somewhere down the hall. Keys jangled, then a door slammed, and the sound of it closing was terrifying in its weight and finality. It sealed off the air, the outside world. Freedom. It clanged shut with the unmistakable message that Tarvis was in and the rest of the world was out.

Then he had more company. The room seemed to fill with deputies and the smell of doom, all of it a frightening mix, everyone yelling and *laughing* at once, all together there to welcome Youth James home to Alpha Juvenile Correctional Center.

CHAPTER TWO

Jagged

CAROLINE MCBRIDE PULLED INTO THE PARKING lot of Alpha in her 1994 DeVille. It shimmied when she turned it off, just to remind her that the old beater had some life in it. She was relieved, as she was every Monday through Friday driving out to the prison, that the seventeen-mile drive from home hadn't done it in. It was on its last tire and eight years old—at nearly 200,000 miles—but she couldn't part with it. She couldn't afford a new one, and she couldn't bring herself to give away her dad's last Cadillac. It was the only material thing she had left of him, and she missed him, every crazy lovable bit of him.

Her hands still hugged the leather steering wheel. She picked at the worn stitching, pieces of it falling off onto her lap. What would he say if he knew his Irish Catholic daughter from the burbs spent her days with the boys from the hood? If he knew she went to prison every day and taught English to a bunch of young robbers, murderers, drug dealers, and con artists who had ingenious reasons for being there? She had no idea what he'd say. Maybe, "Hey, team fight!" In his rocker on the porch with his wild white hair, punching the air with his cane. He'd said a lot of strange things after the stroke. His head didn't work quite right, but his heart was always fine. He was always on her side.

Sides. That's the thing. Education built thinking skills, and on the other side, the deputies engaged in force. She had to believe they were all on the same side. For rehabilitation. She also had to remind herself that some of the boys were beyond it. They were criminals, sent to Alpha maximum security for committing a crime with a knife or gun, and some were already hardened at such a young age.

Yet, she loved being in prison. With Will there, too. William Lincoln

Bonner, the counselor at Alpha, was a regular beacon on a dark sea. He and Caroline were in it together. They were on the same side.

She glanced at the grey squat building. It was a depressing sight. Even though the ride out to the correctional center never failed to give her a lift, that feeling didn't last long. She'd just driven over the low, mile-long bridge, the water sparkling, the sun smiling down on her adopted home state. The bright morning opened up to her. She held on to that snapshot in her head and locked it in. Once inside her nine-to-five home, it would be curtains, literally. Like stepping into a dark hole.

She climbed out of the car and closed the door carefully. It whooshed shut like it was sighing. *How appropriate.* It was a desolate place out here in the boondocks, humid and heading toward a blistering ninety-degree high. They were a good twenty-five miles north of Sarasota in the unincorporated scrubby wetlands near the Gulf of Mexico where the main inhabitants were alligators and snakes. She could almost smell the salty Gulf to the west. In the east, Highway 41 and the tracks ran around the vast acreage. Palm trees ringed the correctional center compound, enclosed with razor wire effectively hemming them in. The only movement she ever saw on the grounds was the occasional tractor mower, or a fox or weasel from her classroom window.

A police car zoomed down the road toward the county jail where the adult population of drug offenders, burglars, and the occasional murderer cooled off, serving out sentences or awaiting trial. The cars of her co-workers were neatly lined up, the only color against the green of palm trees, tall grass and scrub. She hefted the pile of books and hurried across the parking lot.

A door slammed behind the complex. The ragged yelling of male voices caused a tremor in the peace. Caroline's gaze shot off in that direction, but she couldn't see much except for the corner of the concrete block building and the back of a police van. The yelling kept up. Someone was having a very bad day; had to be, *intake.*

Classes would be on hold with an intake. If that's what it was. She set her shoulders, ground her teeth. She'd gotten used to the violent outbursts, the venom bubbling up out of the limitless cesspool of misery at the correctional center.

She headed for the gate set in the chain link fence. A short distance away under a sally port, Deputy Susanna Bettinger was sitting on a bench outside the main entry, smoking. Taking a break.

Great.

Caroline didn't relish running into the prickly deputy, but there wasn't any way around it. Caroline had to use this entry, and she had to go past the deputy who didn't look up from her paperback when Caroline pressed the buzzer mounted in the chain link. The shouting started up again, and Caroline winced. The deputy kept her nose in the book. She'd surely heard the commotion. Who could miss it?

Caroline waited at the gate, her eyes on the concrete, counting to ten to avoid yelling, *"Shit,"* at the top of her lungs. That would not get her access any faster. In fact, it would only bring a smile to Bettinger's face, and to whomever was sitting at master control. But she had dozens of essays to correct and the classroom library to organize, and she meant to start on a grant to get a bookmobile sent out to the jail site. She needed to get after it. She took a deep breath.

Deputy Bettinger's black boot swung back and forth, the cigarette forming a cloud at her ear. She puffed with gusto, deep into the paperback lying open on a broad thigh. Her long blond hair was twisted into a tight bun, and she was wearing the regulation green serge pants and matching blouse that strained to cover her frame. Bettinger wasn't exactly fat. But when she walked, her rear looked like a large animal trying to get out of a sack. "The Amazon," they called her. Not unkindly. She was a big, good-looking blond, and she knew it. She liked the nickname; it gave her stature in the jungle.

Caroline hit the buzzer again. Sun glinted off the coiled razor wire far above her head on the high chain-link fence. The gate was the first of four entries on the way to her classroom. She waited for the deputy inside to buzz her through once he identified her on the monitor. The gate finally popped open, and Caroline headed down the short walkway to the entry.

The deputy finally looked up, and the two women nodded at each other.

Caroline hurried past Bettinger toward the main door, reached for buzzer number two and then turned. "Good morning." It was a distracted, half-hearted greeting.

Again, the shouting and sounds of pain reverberated off palm trees and concrete. Off behind the building, a door slammed with echoing thunder. Loud voices came in vicious bursts like that of a pack of animals.

Now it struck her—for sure—intake. Another young one coming in to be processed and locked up, to get his mistakes ironed out.

Bettinger placed her finger in the book and held it against her chest. *Valley of the Dolls.*

Well, at least she's reading classic crap. Caroline nodded. Bettinger smiled and didn't blink at the noise coming from the back of the correctional center.

"How you?" Bettinger had a strange vestige of southern drawl that was both direct and incomprehensible at times. But Caroline got the message.

"Good. You?"

Bettinger puffed, swung that boot. "Hangin'."

Caroline was about to reach for the button to gain entry, but then she shrugged in the direction of the back of the building.

"Intake," said Bettinger. Smoke curled above the blond bangs. She squinted up at Caroline.

"I figured. Any info on the young recruit?"

"Not much, except this. He's some idiot who thought he'd stick up a convenience store and get away with it. Dumb ass."

Caroline cradled her books and considered the deputy's remark. Not in all the years that Caroline had been teaching at the prison had she met a student who was a "dumb ass." All of them had done something dumb to get in there, but many of them were smarter than Bettinger and Caroline put together. It was dumb not to remember that.

And to Caroline's amazement, during her years at Alpha, she hadn't met a boy she didn't like. Some were strange, some were scary. They probably thought the same of her. But she still *liked* them. They'd been drunk, stoned, sick, beaten down in every way possible when they came into the system, and now they were clean, ready to start over.

Bettinger blew a plume of smoke skyward. Caroline caught a whiff of the noxious poison. "What else do you know about him? Besides the fact that he's a dumb ass," said Caroline. "Which I'm sure he isn't."

The deputy measured Caroline and seemed to ignore the sarcasm. She picked up "the Dolls" and shrugged. "Well, he is a dumb ass for waving a gun at a poor old half-blind store clerk."

"You're right about that," said Caroline. "Very bad way to shop."

"Yeah. It's going to get him at least three years. If he's lucky. Next time he might want to say please and thank you with those Fritos."

"Do you know what level?" Caroline's answer to the woes of Alpha—at least as a first step—was a passing grade on the Graduate Equivalency Degree program. But she wouldn't discuss that with Bettinger who'd made it clear on more than one occasion that efforts to rehabilitate the inmates were a waste of time.

"This scholar? He's sixteen or so. Think he dropped out of grade school, like a lot of them." Bettinger spoke out of the side of her mouth, and therefore, only small, jagged shards of information fell out. She didn't look Caroline in the eye.

Caroline kept her tone level. She'd already made a mental note to get background on the new inmate from his records. She'd get him into class as soon as possible. Otherwise, he'd be sitting in that jail cell with nothing to do but read the handbook for Alpha Juvenile Correctional Center, a specious piece of writing that had been put together by a few alligators and one Neanderthal.

"Let's see how many books we can get him to read," said Caroline. She couldn't resist.

"Whatever," said Bettinger. She uncrossed her leg and the boots hit the concrete. She picked up her paperback, dismissing Caroline. The book feud with the deputies was ongoing, especially with Bettinger, who always had a book in her hand. The irony struck Caroline.

"Ever read James Lee Burke?" She wondered immediately why she kept at it.

Bettinger's lips puckered in thought. "That trash?"

Caroline eyed the paperback in the deputy's hand. "Hmmm. Trash?"

"Well, his books are about a degenerate police officer and a bunch of pimps he hangs out with."

Caroline smiled, tightly. "They're a little more complicated than that."

"You don't say." It wasn't a question. Bettinger deflated like a large green balloon. "Look. I get it. You're an English teacher, and I'm The Man. Or Woman, I guess. We have different ideas. Missions…"

Caroline had to concede that, but it was a long day to be locked up together. The feud continued. Deputy Bettinger had confiscated Caroline's novels and thrown them out, including the brilliant work of James Lee Burke—stories about the broken-down Louisiana detective and recovering addict who found purpose in saving others.

"I went looking for those books. I found them in the trash can outside the kitchen."

The deputy's brows jumped. Her large square hand clutched the paperback while the other twiddled a pencil. "Well, why you look at *me*?"

"What right do you have to throw books away?" Caroline could barely talk through gritted teeth. She kept her voice low and level.

Bettinger cocked her head. "Rights? Whose rights?"

"Well, mine, for one. I bought most of those books for the classroom library. For the boys."

"Fine. But the boys got no rights. They gave 'em up when they took others' rights." Bettinger stood up and stretched. Caroline was reminded of an incredible Hulk-ette. "And besides, that guy who writes those books uses the 'n' word," Bettinger said.

"So does Mark Twain." Caroline was steering into mushy territory.

"Well, then get rid of Mark Twain, too," said the deputy.

Caroline backed off. Bettinger had the prison administration on her side, and Caroline had the powerless education department on hers.

"Well, that's not going to happen." She punched the buzzer.

"Whoa," said Bettinger.

"You have a nice day." Caroline choked on the remark. She wanted to kick herself for starting something she was not going to finish with any degree of success.

Caroline pressed the buzzer again. She was still three locked prison doors away from her classroom.

CHAPTER THREE

Dark In

THE YELPING BROKE OUT AGAIN. It came from the back of the building at the delivery bay where justice was processing an inmate. With intake, classes would definitely be delayed. Caroline was relieved to have the extra time, but she was tense and sad at what that kid was going through. She never knew how long it would take; it depended on how long it took to bundle up, record, shake down the new inmate, and the difficulty the deputies wanted to make of it.

The door to the main entrance slammed behind Caroline. It was dim and quiet inside the long hallway. The cold smell of disinfectant and old food hit her. She blinked to adjust to the low light after coming in from the sunny Florida morning and her salty meeting with Bettinger. Such a contrast. The daily initiation of walking inside Alpha every morning was like being dumped into unreality. The walls were painted a classic, institutional beige, a color so nondescript it could only be compared to parched earth. But the floor gleamed. One or more of the boys had been at it again. It was shiny as a new dinner plate, the boys' pride and joy. They begged to get out of their cells and get at the huge bucket with mop and rollers and inhale that Pine-Sol, finish it all with wax. She wondered who the lucky one was who'd earned the privilege. They needed to be busy. They *liked* being busy. It made the time pass. And with nearly sixty boys at Alpha, there was always work to do.

She walked past the huge, white and stainless-steel, empty kitchen. Deep double sinks, walk-in freezers, stoves and ovens, enough space and gadgetry to prepare for a town-size feast. But nothing was cooked in that kitchen, not even the boys' meals. Breakfast, lunch, and dinner were delivered from the main jail where the adult population of non-violent offenders prepared a special menu—mostly a tasteless offering of oatmeal, soy burgers, and canned vegetables cooked so long and hard that it all tasted the same. The hint of those daily deliveries still lingered in the air.

Caroline peered into the kitchen, at all that counter space and those appliances. What a letdown. Prison administration hadn't had all brain cells clacking when they proposed and then constructed the up-to-date, commercially outfitted kitchen. Its original purpose had been to provide training in culinary arts. Caroline had even offered to teach a cooking class. Only problem was, the inmates could not be trusted with knives and sharp utensils. (Forks, spoons, and knives were collected and counted after every meal.) What was staff thinking? They weren't. The bean counters spent money and adjusted the bottom line later, and the kitchen at Alpha stood as a testament to bad judgment and waste.

Caroline was startled to see Youth Jesse Allen pushing a food cart out of a recess in the useless cavern and into the hallway. "Jesse!"

It was definitely an infraction for him to be in there. But she hesitated. How was she to know the boy's schedule? Education staff was the last to know about work details and intakes, even class changes. Caroline flexed her own schedule every day to accommodate prison life.

"Miss McBride. Ma'am." He smiled, and behind the arresting green eyes was surprise. His hands remained clenched on the cart.

Caroline sized up the look on his face, like he'd gotten all of himself caught in the candy jar. "What's going on, Mr. Allen?"

"Nothing, really, ma'am. Just getting something out of the kitchen." His words ran together. The eyes sought hers. For approval? Complicity?

She checked around for a deputy, but most of them seemed occupied with the intake. She could hear scuffling and yelling out back of the prison. "Getting what? What are you doing in the kitchen?"

"Just pickin' up some paper towels." He jerked his head toward the huge double sink. "On the wall. There." She eyed a roll of paper towels fastened above it. Glanced at the food cart. *Then, where are the paper towels?* Caroline's radar flipped on.

Allen smiled and wheeled along, eyes straight ahead. He was risking trouble, carrying on with a staff member without permission, but he could never help himself from getting chatty. He turned green eyes on her. "I sure am enjoying that book you gave me." He measured his words for the English teacher, and his gaze demanded a response. It reminded her of what they were. A bunch of chameleons who could switch on a dime.

"Well, now, what book would that be?"

"The bio. On Jackie Robinson."

"That's a good one." She dropped the discussion of Allen's kitchen detour and patted her pile of books. "Got some new ones here." Among them were *The Chocolate War* and *The Outsiders*. She'd picked them up at Books-A-Million, and now they were going into the classroom library. She'd been surprised to learn the boys preferred nonfiction, and there was plenty of that. But she liked to push the good fiction writers, like Cormier and Hinton. They offered complex characters and lessons about struggle and doing the right thing.

Allen slowed the squeaky cart with the remains of gluey, grey oatmeal and a stack of toast the color of old, dried brick. It had been delivered from the jail before the boys got up. Allen usually had the duty to load the food cart at the delivery bay and wheel it to the day room at mealtime and back again. He should have been headed back to his cell by now.

"I can't thank you enough," he said, stopping the cart. He touched her arm, his expression tense. "I'm telling you, Miss McBride, when I'm reading, sometimes I suffer from a shortness of breath and an overwhelming desire to continue to read."

Caroline's eyebrows shot up; she took a half step back. The radar needle zipped to full alert. "Well, you'd be the first cardiac arrest from reading a book." She gave him a crooked smile.

Allen put his hand over his heart and rolled his eyes. "Ma'am." He turned back to the remains of breakfast and began to sort out the cart, bagging up bread, sliding metal lids in place. He'd touched her arm. Lightly, but still. *Isn't anyone watching him? Where's deputy staff? And why the hell was he in the kitchen?*

At the end of the dim hallway, the windows of master control were dark. No sign of activity, but there had to be a deputy at the desk. The rest were probably out back with intake. Allen knew that.

She turned her suspicion down a notch, but she was reticent to leave Allen alone in the hallway, unsure of what he was up to. "Your love of books is a good choice. Glad to help. Remember when I gave you Hurston's *Dust Tracks on a Road,* and *Colored People* by Henry Louis Gates?"

Allen grinned. "Ma'am. You were playin' me, Miss McBride. Ma'am."

"You know I wasn't. *Responses.* I asked you to read those books and respond. React," she said. "And you did."

Allen held a ladle in one hand, his expression calm. "Ma'am. Thank you."

She shouldn't be so wary. He was one of the good students, wasn't he? So far, he'd read a hundred books and passed the standardized reading test for high school graduates. He'd been at a fourth-grade reading level when he landed in prison for his involvement in a knifing that killed a security guard. Jesse Allen, an admitted drug addict, came from a poverty-stricken trailer park in the Florida Panhandle where his father left the family so long ago, he wasn't even a memory. Someday Allen would leave Alpha and go back to the same old surroundings and temptations. In the meantime, he was reading about other options.

Allen was kissing up. No doubt about it. His remarks, and manner, were too perfect. And perfection of any sort was not the order of the day at Alpha. In fact, in addition to the usual run of misery, lately she sensed an undercurrent of tension in the air; shifty behavior in the classroom—sly looks, note passing, odd graffiti. The deputies seemed particularly keyed up. Something deep in her brain made her question all of it, and the feeling wouldn't go away. It was faint, and stayed, like an unidentifiable whiff of something going bad.

The door to the day room shot open.

"Allen! I'm gonna stroke you if you don't get a move on! Quit your yappin'. Breakfast club is *done.*" It was Deputy Guy Hathaway, and the chords in his neck strained at the violence of his words. He stomped down the hallway, ignoring Caroline.

"Good morning, Deputy Hathaway," she said. "My fault. We had a classroom matter." *Why am I defending him? I should be reporting him.*

The deputy nodded.

Her lips sealed in a firm line. Allen straightened up, a hard look on his face. Hathaway yanked his head in the direction of the delivery bay. "Get rid of that cart and get your ass back to the cell block."

ALLEN SCOOTED OFF. Now he'd caught the eye of deputy staff, and he'd surely get marked up in the disciplinary log. A big fat red check next to his name in the book, one that Allen had no desire to read or be a part of. From the back of Alpha came the deep bellow of an angry male voice. The loud bursts were intermittent. From the sound of it, someone was getting an earful.

With a glance toward master control, Allen shoved the cart into its cubby off the hallway with extra force. He headed back toward the cell block. A new one was coming in. It always sent a thrill of shared misery and tension through the cell block. He tried to hide it, but Miss McBride caught the hint of a smile on his face.

CHAPTER FOUR

A Donut a Day

TARVIS SAT IN A COLD, GREY ROOM. It smelled faintly of dirt, and he had the panicky feeling he was buried. *Buried alive.* The muscles in his legs tightened. He tried to push himself up, out of that deep hole of depression, but he was way down in there, and he'd have to endure it. He focused on the high narrow window that let in a patch of gold Florida light.

I'll keep my mouth shut and do the bullshit and get the hell out of here. What else can I do?

The deputies weren't hassling him right now, but he could hear shouting and occasional laughter. *Yeah, this place is a laugh a minute.* He couldn't tell what they were saying, or what was so funny, and the empty feeling of not knowing *anything* smothered him. How long had he been sitting here? An hour? Time sludged along, then sped up with the racing of his heart. He twisted the hem of his crusty t-shirt and found a clean spot to wipe his face. The clammy sweat and the smell of vomit made him gag. He sat up on the metal chair, his back straight against the curved slab that hit him in the small of his back. He took a deep breath. He'd thrown up in the van, and the sourness lingered, but he was suddenly hungry and so parched his tongue stuck to the roof of his mouth.

The door banged open and framed an enormous human in a green uniform. Tarvis read "Grappler" above the pocket. The deputy took two strides into the room and kicked the chair out from under Tarvis. He sprawled on the floor. He didn't look at the deputy. He sat up and stared at the wire mesh set inside the glass panel of the door. He felt like a spider caught in a web.

"Get up," said the deputy, his voice a hoarse command from deep in his throat.

Grappler's face reminded Tarvis of an uncooked pork roast, pink and uneven.

Tarvis scrambled off the concrete and stood at attention. "Sir, yes, sir."

Grappler smiled, revealing a row of surprisingly small teeth. "Guess you learnt somethin' already. The 'sir' business, and the 'ma'am.' And if ya forgets it, I will personally come and make you a gift of a bar of soap with 'sir' writ on it. Straight to where the sun don't shine."

At that, Tarvis was drawn to the waning light at the window. A thirst for freedom so overwhelmed him, he thought he'd scream. He didn't. He recoiled from Grappler's thin, curling lips. He stood with his hands at his sides, in military formation, and waited. It was going to be a long wait when he considered the scale of things. At least three years' worth, with good behavior.

Grappler stuck his huge thumbs in his belt and gave the chair another kick. Tarvis was glad it wasn't him on the receiving end of that boot. He almost choked with relief but held himself steady.

"Get your ass out of here and go next door," said the deputy. "Paperwork."

"Sir, yes, sir."

CAROLINE AND ART MULDOON, the math teacher, stood in the day room behind master control. It was eerily quiet again. The day room was the heart of Alpha, if such a place had a heart. The smell of breakfast from the food cart still hung in the air, and the boys were back in their cells. One tutor sat at the far end of the day room, her large rump spilling off the metal stool bolted to the floor. Young Wesley Pautz leaned on the metal table repeating formulas from a math book. "M-C-squared," he said, levelly and loudly. Soon the boys would file out of the cell block and into the day room and head from here to the classrooms. Caroline wasn't here on weekends, but she knew this was the place of meetings between inmates and visitors, mostly godmothers, grandmothers, aunties, and very few parents.

Generally, the wide-open, sunny space was a pleasant spot. The boys liked to be in there, an atrium of sorts with high, narrow rectangular windows. On one wall, a glass panel of windows overlooked master control and a view of the hallway beyond. On the other walls, doors opened to the classrooms. And next to the classrooms, three-inch-thick, three-hundred-pound metal doors opened to the cells of Alpha in three wings—A, B, and C, which shot out from the day room like spokes on a wheel.

"Another pupil coming in, eh?" Art turned to Caroline.

She stared through the windows of master control and beyond. "That should put the place at capacity. About sixty or so. Right?"

"Yeah, full up."

"What luck, huh?" Caroline grimaced. Luck is not what put them in prison; it was their luck that a judge had seen fit to send them to the juvenile facility instead of into the adult jail population. But the boys told Caroline time and again that they didn't see it that way—even after they'd heard about the horrors in adult prison. Many of their fathers, brothers, relatives, and friends had been there, and spoken of it. Prison was prison, and for the young, especially, she could see the toll on their faces. It dragged on forever, wore them down. *Is that the point of it? Aren't we supposed to build them up?* They stood silently, and watched, expecting their new pupil to appear in the hallway.

"Wish there was something I could say or do." Art mumbled and crossed his arms. It was useless, and they both knew it.

"I hear you," Caroline sighed. "We'll get a chance. Soon."

"Yeah. That's what the kid needs. A chance."

Tarvis's intake dragged on to another cold room at the back of the prison. Deputy Pilson stood nose to nose with Tarvis, a clipboard in his beefy fingers.

"Sit down, asshole," said the deputy.

Tarvis stumbled backwards into a chair next to a long folding table. An empty room, except for the palatable misery. It pinged off the concrete block walls, rumbled in the deputy's throat, hung in every breath Tarvis took. He couldn't wait to see what his cell looked like. He needed water but was afraid to ask.

"Name," said Pilson.

Tarvis thought he was joking. His eyes widened, but he caught himself.

"Tarvis Philip James."

"Tarvis Philip James, what?" The deputy's eyebrows knit together in a menacing black line.

"Sir, Tarvis Philip James, sir."

"That's better." Pilson spit the words as he scribbled on the clipboard. To Tarvis, it looked like a bunch of spaces and boxes. His life reduced to this.

"Do you know why you're here?"

"Sir, stuck up a Seven-Eleven, sir?" Tarvis's voice broke.

I know why I'm here. Don't you?

"Age? Height? Weight? Race? Last known address?" Pilson's sneer settled on Tarvis. "Routine."

He didn't dare say a word, but he could think it. *What a bunch of dumb fucks.*

"Nurse'll see you next," said Pilson. "Sure there's nothing wrong with you." He laughed as the door slammed behind him.

The hallway was dim, but Art and Caroline could clearly see the shadowy figure of the boy alongside the burly deputy. The boy bent over, then shot up, like he was on strings. He was tall, handsome, wiry with broad shoulders. He stumbled along, coming closer to the day room. Huge eyes and high, chiseled cheekbones, his expression was frightful, his shirt ripped. He clutched his jeans with one hand and held the other up to his face. Deputy Harold Pilson, a fire plug with a blond crew cut, dragged him along. "That's right, fucker. I don't want to smell your stinking breath."

Caroline flinched. *What a welcoming committee.* Pilson was a difficult person to deal with. Always the foul mouth. He lounged in the classroom and chewed tobacco or ate chips, crackling and chomping and leaving crumbs, and he regularly interrupted the lesson.

"We'll teach you what to do with those hands. You won't be shootin' up some old man in the Seven-Eleven for a while," yelled Pilson. He was hoarse from all the screaming. The boy and Pilson disappeared into a room off the hallway. A thud echoed in the day room. Deputy Hathaway appeared and went into an adjoining room. Doors slammed.

"Jesus, I hate this," said Art. "What the hell can be so hard about simply bringing the kid in, giving him a shower, and putting him in the cell?"

Caroline murmured. "I don't know, Art. And it seems to be getting worse."

"What?"

"All of it. It's like a damn bomb around here."

"What're you thinking?"

"Feels like something's going on. Just now I caught Allen coming out of the kitchen with the cart. You know he's not supposed to be in there."

Art gave her a quizzical expression. He was retired military, but a softy, and he didn't miss much. When young men were out of line, he had a way of nudging them back to base. "The kitchen? What the hell's he doing in the kitchen?"

"Said he was getting paper towels. There weren't any paper towels on his cart."

"I'd keep an eye out." It wasn't their job. The deputies were there to enforce order, but the education staff added stability. Caroline tried to build trust but reminded herself that trust only went so far in prison. The boys hardly knew the meaning of the word since they'd gained "trust" with a knife or gun.

"Something else, Art. He's been buttering me up."

"I can only guess."

"The usual. How wonderful the books are and class and all that business." She frowned. "And, by the way, don't you think the deputies have been extra pinchy lately?"

He shrugged. "What's new? It comes and goes. I'd say, definitely, keep an eye out." His shoulders slumped.

The boy was back in the hallway, bouncing along with the red-faced deputy. He had a handful of filthy t-shirt up around the boy's throat and was steering him into the day room. The young face was a mask of fear and rage, the deputy disgusted and angry. Caroline saw it sizzle from where she stood.

What could make two people who barely knew each other show so much hate?

It did seem to be getting worse, but maybe it was just her. Maybe she'd had enough. To get used to it would be to condone misery, to say in her heart and head it was all right to "correct" human beings like this. There were success stories, but long term, she didn't see much correction through abuse. They had been horribly abused to begin with, and now they were in for more of the same.

Pilson ripped the keys off his belt and shoved the youth against the wall next to the door of B wing. Spittle ran down his front, the pants sagged below his waist. "Get your ass in there. You need a shower. And clothes. You ain't gonna see that t-shirt and jeans no more."

Tarvis looked around with wild fury. His liquid brown eyes locked on Caroline. She raised her chin, tried to smile but none would come.

Pilson shook the boy. "Eyes front." The deputy fumbled with the keys. He didn't acknowledge the teachers. He shuffled to stay on his feet and maneuver his tall, rangy prisoner through the door. Caroline thought of a tugboat pulling a sleek ship. It was ludicrous.

She inched toward her classroom door. She wasn't supposed to be there, to see this. Be witness. But she wanted to be there. She hoped her presence would mitigate some of the language and abuse, but she was reminded once again it didn't matter if she were there or not.

Art sidled next to her, raked a hand through his white hair. Caroline murmured, "Maybe we can get him into class. Soon. That initial lockdown is such a waste. Spending those first weeks in the cell with nothing to do."

"I don't know. With the way things are going, they'll probably tighten up." He turned to her then. "I'm thinking. The kitchen. You probably ought to mention it to the sergeant."

"Yeah, Art, but I hate to. You know what that would mean."

"Drama. He's been on a rampage lately. Maybe save it, wait a bit. You know, nothing ever stays the same around here." Art rolled his eyes. "Think you ought to mention it to Harv?"

Caroline's response was unenthusiastic. "Right on."

Harv Sanders, the education director, was a long shot. He fenced with the deputies over education's mission: rehabilitation through reading, writing, and arithmetic. The deputies had the power, and they never let education forget it. But Art and Caroline pressed and Harvey tried. His usual response began, "Well, the problem is…"

It was a constant dance, a push and pull to extract money for books or computers or bid for more class time. They needed a head's up when the deputies changed the schedule or policy with no warning. But it didn't happen. They all loved Harvey, but education was the orphan, and Harvey was in charge of the orphanage.

"I'll tell him. Eventually," Caroline said. "Will you let me know if you see anything funny?"

Art gave her a wry smile. "Funny. Right."

"Sad, that's what it is."

"It's getting to you?"

"Ya think?"

"Don't let it." He had very blue eyes, and they'd seen it all. She felt like the sky opened up when he smiled. He patted her arm.

A door buzzed and Nurse Carmen Rainer bustled into the day room in a cloud of rosy fragrance and talc. Her short curls bounced and her cheeks were red as apples. She was carrying a sheaf of records.

"Already been past the sergeant. He says I can give you these," said Nurse Rainer. "New one's exceptional needs. Tarvis Philip James, sixteen. Been out of school a while now, used to have something of a home life, but, apparently, trouble there."

"Great. Thanks," said Caroline. "You already have his records? For us?"

"Yeah, deputy staff wanted us to be ready for this one," said the nurse. "I guess the kid likes music—and math, Art. So, he'll be your whiz kid. Deputy made him sing nursery rhymes all the way out here from the detention center, and it didn't go well. Boy said he didn't know the words. Puked on himself, too."

Nurse Rainer delivered the news in a one-note monotone, but Caroline knew she was one-eighty out from bored. A plump woman in a blue smock with bears on it, she looked like someone's kindergarten teacher. She was strict and hardworking, especially when it came to discharging meds and vitamins, watching their weight and nutrition against prison standards, checking for diabetes and high blood pressure, which was unusually high given their history of bad nutrition, stress, and luck. She didn't take nonsense from any of them, and it worked. They invented sore throats and headaches so they could visit her office for some mothering. She cleaned ears, which they resisted, and she nagged them to brush their teeth and eat their vegetables. She made it clear she didn't like the wholesale distribution of meds for behavioral problems because she'd seen too many of the boys come in with alarming records and charts full of over-medication. Attention, not medication, was the best prescription for these boys, according to Nurse Rainer. She didn't have children of her own, but she did have "a family of sixty boys," and over the years, hundreds of them called her "Ma'am Mom," when they could get away with it. If a deputy heard them, they got "stroked" a red in the book, and "Mom" usually rebuked the deputy for butting in.

Despite what anyone said, she was mother to the worst of them, some for up to eight years. Like Youth Jason Bentwich. He beat his neighbor to death after he lost to him in a craps game, and then he set him on fire. Youth Bentwich had the face of an angel. His father had chained him up in a shed and beat and starved him. He ate more dog food than real food growing up, that, and Cheetos and stale beer.

"At least our new one's not a Bentwich." She handed the folders to Art and Caroline; checked the clipboard and shook her head, a crooked smile forming. "That's a start."

CAROLINE PRESSED A BUTTON AND THE DEPUTY in master control buzzed her out of the day room and into the hallway. Another deputy was just leaving master control and she entered before the door slammed shut. Deputy Tommy Swanson was eating a donut as he manned the board. A large flat box of glazed and frosted goodies lay open within easy reach. Huge windows rose from a desk panel studded with red, green, and white lights and a number of switches. The long, built-in shelving was piled with binders and records on all the inmates. The windows looked out into the bright, empty day room with sun streaming in the high windows. She could even see the doors to the cell blocks and into her classroom from where she stood. She could see a lot from where she stood, but, after all, she could see very little of what really went on in the prison. It was a place of yelling and commands but also a place of whispering and secrets.

It was dark in master control compared to the day room beyond. All the better to read the computer screens. The sloping desk under the wide windows constantly blinked signals from the cell blocks and all-around Alpha. The board had so many toggles and lights, it looked like the *Starship Enterprise*.

A speaker crackled. A young inmate in his cell reminded the deputy on duty that he needed his meds.

"Hold on there, Pepino. Nurse is making the rounds." Deputy Swanson switched off the intercom.

Caroline peered up at the video monitors suspended above the board, which showed all the doors, inside and out. She could see the sidewalk to the parking lot and inside her classroom. It gave her a tug of relief. But, still, they couldn't begin to cover it all. She knew the cameras only recorded fifteen-second intervals with fifteen-second breaks between. It was a secret kept from the boys, but, really, she wondered, *How do you keep secrets from these boys? You don't. You can't.*

She turned her attention to Swanson. "Pepino? Who's Pepino?"

"Pepino, Pedro, Pecker-head. All the same." The deputy chuckled to himself, then looked up at Caroline.

She ignored the observation—with the hint of a smile. It wouldn't do any good to get into a pissing contest.

"What can I do you for, Miss McBride?" But Swanson went back to the board. He flicked a switch and reminded Deputy White via radio it was time to make a mandatory check of the cell block. Caroline knew this was crucial. Several boys had attempted to hang themselves, one with a shirt wrapped around a pipe in the shower room, another using the metal end of a pencil to slit his wrists. She was always relieved to know the success rate was zero. So far.

"I hear we have a new one," said Caroline.

"How could you not? I suppose you could hear it all the way to Miami," said Swanson. He looked like one of her "students"; he could have been one, growing up on rough outskirts of Palmetto. He wasn't much older than the oldest prisoners of twenty-two, a fact he kept to himself. He often complained about his job at the correctional center, but he and his wife had just had a baby girl and he needed the work. He said Alpha was better than working downtown, listening to the screaming adult population. He preferred whining "babies," he said, because he was used to it at home.

Caroline casually chose a glazed donut from the box on the desk. She really didn't want it, but Swanson was enjoying his, so she'd join him. Maybe they could share one damn thing together. Swanson flicked a toggle on the board. His mouth was full of crumbs, and he had pink sprinkles on his moustache. Caroline pointed to his lip, and he dusted it off.

She came around closer to his chair. "Do you suppose I could test the new kid this week. So we could get him into class?"

He looked up at Caroline in mock surprise. His eyes were bright blue, and he was bald as an onion. "Now how do you suppose I could do that?"

She knew Swanson didn't have the power, but she liked to grease the wheel. He went fishing regularly with Sergeant Daryl Miller, the head honcho at Alpha. "I know, but you could say something. Will you put in a word with Sergeant Miller when you see him?"

"Pulling rank?" He reached for another donut, and after a bit of contemplative munching, he smiled. "The sergeant will get to the little twerp when ready."

Miller would sign off on enrolling the new recruit in class, and that could be anywhere from two days to two months, depending on the boy's behavior and the whim of the sergeant. She wanted it done sooner than later. Education staff could pull a string here and there and hurry up the process. Occasionally. A big part of her job was prodding and pretending. Just like they all did. Right now, she smiled and pretended she liked donuts. A regular donut-eating girl, hangin' with the deputies.

Swanson went back to the board and buzzed in a visitor at the gate with one hand, waved the donut with the other. "Be a better idea to take that little shit out back and shoot him. He's a waste of your notebook paper." He seemed amused at his little joke.

Caroline stiffened. *Why would he say such a thing?* It was an unusual remark for Swanson.

"Really," she said. She waited, hopeful he'd soften up, but he swiveled in the chair, chomping away.

"Yeah, really. Worthless waste of air space. You can pound all the math and books you want into that little shit bag, and he'll just go out and do it again."

"Well, I hope not, at least not any time soon," she said. "Ask Miller if I can start pounding him with books."

"Don't I wish. Want me to take that big old dictionary you have on your desk and give him a good whack?"

She frowned. He was making her tired. "You do not have your teaching certification for administering reading material."

"All right already." Swanson laughed and stuck the rest of the donut in his mouth. He licked his fingers.

Sometimes he surprised Caroline. She'd heard him telling Youth Conroy to finish his homework, and when no one was looking (except for Caroline), Swanson helped Youth Allen practice algebra for the GED. Both boys had seemed to enjoy the positive attention. Swanson didn't wear his harsh words well. He was a prisoner of his self-inflicted employment, and the hard talk didn't suit him. It didn't even sound like him.

"What's his name? Tarvis? He'd do well to get out of that cell and into class." Caroline pressed on, managing a light tone. "It's a waste of time sitting in there all day doing nothing. And just think. Sir. You could practice your algebra."

His head shot back. "Miss McBride, ma'am, far be it from me to ascend to the office of math teacher."

"Oh, don't bullshit me," said Caroline.

"Ditto. Ma'am."

"Touché."

Swanson hit a toggle with the palm of his hand. "Ain't he usually supposed to be in his cell for at least two weeks? For a cool-off time?"

"Miller could let up on that," said Caroline. "Let's give it a try." He glanced up at her, and she looked him in the eye. It helped that she felt tall with him in that chair. She wasn't about to intimidate a deputy, not that she felt she could, but she liked the edge. Her wishful thinking sometimes made it true. "I need to get that testing done, before the county board comes end of the month." She played the oversight card. They all hated the auditors. Here she was, wheedling and manipulating, just like the rest of them. A prisoner of the system.

"Yeah, right," said Swanson. "But like I said, be better to take him out and shoot him. That's what they do anyway, to each other, on the outs. They don't care about nobody."

"All right then," said Caroline. "Don't forget to ask the sergeant." She hated that kind of talk, the hate talk. Swanson's flip attitude held little conviction, with no promise of good consequences.

"Here." Swanson got to his feet and pointed at the desktop. "For your collection. Some of these pea brains can't have books yet. We took 'em out of their cells and should have dumped 'em." Caroline picked up the autobiography of Ben Carson, *A Tale of Two Cities,* and several histories of American wars—glad to find them here instead of in the trash can.

"Thanks," she said. "It was the worst of times…" The chaos of intake and the deputies' methods, and Swanson's harsh words. The business in the kitchen with Jesse Allen, and the incident in the hallway with Deputy Hathaway. It was a major infraction to dawdle on duty and chat up the staff, and it was a sure thing the deputy would make the youth pay. She couldn't shake the feeling that something was going on.

And it wasn't even nine o'clock in the morning.

She'd have to think about it later. She had to focus on getting ready for classes, with no idea of when they would start.

"Any idea when we can have class?"

"You askin' me? No i-de-ar. You know the drill, each one of them so different and special. Could take all day." His lip curled. She dropped the discussion. Swanson was acting like a twit.

She shifted the stack of books. She'd get on with it. Make the most of the interruption. Organize the bookshelves and catch up on correcting papers.

She wanted a vat of coffee to go with that rush of sugar donut. That would do her up just right, send her spinning through the rest of the day.

"You have a great day," she said. He grunted and pushed a button to let her out of master control and into the hallway. Where she ran straight into the gleaming-white shirt front of William Lincoln Bonner, counselor and director of the psych team. His dreads were pulled back neatly with a leather thong. He was tall. Her eyes hit just about the level of his collar.

"Sista Soul," he said. Caroline smiled whenever he called her that. She looked up into a grin that started slowly at his wide mouth and ended up playing around his eyes. Her face grew red hot, and something inside her, like a cold weight, started to melt. Will knew exactly where to find that spot and work it.

"Hi," she said.

"Where you off to in such a hurry?"

"I have class. I guess. Later. Who knows when."

"Intake. Probably be at least a couple hours 'til things settle down." His voice was just above a whisper, and somehow intimate, even when he talked of prison business. She felt soothed around him, and she wasn't the only one. Will was everywhere, trying to mitigate the abuse, calm the place down. The deputies pretty much sidelined him, but Will never let go.

"I need to talk to you," she said.

"I like that."

"No, I mean, about a weird vibe I'm getting."

"Around here? Weird?"

"Don't let it ruin your day."

"My day just got better." Again, he smiled and Caroline did all she could do not to drop the books and throw her arms around his neck. It was the same feeling she got when she stood on top of the Empire State Building and imagined she could fly.

"See you in a minute, or two?"

"For as many as you like." He had a musical way of putting it, almost an island cadence. She felt centered when she was around him, reassured she was doing the right thing. He said the same about her. Each was a compass for the other.

He took the books from her, and when he did, his hand brushed her arm.

She felt it to her bones. She took his hand and held it, with the boys waiting in their cells to get to English and the hot Florida sun peeping through the high windows, with the screaming of the new inmate and the deputies fading away in the background. Caroline shut out the prison.

Swanson at master control pointed at the door and shrugged impatiently toward her classroom. He leaned on the buzzer. She shot him a look of irritation. She'd go when she damn well felt like it.

"What's up with him?" Will murmured, but he was still smiling. "Sometimes they're worse than the boys."

"Same old thing. They don't like to see us talking, or anything."

"Or anything?"

"You know." She deftly ran a finger over the smooth skin on the back of his hand.

"Let's go."

"Don't I wish."

Will produced a key. He ignored Swanson and unlocked the door into the day room, and from there, the two went into her classroom. He followed her to the desk and put the books down gently where they cascaded like a deck of cards.

"Thanks. You," said Caroline. "When you free?" She slowed her pace, giving herself the luxury to unwind and spend these few minutes with him. He grinned back. His teeth were impossibly white, his skin rich and smooth. Caroline wanted to touch his cheek. She thought better of it. She'd already let herself go and shown her affection. Right under the eye of the camera.

"Soon. Got a meeting, then we talk." Will turned to leave but not before squeezing her hand. His gaze flicked to the tiny office/storage space at the back of her classroom, and she followed with her eyes.

"Hmmmm. Yeah," she said. "Soon."

CHAPTER FIVE

In the Way

ART LOOKED OUT OF A WINDOW IN THE classroom door. He didn't see anyone in the day room, but he could hear faint rumbling. The new inmate was somewhere in the prison, getting settled in a most unsettling way. Art was thinking the boy had made his way into the showers and back to his cell. A deputy was still yelling.

Art's ruddy-Irish face broke into a grimace every time the deputy swore at the kid. Initiation at Alpha was a loathsome procedure. Art had been a captain in the Navy, and he knew about initiation, and hazing. But he didn't like the degrading way the deputies handled the new "swabbies." He ran his classroom like a taut ship. Veered more toward indulgence and trust than the deputies would like. Art answered the boys' questions about the military, and occasionally gave them candy. He was consistently positive, and they responded well. At least, it appeared so because they were learning algebra.

He went to his desk at the front of the classroom, sorted a stack of calculators, and at once shuddered at the thought of where the boys had come from, at what they'd done to get in here. Calculators and protractors were completely foreign to them when they'd grown up with guns and knives. He put that thought out of his mind and got down to business. He had to teach the best way he thought, regardless of his students' criminal behavior and the intimidation of the deputies. He was constantly at odds with the deputies, especially with Sergeant Miller.

Art was sorry he had conjured thoughts of the sergeant. Bad luck. Here was Miller, shouting in the day room and pounding toward his classroom with that unmistakable march of his. Suddenly his burr cut was framed in the window.

Art heard the jangle of keys as the sergeant popped the door open. Art leaned over his desk, busy at arranging calculators, papers, and folders.

"I'm shuttin' it down, Art." The deputy planted his feet.

"Good morning," Art said, without looking up.

The sergeant puffed out his cheeks. "And to you."

Art straightened up and stared down the sergeant. *What new hell we got now?*

"This movie business. Shuttin' it down. This isn't the local Palmetto Ghetto Cinema, or whatever you want to call it."

Art was perplexed, but not all that surprised. He barely hid it. He always found it best to let Miller sputter on until he ran down.

"You can't be showing movies in here," said Miller. "At least not as much as you're up to."

"The films are instructional, Sergeant Miller. For math class." He intended to keep the conversation short, maybe to avoid a pissing contest, into which his meetings with the sergeant often plummeted.

"You're showing them *Band of Brothers*. That's war business, and, I might add, unnecessary entertainment for these scum bags."

Art winced. *Here we go again. Incarcerator throwing lesson plans into the incinerator.* "Well, besides the lesson in compassion and camaraderie, and working to save one's own skin through teamwork, the series *is* a math lesson."

"How's that." It was not a question. The deputy always seemed to have his guard up with the educators. It was rumored that he'd barely made it out of two years of community college with an associate's in criminal justice, and even that was due to the diligence of one of his girlfriends—he couldn't ever come up with her name—who tutored him through three rounds of algebra.

"Relative to the film, I use the battlefield situation to illustrate geometric calculations. For example, the placing of mortar rounds. Azimuths for angles of attack and parabolas…"

"All right, all right. Why don't you stick to the textbook?"

"Well, I do. But the boys are visual learners, you see, and the use of the film…"

Miller checked his watch and clomped back to the door. He perpetually gave the appearance of being pressed for time, overloaded with the duties of running the correctional center—and fully in charge. Maybe he was all that, but he gave precious little opportunity to gain support in the accomplishment of his goals. He had a smooth pink face, full jowls for one so young, and he always seemed to be in a sweat.

"Just this time. Lay off the movies. Next thing you know, you'll be bringing popcorn in here. Nice and cozy."

Miller let himself out with his key. Art couldn't resist a smile. *Popcorn. Now, there's an idea.*

MILLER MADE HIS WAY AROUND the day room. Checked the doors to the cell blocks, flipped a textbook closed that had been left on a table. He yelled into the hand-held radio and then clipped it to his belt. Through the wide windows of her classroom, Caroline saw him stomping away from Art's door and headed toward hers. She'd hardly put her bag down, and now she had to deal with Sergeant Blowhard. She could just imagine what pain he'd inflicted on Art. She steeled herself. She admired Art's creativity, and she had a good jot of her own. But they both had a problem keeping their heads down, getting after it, and avoiding confrontation with the sergeant. He flared easily. The teachers were considered interlopers in Sergeant Miller's correctional center. They got in the way of his "Alpha policy."

Caroline's green pen flew across the essay on her desk. *He must know I've got prep for class. Maybe he'll leave well enough alone.* Her hands flicked from a stack of essays to a raggedy textbook, and back again. But she couldn't concentrate. She eyed Miller threading himself among the tables and chairs in the day room.

He had a mean glint in his eye. She could see it even from where she sat. "Oh goodie," Caroline muttered, just as the key clicked in the lock.

"Morning, Miss Caroline." Miller stuck his thumbs in the waist band of his uniform and flexed his upper arms. His shirt was tailored tight on his bulging biceps. Caroline would have chuckled, but he might have taken it that she was pleased to see him.

"And good morning to you. What can I do for you, sergeant? Sir." Just a tinge of sarcasm.

He cleared his throat. Caroline often wondered if he enjoyed this job of badgering the education staff.

"Letters. What's with the goddam letters?" Acid in his tone.

She dropped the pen and stood up. *Now. What?* She shoved the chair away from the wall and crossed her arms. "And to what do you refer? Sir."

"You know damn well. Those letters to all those authors."

She sat down at her desk and studied him. Unblinking, steady as could be, but her mind was going round and round. *Oh, that! Those damn authors! God forbid!*

"It is your censorship directive, Sergeant Miller, that all correspondence go through your office," she said. "I am following procedure." She looked him in the eye, a happy little bubble forming way down deep. She'd gotten to him with the writing project. The boys were asked to write letters to their favorite authors, dead or alive, and tell them what they were learning and what they liked about the writing. So, Miller was stuck reading dozens of letters to Charles Dickens, J.K. Rowling, Langston Hughes, and W.E.B. Du Bois. He was not amused, especially when he had to read letters to dead people he hadn't even heard of.

"It's a waste of time," he said.

"What? The rules?"

"You know." He clamped his mouth shut. Caroline suspected the young sergeant with closely set eyes and raw fingernails was not a reader. "What do they care about Dickens?" Now it was almost a whine. "And that Mary Clark business."

"What's the matter with Mary Higgins Clark?" She feigned ignorance, knowing perfectly well he objected to murder in high heels with the occasional sterling-silver carving knife.

"Too much entertainment. Murder mysteries." He spat the words. "Stick to the textbooks, or whatever."

"Sergeant, a novel is *meant* to entertain. A mystery presents a certain amount of intrigue and puzzle, helps the reader focus on story line and writing. Art is…"

"I've just seen Art. Had it out with him, too. He's showing movies again, and next thing you know he'll be passing out the popcorn and candy. Why do I have to keep after you people?"

He didn't wait for an answer and opened his mouth to continue. She shook her head. "And why do we have to keep after *you*?" She bit her tongue. It did no good to antagonize Miller, but sometimes she had to bite back.

Did he hear me?

He swaggered over to the bookcase and picked up *Skin Tight* by Carl Hiaasen. It was among Miller's censored books. She waited for the book review she knew was coming, and she was slightly amused. When it came to books, she was in familiar territory and she liked to spar with him. She was always looking for a convert.

"And this guy…" He shook the paperback, flapping its leaves. "This guy makes fun of the governor and the tourists and industry…"

"Well, maybe he should. Look what they're doing to Florida."

He dropped the book on a student desk. "Who?" He was sputtering again, restless on his feet.

"You know, great sugar and ag pollution. The politicians. The greedy, carpet-bagging developers and money launderers and drug dealers. People who just don't care, except for themselves. All of it."

"He's just too hard on 'em."

Caroline stood up, hands on her hips. "Do you hear what you're saying?"

"I hear myself just fine," he said, planting his feet farther apart. "Now you hear me. Enough is enough with these crazies. And that Alice Hoffman is spooky, so is Stephen King…" His arm swept the bookcases, his face set in a disapproving frown.

"What's the matter with spooky?"

"They got enough to be spooked about. They don't need rabid dogs and creepy people and ghosts and such."

"I guess you're right," she said, but the wry look said otherwise. "On the other hand, reading stories helps to objectify their fears. Put them in their place. Make them realize they aren't alone and that there's always a way out."

"I don't know how you can leap to that, Miss Caroline. You making some objectifying conclusions there. To which I objectify."

Caroline laughed. "You know me and books. Always making my pitch." She felt a bit more relaxed. He had picked up the Hiaasen book again and was turning it over to the blurb on the back cover.

Miller shrugged. "Suppose this won't make mass murderers out of 'em. But who knows?"

"No, it won't. And while we're on the subject. You've even banned Stephen King's *On Writing*, which is a classic on inspiration and technique..."

"Come on. Stephen King writing about writing? That's like Charles Manson writing 'bout how to be charming. You got better stuff to give 'em." He was pacing, frowning again. She shook her head. He came back around to her desk and toyed with the corner of a peeling textbook. Caroline moved the book out from under his chewed fingertip.

"You know the policy around here," he said. He seemed to fish for the right words. "Lay off the *entertainment*. Give 'em the Bible."

"The Bible?" She threw her head back. "OMG. What about the separation of church and state?"

"We are God-fearing, God-loving people here."

"Oh, really? As compared to the heathens on the outs?"

"Something like that." A smile played around his lips.

Caroline said, "You know, most of these books are *based on the Bible*. Trust. Love. Kindness. Even an eye for an eye and anger, the righteous kind of anger. They say, every story ever written is right out of the Bible. Or Shakespeare."

"Zat so? Well, I don't need no Bible stories cooked up by Mary Higgins Clark. You gotta be careful, Miss Caroline. All's I'm sayin'."

Caroline walked over to the bookcase. "Why don't you give this a try." She picked up Hiaasen's *Lucky You*. "Try it, you'll like it. He's hilarious, and he does have a point."

A smile remained, but he didn't look happy.

"Books *are* a way out, sergeant. New beginnings, sometimes even happy endings. Ideas. The way to a better future. They have to see that there's another way—kind of play it out in their heads through the stories. Get them thinking. Know what I mean?"

"These books are reward. Privilege. Worst of all, they're an escape for their sorry asses."

She wanted to shout at him, "*If they learned to read and enjoy it, they would be free to start over. To dream…*" But he would never agree with her. Out of principle, and "policy." He'd made it plain that he didn't believe that an inmate who was reading wouldn't be thinking about how to dissemble the plumbing, or worse. Knowledge was dangerous; it was one more thing he could not control.

"They are here to suffer for what they did," he said. "Not get rewards. Of any kind."

"'Suffer the little children…' There's your Bible for you." But she wasn't in the mood for biblical quotes or charitable deference to Miller. He brushed off her reference. "I don't know what you're thinking, but these people are hard core. *Lost.* They can make more money on the streets with their drugs than they can with a high school degree, and they know it. You know it. They're playing a game with you. And with me, and I don't like it. Enough already."

"I can't argue with much of what you say," said Caroline. Under her breath she added, "But I have to try."

She had that vague buzzing in her brain again. *Were they playing a game? Of course, they were. But what?* Miller's rampages came and went, like storms blowing through, but this latest bit of stomping and protesting seemed overboard. He seemed frazzled about something. She should trust him and that staff. They knew what they were doing to keep the place locked down; she didn't. She should shake off her concern and preserve her sanity, go about her classes and such. Get to the work of teaching. But it was hard to concentrate with the interruptions. With the tension. And with that damn buzz, that odd undercurrent every time she turned around.

She persisted. "Do you know something, sergeant? Any news?"

"Yeah." He stopped pacing and looked at her. He wasn't intimidating. She had a sudden wave of empathy. He had a job to do, and it wasn't all that much fun.

She coaxed, lowered her voice conspiratorially. "What's going on around here, sergeant? Any new mischief?"

"There's always that, Miss McBride. There's always that. But you tend to your business and we'll tend to ours."

"You won't share?" She forced a smile.

All she got was the stink eye.

She took a last stab. "About those books. Daryl. We need the books. The books help. They need to know they have choices."

"Not this again. You just don't stop." He put up both hands in mock frustration.

"I know. It sounds like the same old thing to you. But, come on. They have time now. In their cells with nothing to do."

She thought of Tarvis in his cell. She had to get to Tarvis, put in a word for the new student.

"They should read that rules book," said Miller. "That's what they should read. Maybe you should add that to the vocabulary lesson: the word 'rule.' They sure as hell aren't familiar with the meaning of the word."

"Let them have books." She could hear the pleading in her voice, but she stood up, straightened her shoulders. "Books show them there are consequences. You know that."

"Consequences. Huh." He turned on his boot heels. The keys twirled around an index finger. He wore a crooked smile as he went for the door. *Always leave them laughing or smiling. That was our Daryl.*

Finally, he hadn't said no. And then she smiled. He'd carried off Hiaasen's *Lucky You.*

She hadn't asked about Tarvis. First things first, seemed to get pushed to last. *Again.*

CHAPTER SIX

Again. Why Am I Here?

TARVIS PRESSED HIS FOREHEAD AGAINST the concrete block wall of his cell. The cool rough surface gave him a moment of relief. Pebbly. Like the sand under his feet along the Withlacoochee banks in winter. He shut his eyes tight and tried to imagine. The river might as well have been on the moon for all that he could see and feel.

He glanced toward the cell door. That deputy was gone, sure to return. The devil. He'd ordered him to strip and shoved him under a rain of cold water in the shower room. Slipping on the scummy tile floor. He'd never felt so sick and cold, and humiliated.

At least he was alone now, and clean. The sharp, smell of the soap was like the lye his grandma used in the washtub but it wasn't comforting and homey. The scratchy prison shirt rubbed his bruised back.

He was almost afraid to move. If he held still and just breathed, in and out, against this wall maybe he could calm down. Live out this minute of peace with no one yelling at him. He clenched his fists and stifled a sob.

He heard shuffling in the cell block and stiffened. The deputy yelled at the inmates to pick it their feet and get to class. It gave Tarvis an odd sense of relief, and hope. Deputy Pilson had someone else to torture. And some day, Tarvis would get to class. *At least I'll get out of here. Feels like I'll never get out of here. How did I ever get here?*

CAROLINE HAD A SHORT STRETCH to sit and stew, now that Miller was gone, and she was left alone at her desk. The paperwork for intake was finished, the new inmate was back in his cell. She often wondered what took so damn long for the processing. No doubt, deputy staff cranked in time for the settling of nerves following the harrowing experience, but she figured, if they made it less harrowing, they could all get down to business faster. She sighed. Classes would resume soon. She checked the clock. Just past ten. She opened a drawer, and slammed it shut. For no reason. Again, she asked herself: *Why am I here putting up with this shit? To do some good?*

She'd heard over and over from staff since she started teaching at Alpha: *These boys don't care about consequences, and that's the main reason they are in prison.* It was always the same refrain. The inmates wanted what they wanted, and they went after it, no matter what and no matter whom they stepped on to get it, the drug dealer, best friend, or grandmother. They had made some bad choices, and they kept making them.

But Caroline bet on second chances ... or what was the point? After they served their time, their records could be expunged. They could start over if they chose to make it happen. Sometimes decent food, shelter, and a regular schedule worked wonders.

Still, she often questioned why she stayed. She sat back, shoulders slumped, and remembered how she arrived at Alpha in the first place.

Harvey Sanders had talked her into it, and once she made the commitment, she couldn't let go. From the first she'd heard of it, Alpha Juvenile Correctional Center had been enticing—a brand-new charter school for boys, thirteen to twenty-two, and she'd be the first teacher hired. She could make the classes her own, design them the way she wanted them run, five days a week, fifty weeks a year, except for holidays. It was also a twenty-five-thousand-dollar-a-year pay raise over her Catholic school teaching job. She couldn't afford *not* to go to prison.

Harvey drove her out to Alpha one sunny afternoon in his truck, all the windows rolled down, the soft Florida breeze blowing in her face. He didn't look like he belonged in prison in his pressed, white guayabera and amethyst necklace, one casual hand on the wheel, his carefully combed and gelled hair not moving in the wind. She enjoyed the carefree moment as they sped along past the palm trees, but then she remembered where she was headed: a correctional center for the worst young criminals. The thought was deflating, but then she looked at the smiling Harvey beside her.

"Oh, you'll love it out there," he said. "It's a great gig. But I warn you. You'll gain ten pounds the first year. Good grub at the county jail where we have lunch."

"Really? Good grub at the jail?"

"So happens," Harvey said.

He wasn't kidding. As it turned out, the county jail was a short walk from Alpha, and deputy and administrative staff gathered in the huge cafeteria in staggered shifts for lunch, Monday through Friday. Somehow Sheriff Ron Wellston managed to get "dented" boxes of frozen lobster and crates of steaks that "had fallen off the back of a truck" for the daily menu. The inmates who were incarcerated for nonviolent offenses at the jail did the cooking, and many of them had baking, prep, and fry credentials on their resumes next to the drunken-disorderly and drug charges.

Harvey winked. "Lobster and steak for a dollar? You betcha. And Starbucks. Fried chicken Thursdays."

Harvey won her over easily. Not so much on food. Somehow the idea of a burglar boiling her a lobster never had much appeal. Besides, she was always counting calories and wary of gaining that "freshman fifteen" that had crept up on her in college and just might find its way back. Harvey had won her with enthusiasm, and his passion for doing something for "the youth." Harvey was all out there, a regular cheerleader for the correctional center. He didn't seem to fake it.

"You can make a difference here. We all can. We're a team." He beamed and waved an arm over the landscape, taking in the expanse of desolate Florida swampland like it was mecca.

Harvey slammed the door to the truck. For the first time, Caroline looked at the grim, grey building. Really looked at it. The surrounding greenery was lush in contrast, and peace was in the air. Oddly, there was something about the tangle of Florida palms and sea grape, cawing birds and intermittent quiet that lulled her. The lullaby of prison, thanks to Harvey.

"I desperately need a language arts teacher," he said. "You have the chops. Besides, Mary Ann says you are pretty sick of your, er, situation."

He was too diplomatic to elaborate on the "situation," which was teaching privileged, whining middle-schoolers. Her friend, Mary Ann Cruthers, had told Caroline about the opening at Alpha: "Caroline, you'd be perfect in prison," she said, standing in the kitchen of St. Michael's Middle School.

Harvey pressed the buzzer at the gate and several buzzes later they stood in an empty wing of Alpha block, not a soul around except for a deputy or two. All the boys were gone for the day. The sheriff's department had bussed them to a processing center. The door to a cell swung open, and Caroline stared at the tiny grey room with stainless steel fixtures bolted to concrete. It was not exactly homey. A cot, a sink, a toilet, a small table and stool. Above the cot, a small rectangular window framed the warm gold sun and lush green of a palm tree. It was a horrible tease, that window. The boy who lived here could get a glimpse of the thriving world, but he couldn't touch it.

Harry led her to the empty classroom for language arts. A blank slate. Twenty desks and separate chairs were arranged in precise lines. A long, high stretch of windows let in plenty of light. A huge beaten-up desk was angled in the corner, and a blackboard ran the length of the wall. Sterile. It needed people, and plants. Books!

"Here 'tis," Harvey said. "Go for it."

"Is that a Florida state standard in education? Go for it?"

She started imagining what she would do with her first classes of inmates. She didn't have a clue.

"You can do this," he said. "You're a natural."

"I'm a natural with criminals?"

"You'll figure it out."

"Me. Figure it out. White girl from the burbs? And these... guys?"

He laughed. "Just get down to the business of teaching. Remember the job. They're coming in at grade school reading level, some of them at second grade, and you need to get them up into high school to pass the GED. That's the mission."

They got back in his truck, and she was already warming to the challenge. He put both hands on the wheel and stared straight ahead. "Pretty place, isn't it?"

She looked around at the jungle of palm trees under the blue and white sky, a gull swooping, the breezy afternoon belying the location. Her mother used to say, "Pretty is as pretty does."

Then he sold her. "You know. All kids are the same. Deep down. Doesn't matter where they are or what the deal. They're just kids." He gave her a thumbs up and started the engine. "And by the way. If you—the girl from the burbs—do figure it out, please let me in on it."

CHAPTER SEVEN

Class Time

IT WAS ALREADY LATE MORNING. Enough with the donuts. She wanted a beer. Or a nap. But more than that, she wanted to see Will, and it was probably too late for that now. She glanced toward the door hoping to see his broad shoulders framed in the window walking toward her. They had to talk. That unsettled feeling lingered, and she wanted to know if he'd heard anything. The thought buzzed in her head like a bee in a jar.

She stacked essays and lesson plans. She needed to assume the positive, forget about Miller. He'd left a bad taste, and doubt. He hadn't answered anything about Tarvis and the reading policy with the books. He'd just complained... and more. He pretended like he wasn't aware of any new strain of tension.

The buzzer sounded. Hathaway appeared at the classroom door, and behind him, a neat line of boys. They shuffled in, their binders under their arms, bringing with them an air of testosterone and soap. "Sir, sir," they whispered. "Ma'am, ma'am." Caroline nodded, always amused at the faint whisper of their greeting—a quiet acknowledgement in the presence of authority.

Will came in behind them, holding up a manila folder. She brightened. "Miss McBride." He turned his back to the classroom and winked at her. "More records on the new kid, Tarvis Philip James. Just wanted to let you know."

She moved inches closer to him. "You think we can get him into class? Without a long wait?"

"Maybe so. Good sign we've got these already." He fanned the pages of the records.

Hathaway sauntered up within ear shot. "Sorry to interrupt." Clearly, he was not sorry. He looked from Caroline to Will, who backed away but not before he squeezed her hand. He stared back at the deputy, a hard, cold light in his eyes.

Hathaway snickered. Caroline ignored him. The deputy didn't like to see them together, a Black man and a white woman. She'd heard the gossip, from Hathaway and the rest of them, but nothing could draw her away from Will. Certainly not the sneering. It only seemed to make her stronger in the face of it, pulling her closer to Will.

Will put Tarvis's folder under his arm and headed for the door. "I'll be back," he whispered to her.

The boys waited, standing, next to their desks, most of them gazing at Will. They always wanted a piece of him, of his toughness and wisdom. They wanted to be him. He'd been one of them, and he'd gotten out of the game. To see their blatant longing and adoration always gave Caroline a sense of pride, and hope. Will glanced once more at Hathaway on his way out the door, an unreadable look, not so much of disgust as benign resignation.

She took a deep breath. The rows of desks were neat, the room in immaculate condition, thanks to the boys, and hundreds of books lined the walls. She'd scrounged bookcases, and now they were crammed with encyclopedias, reference, self-help books on the back wall and under the windows, and behind her desk, novels and nonfiction, all of them arranged in alphabetical order. Another task her students begged to do. She'd donated most of the books. Friends had given her piles more and Art's Shriners club held book drives. She was addicted to books, and she hoped her students would pick up the best addiction they'd ever have.

"Be seated," said Hathaway. "And pick up those chairs, don't be scraping the floor up, or I'll have you down on your knees with a toothbrush cleaning it up."

He never seemed to notice how his boots marked up the floor with black streaks, that he left a trail of crumbs from the chips and the wrappers, newspapers, cups.

The deputies only saw what they wanted to see.

CHAPTER EIGHT

A Safe Place

THE BATTERED LITERATURE BOOK FELL open to Hemingway's "A Day's Wait." She considered this short story by one of her favorite writers. *Discuss the "verb"—most important part of speech.* Her students weren't crazy about all the grammar rules, but they liked reading "real adventure." They had questions about Jack London, Richard Wright, and Ernest Hemingway, and they liked hearing about what these writers had done with their lives. Boxing, fighting, flying, living in Paris, and surviving. The classroom was a place of escape. A safe place to run away, at least in their minds. When they opened their books, they traveled. It didn't matter what Sergeant Miller said or did to discourage that notion.

The Florida sun poured through the high, narrow windows, the buzz of a power mower started up, the chopping down of the world around them. The growth constantly needed to be trimmed for security. She could just barely see the coil of razor wire rising above a palm tree.

She stood at the blackboard. They settled in their desks, got out their notebooks and pencils and sat military style, arms straight in front of them, feet flat on the floor. The deputy gave them the usual disapproving once over.

Hathaway took a seat in the corner, his feet crossed on an overturned waste basket. He'd brought the usual comforts, his newspaper, coffee, and something disgusting, sweet or salty, in a wrapper.

Language arts at Alpha Juvenile Correctional Center was finally off to a start.

Caroline wrote the "word for the day" from the GED list of spelling words on the board: "abominable." They were to write a sentence using the word. Out of the eighteen students in the class today, she was sure to get eighteen versions of "abominable" in a sentence. They picked up their dictionaries from the racks under their chairs, looked up the word, and began writing the definition in their notebooks.

Deputy Hathaway opened the junk food and the crackling began. She should be glad he was there. She certainly had no management problems in the class. His very presence put a stop to that. He ably prevented disruption even while he invented his own.

Caroline walked around the room. "Finish the sentence and then take out your homework, please." Some had already done that, and she began to collect the neat stacks of notebook paper filled with essays, pleased, once again, at so much writing. They'd been sitting in their cells during intake for hours, and this is what they did. Mostly write. They weren't allowed to nap or exercise. They weren't even allowed to sit on their beds, a ridiculous rule that was impossible to enforce. And, worst of all, reading was limited, a policy she'd been fighting for years.

They were ready for class, their uniforms rumpled clean from the dryer, heads bent to the task. The odor of soy burgers and macaroni from lunch did not yet hang about the room as it did in the afternoon classes.

"Mr. Gomez, please put your sentence on the board and diagram it for us. Using the word 'abominable'."

Youth Ronnie Gomez sprang out of his chair. "Ma'am, yes, ma'am." He liked diagramming sentences, a tedious grammar exercise that only a wordsmith, and a visual learner, could love. She had once asked him why he liked diagramming. He'd said, "I like putting things where they belong." She was glad to know of his appreciation for order and placement. Except for the bundle of jackets he'd lifted from Marshall's in orderly fashion and placed in the back of his van.

He finished writing the sentence on the board in florid cursive, underlined it, and then separated subject, predicate, and predicate adjective: "The deputy staff is abominable." Caroline froze. She eyed Hathaway who was engrossed in the newspaper and snacking and didn't look up. She reached for the eraser. "Sir, that does not define the word," she said, quietly.

Youth Gomez's eyes grew larger as he glanced at the board and around the classroom.

She heard the snickering, the random cough stifling a laugh. They were careful to maintain the proper posture, hands flat on the pages, some clutching pencils.

Deputy Hathaway had come to. "Sit down, asshole."

Caroline erased the sentence but not fast enough. Ronnie Gomez would get a big fat red mark for that one, maybe two weeks loss of privilege.

From his desk, Youth Gomez shot Caroline a look of amusement. Or was that triumph? That look said: *It doesn't matter*. For a minute or two, he'd gotten over. He was here for days and months that stretched ahead of him for what seemed an interminable time, so, really, what did *abominable* mean to Ronnie Gomez?

They rustled their pages. Eyes flicked left and right. She could feel the current like she'd stuck her finger in a light socket.

Gomez remained remarkably calm.

"I might have chosen another subject for that sentence, Mr. Gomez, and done a better job at definition." She kept her voice level, tented her fingers on the desktop.

Now, Eliot Sampson was waving a piece of loose leaf at her. It might as well have been a red flag. He would get into trouble for interrupting the class. Too late. Before she could signal him to stop, Deputy Hathaway had the binder open and he was certainly slashing a red mark next to Sampson's name.

The deputy stood up, leather creaking, and walked over to Gomez, but he directed his remark at Sampson. "One more minute, I'm gonna put you all back in the can. Knock it off, Sampson." But he stared a hole through Gomez. The deputy returned to his seat and whooshed the binder shut.

We haven't even started and already, trouble.

She made a note to pick up Sampson's paper. An adept writer, his poems full of hearts and flowers for his girlfriend and baby, he continually vied for Caroline's attention.

She nodded at Sampson. "Get your textbooks out, please. We're going to look at poetry today." A few groaned. Hathaway didn't move except for one eyebrow. She expected their reaction but she plowed ahead. They had just had this discussion. They liked poetry, they wrote it, but they weren't so happy to read the classics. They said they couldn't understand the meaning. Caroline answered, "Well then, *feel* it! Feel the words."

She heard the key in the lock. Another interruption. And surely more commotion. The deputies rotated through the classroom during the lesson, but here was Deputy Haver pushing Youth Julius Duval through the door. The boy was shackled in handcuffs, scowling and shuffling across the back of the room. Haver led him toward a desk in the corner and shoved him into the chair. Duval had no books, no notebook. He wore black and white stripes, and his face was pinched and hard with anger. He scooted the chair against the wall with a slide and a crack. Haver stood over him. Duval began tapping his feet nervously under the desk. He dropped his cuffed wrists on the desktop with a resounding clank.

"Quit that tapping and noise with the cuffs or I'll put 'em on your ankles," said Haver. "And maybe a bag over your head." Duval turned his face away and sneered. Haver went to the door, not looking back.

Duval sat still as stone.

Caroline sighed. She waited until the shifting and questioning looks leveled off.

"Eyes front," Hathaway said, not moving a hair. He snapped the newspaper for emphasis. They did as they were told, at least the ones who knew what was good for them. She turned to the textbook, but she kept glancing at the handcuffs. The sound of them, the look of them grated on her nerves. The boys wore cuffs occasionally for transport, tutoring, and mental and physical assessments but hardly ever in class. The law mandated that the boys be brought to class in nearly any condition, and so here he was. Cuffs could always be removed at the discretion of staff, and where was the discretion today? Given the look on Duval's face, the deputy had made the wrong choice.

Now Caroline was infuriated, and it was all she could do to tamp it down. Once again, deputy staff was thumbing its collective nose at education. Their message was clear: You want him, you can have him. *Good luck.*

The air around Duval fizzed like a bomb.

He stole a glance at Hathaway and became more agitated. The feet tapping, the clenched fists. His eyes darted around the room, like a cornered cat. Caroline shot him a look, but Duval's mind was not in English class. He was somewhere else. He hated authority and made it known in his lack of cooperation and brooding. Truth was, he'd gotten off to an extra bad start when he came to Alpha. He'd robbed a liquor store, and when the chase began, he'd produced a gun and shot the pursuing officer in the leg. Once captured and settled into the back of the police car, he'd fouled the interior. There was a special place in the system for youth such as Duval, and didn't he know that? Why did he make it harder on himself? Duval didn't give a rat's ass. He let that be known, too.

He was closed down again, his hate cutting off communication. She wondered what he'd done now. It gave her a sinking feeling, but she remembered what his case worker said. Duval cared for animals. A mark in his favor. Treatment of animals had become a signpost in the pathology of criminal behavior. Those inmates who had set bunnies on fire and hung dogs by their tails had often graduated to doing worse to humans. Duval loved animals. He'd built a makeshift kennel for stray dogs, and the condo he'd briefly shared with an uncle was also home to a dozen cats that ate better than Duval had as a young child.

The judge had seen something redeeming in him, and here he sat instead of in adult population. But Duval clearly didn't buy it. He was a miserable, poor boy from Depot, Florida—a place so bereft and humid and mosquito-ridden, it hadn't even gotten a proper name. Duval hadn't gotten a proper name either; his mother took his name from her French Haitian pimp because she'd liked the sound of it, not really knowing who the father of her baby was, not having family or anywhere to go with the baby. She'd died of heroin addiction and AIDS. Duval had seen most of it from the closet where he spent a great deal of time locked away. His mother's boyfriends abused him growing up, but his anger was not directed toward his errant mother or a spurious close connection. Not a bit. He wrote in his journal without punctuation, without end, page after page in his composition book, about his visceral hatred for authority and how he was going to get out of prison and kill the first cop he got his hands on.

Duval fumed. He hurt all over. Caroline couldn't stand to read this on his face, and, at once, it's what fed her determination to fix it.

She needed to get it across that this was a safe zone.

She faced the board, shut her eyes tight.

They all needed something different, especially in this climate that buzzed with tension. They were careening toward a dead end, and she needed to turn this thing around. They needed something calming. They looked up at her, waiting expectantly. She was the teacher; she was supposed "to lead."

She flipped through the literature anthology looking for Robert Frost's "Blue-Butterfly Day." A poem about nature. Something hopeful. She wrote the page number on the board. She thought of putting a textbook in front of Duval, opening it to the poem about butterflies, getting him into the reading between the flashes of anger and the faraway look on his face.

What the hell? Who am I kidding?

"Open your books, please." She looked down at the neat even lines on the page, the drawing of wings sailing over goldenrod and a picket fence. She'd salvage something of a blue-butterfly day. She forced a smile, checking around the room for the right someone to read the poem.

Pick carefully.

Their rough looks and furtive glances gave the lie to poetry.

Caroline smoothed the page, soft and faded. *I hope this flies. On a wing and a prayer.*

CHAPTER NINE

Flurry on Flurry

CAROLINE NEEDED TO GET THE HANDCUFFS off Duval. The classroom was a free zone. A safe zone to learn. This wasn't Caroline's policy; it was correctional center policy, despite the reluctance of deputies to go along with it. *Any* show of freedom or privilege, mandated or not, seemed to come slowly and with a grudge.

How to get the deputies to accept their own damn rules.

Hathaway sometimes allowed the boys to relax in the classroom, but Caroline wondered if this were out of laziness. His feet up, his nose in the newspaper, he didn't seem to pay the least bit of attention to Duval's seething anger. The youth was still, and slumped at the desk, staring straight ahead.

Hathaway grunted. "Eyes front. I mean it, and feet flat on the floor. No speaking out and no more interruptions." He continued reading.

Caroline worried that if she didn't insist that Duval be free to write and use the textbook the handcuffing business would become a default method of containment. It seemed the deputies always fell back on ways to *contain*.

The classroom is a comfort zone.

Prison is not a place to get comfortable.

It was good to remember that.

"Will you please remove the cuffs, Deputy Hathaway?" She pointed to Duval's wrists. "He'll have trouble turning the pages, and we're going to write an essay…"

She waited for the deputy to oblige. Instead, he waggled a finger. Wait one minute, the finger said. Smiling, easy as could be, he ambled over to the bookcase, and picked up one of Bruce Catton's volumes on the Civil War.

Now what?

THE BOYS OF ALPHA BLOCK

But Caroline knew where this was going, and she decided to be patient though her teeth were grinding. He fancied himself an expert on famous military battles, and he liked to show off. He swaggered across the back of the room. Another history lesson of the Old South was coming. At least he stuck close to the truth, that the Civil War was fought to end slavery.

Duval couldn't have cared less. The deputy ignored the boy, his eyes vacant and miserable, his expression fierce, but he seemed to have calmed down.

Hathaway rocked back and forth, paging through the book, and at last, he found some manners. "If you don't mind, Miss Caroline, I'd like to say a few words."

She struggled to maintain a neutral expression, looking down at the literature textbook on her desk. "Go ahead, sir. Take a few minutes," she said. "Please."

Hathaway rested the book on his large paunch. He reminded her of an old pol with his thick salt and pepper hair and sonorous voice. Their eyes followed him.

"Most everything in the world has to do with war," he said, puffing out his cheeks, clomping around the room. "Fighting, arguing, warring and killing. One tactic used in military battle is *the element of surprise,* a tactic that often yields victory..."

Jesse Allen sat up straighter in his desk, the look on his face a reflection of brain cells popping like mad. Hathaway repeated himself: "The element of surprise. It has won many a war... Robert E. Lee was a master of the tactic. So were the Japanese, and the Germans, who probably took a cue from the old general himself."

Caroline wondered sometimes at Hathaway's interpretation of history. At least he made it lively. She filed the lesson under historical fiction.

Allen's gaze was pinned on Hathaway. Caroline walked down the aisle between the desks, past Allen who hunched over his desktop. He was drawing. Sketching.

Boxes? No, looks like rooms. Sometimes they draw buildings and such...

She glanced again. Allen sat up and folded his hands over the paper.

Hathaway droned on. "...They may have won some battles but they lost the war. Surprise was on their side..."

Caroline kept her game face on and glanced again at Allen. His enthusiasm was not that unusual, but she couldn't help feeling that something was going on with that kid. She shifted back to Hathaway who was reaching a crescendo of enthusiasm for war. She'd just wait until he ran down. Let him be. This was a war she would not wage. The boys needed male mentors. Even though Hathaway didn't seem to understand the concept that interrupting someone in the middle of a lesson set a bad example. One historical point or two, and then she would wrestle the class from him.

Duval glowered at the deputy. Caroline shot Duval a look. *Not good, sir.* He looked away, shutting out the world around him, his attention straying to the window and the occasional sea gull. He twisted his hands in the cuffs and clinked them on the desktop.

The deputy stopped for a breath, turned a page. Caroline cut in. "Thank you, Deputy Hathaway," she said, checking her watch. "Should we get on with the English lesson?" She could feel the eyes shifting from her to Hathaway and back again. Hoping for a shot of drama. He lifted the textbook, oblivious, while her eyes bore into him, then she pointedly looked at the cuffs.

He didn't seem inclined to remove them. She wanted to avoid a stand-off, but it was going to happen. She wanted her class back.

Hathaway raised one finger. He made one more stab at territory and control, winning and losing. The element of surprise. *What is the point?* Allen was writing furiously.

She folded her hands and waited. "The cuffs?"

Hathaway grunted. Clapped the book down on the bookcase and reached around for the key. "Surely."

He took his time. The cuffs slipped off with a metallic clink, and he clipped them to his belt. A cloud of gloom passed from Duval, but the moment was brief. He resumed staring, darkly.

Hathaway had taken too much time with his history lesson, and now they wouldn't finish the English assignment. She should have been used to it, but she wasn't.

"Back to poetry. Robert Frost." Their eyes were on the page now. Caroline was determined to bring on *feeling*. Good emotions. Empathy? An appreciation for creativity? Through their eyes, she saw things she hadn't seen before, no matter the number of times she'd read the poem or story.

Youth Roberto Clemente volunteered to read the poem. Named for the famous Pirates baseball player who died in a plane crash, Clemente had a generous nature, and he seemed driven to succeed, rather like his namesake. He was always smiling. Caroline had a special affection for him, which she was careful not to reveal. Clemente was in prison because of his association with a gang that had used him as a messenger. And one time, he was caught with a gun. When the incident was discussed during his therapy sessions, he became agitated, and cried, mostly about what he'd done to his mother. And Caroline believed him. Alpha was a time out and a new beginning for Roberto Clemente.

Now he stood at his desk with the literature book opened to "Blue-Butterfly Day." Clemente had a low forehead, and his small fleshy ears stuck out. He squinted at the page. His knuckles clutched the book so tightly that his fingers turned white around the edges. A native of the Dominican Republic, his accent was soft and edged in French, but his difficulty was not so much with the language; it lay mostly in his eyesight, which was poor and made him look sideways at Caroline when he talked with her. She was trying to get glasses for him through medical, but it would be a long wait. When he wrote, he wrote in a precise, slanted script, and he always corrected his work.

The selection was only two stanzas but highly descriptive of butterflies in flight. An escape from the concrete-metal prison, and, of course, that's why Caroline had chosen it.

Clemente's lips were moving, but nothing came out. He had a lisp. He tilted his head, set his feet. She'd gotten used to his quirks as she did for the rest of them through the years of English lessons.

His face twisted with effort: "It is *boo*, I mean, blue..." He spoke clearly, slowly, enunciating each letter. He struggled, but he was doing it.

Caroline heard some restless huffing and sighing, but she kept her eyes on the page. Hathaway looked in the direction of the noise. His boot hit the floor, but then he went back to a handful of tortilla chips.

Clemente kept reading the poem.

...And with these sky-flakes down in flurry on flurry
There is more unmixed color on the wing
Than flowers will show...

Caroline's eyes shifted from the page to Clemente's intense expression. She focused on his struggle with the words. She didn't see the flurry in the corner of the room. Then she sensed it. The desperation and misery on Duval's face simmered. She couldn't ignore it as she walked back and forth, juggling the book. Duval glowered. She looked over at Hathaway, but he had the newspaper over his face again. *Was he asleep, for God's sakes?*

"Thank you, Mr. Clemente," she said. She looked around, determined to engage everyone in the class. "Mr. Duval? Thoughts? On Frost's comparisons in nature?"

Nothing. Her effort was clearly futile.

It startled her to see such frank hate. It wasn't directed at her so much; she could see it went down a great dark well inside him where no one could go. His eyes were slits, his mouth compressed. The rest of the world was out, and he was in his own private hell. She stopped moving, oddly suspended between the beautiful words in the poem and the stark setting of the prison classroom.

Now she wished she hadn't blithely, and stupidly, asked Duval a question, but it was too late to take it back.

I should leave him alone. He's in no mood for poetry...

In the space of a second, Duval slid his hands to the center of the desk. His hands, a platform. She watched him do it. He sprang from his seat with the speed and agility of a high jumper, his arms spread in abandon. A flat trajectory in black and white stripes, his flight in slow motion. Time froze right there. She was stunned. She stood behind her desk, the textbook now clutched against her chest.

His target was obviously Clemente, and his aim was perfect. He landed on top of the unsuspecting student who bent to his textbook, the breath knocked out of him with a loud yelp. He and his book went crashing to the desk and then to the floor. Clemente doubled over, Duval on top, upending chairs and desks all around them. The cascade of destruction was instant.

All eyes were on the two boys. The rest of them sat with their mouths open, and their expressions changed: a little desperation here, joy there. Each one of them was making a decision. It was clear on their faces. Some wanted to break the rules, and some did not. Then, in a whoop, the group next to the windows threw their notebooks and texts into the air.

A desk went flying and knocked Deputy Hathaway off his chair. The newspaper flew up like a kite. His feet flailed as he tried to gain footing, but instead he ended up spread eagle on the floor.

Caroline's arms shot out in useless protest. She yelled. "Roberto! Jul…" But they had already decided. It was too late to run and too late to recover, to salvage some calm and reason. Notebooks and books careened off the bookcases and crashed into the walls and into heads, backs, and desks. Deputy Hathaway was still on the floor, useless in the action. He raised his arms, but it didn't do any good. Pent-up frustrations exploded before her eyes.

How long does it take to kill someone?

No one was dead, that she could see. Everyone was moving, jumping, fighting, yelling. Alive. So far. Two boys worked on separating Clemente and Duval, but their arms and legs were locked together, thrashing around. She held her breath.

Something had burst, and it gave her an odd sense of relief as she backed off into a corner. She'd seen this coming, this explosion, and now the waiting was over. Trouble had been brewing from the start of class. Maybe all day, and well before. Yes, well before. But hindsight was no consolation.

She didn't move. She couldn't. Anywhere she went she'd be stepping into a whirling mass of arms and legs. She'd seen a skirmish or two in the years she'd been at Alpha, but this was different. This time the concentrated fury had everything to do with a built-up, bottled-up rage coming uncorked. Through the litter of paper, she saw the glee and abandon on their faces, and she almost smiled. For one minute they were free.

OMG, what's the matter with me? This is not freedom.

She wasn't afraid. She felt strangely disassociated from the mayhem. She wasn't even in the room. Her mind floated away, and she let it.

Duval pounded away, but Clemente held on, fending off the blows. Legs kicked dangerously close to the heads and hands of those youth who were at once breaking it up and getting in the mix. Caroline yelled, again, and again her words drowned in the noise.

Two youths grabbed Duval's arms. They yanked at him, pulling him off Clemente. Duval resisted, the muscles in his neck straining to free himself, his shoulders jerking out of their grasp. Duval was a big kid. He had the torso of a linebacker, and he used it to break away and once again pin down Clemente who flapped around helplessly.

It seemed to go on and on, but it was all over in a minute.

The room turned green with deputies. Caroline hardly noticed, except for the wave of sweat and fear that swept the room. Her eyes were riveted on Clemente and Duval, and then it was as if she woke up. She started toward them. A reflex, and a stupid one. Pilson was at her side, his arm blocking her. "Don't," he yelled. She stopped and backed up.

The deputies, stepping on the texts and notebooks, grabbed boys while the last of the ragged loose leaf fluttered around the room. Pilson didn't move from his spot next to Caroline. The deputies marched boys toward the door.

Like a tornado or earthquake that brings down a building, it was over fast. She grimaced at the aftermath. At least everyone involved seemed to be upright, walking around in one piece. She was surprised not to see a body or two on the floor. Hathaway had managed to struggle to a seat while the other deputies cleared the room. Shirts and books were torn, faces were strained, sweating, some beet red. A few smiles but more scowls. The room was nearly destroyed.

This would require a thorough sorting, and the realization hit her. Not only was the room a mess, she was a witness, and she'd been helpless to stop it. She may have even contributed to it by insisting the cuffs come off. Even if it were correctional center policy to have unrestrained inmates in class, Duval shouldn't have been in class.

She tried to put the sequence of events in order and lock it all in her memory. There would be questions. She already had some herself, and the number one was: W*hy?*

What was Duval thinking? Why would he do such a thing? He had to know this would lengthen his time, even if it took him all of a second to decide on this mayhem.

Where is Duval? And Clemente?

The deputies were herding the last of the boys out of the classroom. The block would be on lockdown. Now all that remained was a big clean up and hell to pay.

She turned to Pilson. "There were several boys who helped end it." It was a weak defense, given the huge mess they'd made. She tried to remember, and she couldn't. She could barely hear herself think for the deputies yelling and the radio in Pilson's hand crackling orders from master control.

Where had the radio been? Hathaway didn't carry one with his newspaper and chips?

Pilson growled. "Yeah, bet they were all a big help." He clipped the radio to his belt. "There are videotapes."

Even so, video would not show what really happened, the anger and confusion, the pent-up tension. The tangle of arms and legs. Belonging to whom? With a renewed sinking feeling, she thought about how she'd asked Hathaway to remove Duval's cuffs.

Pilson said, "Just, please, stay right where you are, Miss McBride—'til we clear the room." He waved toward the corner.

Caroline backed up farther and remembered a name. "Hardwick." She almost whispered, but she needed to say it. "He yanked Duval off Clemente. At least he tried. Will you remember that? And let me think. There were others…"

Pilson made an unintelligible sound and hustled away, his beefy hands landing on the shoulders of Hardwick and Allen.

Tyce Hardwick was paralyzed, at attention, his uniform remarkably intact, his face as red as a tomato. "Sir, yes, sir," he said. Allen's expression, on the other hand, was strange, calm and *smug*? While Allen was an ass-kissing busy bee, Hardwick was quiet, no showboating, and his physical demeanor and responses were always crisp. That was on the outside; on the inside he was terrified, sometimes tripping over a desk, even stammering. Now she hoped he wasn't sucked into the downward spiral of this mess Duval had started.

And Allen. In the middle of it all, his green eyes had shifted to her for a split second, his hand on Clemente's back. She wondered about that expression; was he helping or disrupting? It was hard to tell. Allen was a sneaky one.

Hardwick and Allen shuffled out the door with the others, their arms pinned behind their backs with Deputy Pilson at their heels. Through the large windows of the classroom, Caroline looked out into the day room. It was a mass of green and blue and black and white stripes, milling about in confusion.

That's all it took…seconds. And disaster.

Not a notebook remained on the desks. Textbooks and pages were strewn everywhere. A real flurry on flurry.

At least the bookcases had been spared. She checked the shelves that lined the classroom and breathed a sigh. They'd dodged that. Now nearly every one of the textbooks littered the floor. She picked up a book and dropped it on her desk.

Caroline moved over to the windows overlooking the day room. She could just barely hear the conversation. Haver gripped Duval by the arm, and Pilson yanked at Clemente who looked thoroughly confused. One minute he'd been reading about butterflies, the next he was under attack. Sheer fright twisted his expression. "Sir, what? What happened?"

"Shit happens, Clemente. Now look alive. For once."

The boy's mouth hung open, a line of spittle wetting the front of his shirt, the back of it ripped from his collar to his belt. One of his shoes was missing. Clemente still had his literature book, clutching it to his chest like a float on a stormy sea. Pilson grabbed it and threw it on a table.

Caroline wanted to reach out to him. She raised her hand and pressed it against the glass. Haver and Pilson hustled the boys into a corner and lined them up. Clemente stared back at Caroline, his lips moving with no sound, and the thought struck her. *What the hell would Robert Frost think? He'd probably call this flurry on flurry and fucked.*

CHAPTER TEN

Dust and Embers

CAROLINE GRABBED BOOKS OFF THE FLOOR and started piling the remnants on a corner of her desk. It was a futile attempt at clean-up, but she didn't know what else to do, and she had enough nervous energy to pick up the whole room. The day room was still a mass of confusion. Most of the boys were back in their cells. A few were braced near the entrances to the cell block. Yelling. Slamming. There was nothing like the slamming of prison doors; it was a thunderclap from hell.

She'd give it a minute, and then she was going out there.

She picked her way through the debris and overturned desks. Half-written essays, folders torn open, broken pencils. A shoe? She nudged aside a tattered heap of textbooks, stirring up a sense of loss that seemed to creep into every day. These were books she'd scrounged from the local public system, old and scruffy but full of classics. Now she'd have to hunt down another set, and good luck with that. The administration often considered getting new books, but that was talk; new ones were near eighty dollars apiece. Out of the question. They could build a million-dollar facility with a useless kitchen, but they couldn't afford literature books. She was sick of arguing the point. The remains of the beaten-up books would have to do with help from some tape.

Caroline's thoughts drifted back to Duval. His emotional outburst would cost him and those he took down with him. They would all pay, probably with months more of incarceration.

And she would pay. The guilt she felt for having any part of it was unnerving. Stultifying. Another push in the direction of the door. Had she stayed too long?

THE BOYS OF ALPHA BLOCK

A radio cracked out commands, Pilson and Haver were shouting. Deputy Hathaway sat on a stool at a metal table in the day room, his big head hung over his chest, and he was shaking.

She buzzed master control and entered the day room. Hathaway gave her a wry smile. "Damn." He rubbed his leg above the leather boot, his eyes roved toward the classroom through the wide expanse of glass, and he took in the mess. "Looks like hell in there."

"I'd say so." Caroline put her hands on her hips. "You okay?" Her concern sounded insincere. He hadn't been much help.

"I'm fine." He looked her over.

"Did you see this coming?" She had the suspicion he'd been asleep, but would he admit it?

"Do you see a tornado coming? Duval. He's a mess. A red-hot rippin' mess," said Hathaway.

"Why was he allowed in class? The cuffs? You know we're not supposed to have that in class."

"And you know Duval. A perpetually dark cloud. He'd bucked, and the cuffs were a little reminder to sit down and shut up."

"That worked well."

Swanson appeared next to them. "Ouch. What happened to you, Doc? You okay?"

"Ain't no tea party 'round here," Hathaway said. "It's that Duval. Regular mad hatter, that one."

Caroline crossed her arms. She'd just shut up, for now. Her allegiance, and worry, was with the boys—abused boys, acting true to form. What would the staff do with them now? Hathaway had seemed oblivious, sunk deep into his comforts or dozing. She'd need to report that, and she'd need to speak up about her part. But Hathaway could count his blessings. They all could. They were lucky no one was brained in the melee.

Pilson held Duval's arm and gave him a good shake. The smiling deputy looked like a rosy ripe pear, his lower half larger than his shoulders, his blond complexion tinged with emotion. An adrenaline junkie, he was there for combat, and though short-lived, today he got it.

Caroline watched Duval. Compared to Clemente, Duval's reaction was the opposite. The awful chaos seemed to have a calming effect on him. It was written on his face. *I am a bad ass. I caused a stir. I showed them.*

The deputy shoved him toward the door. Duval shook his shoulders out of the grasp, and a whole range of emotions played across his face. His gaze changed like the whipping of dark clouds in a storm. He seemed to realize what he'd done. Defeated. A pleading look around the eyes. *Despair.*

Prison for the young was a damnable punishment. But worst of all, it was a consequence of all the horrors that had happened well before they even arrived. It never seemed to stop.

NEXT MORNING, DEPUTY HATHAWAY stood over the coffee machine. He'd suffered a bone bruise as a result of the classroom brawl. It would be weeks to full recovery but he was back, to Caroline's amazement.

"I should retire," he said, pouring the black liquid they called coffee into a foam cup.

"Now's as good a time as any," she said brightly, taking her turn with the carafe. She gave him an encouraging smile.

He cocked his head at her.

Well, he was always boasting about his ranch in the middle of nowhere. Golden scrubland in central Florida where he sat on the front porch and watched the sun set into the Australian pines and oaks—a pastime he preferred to "babysitting" young criminals. He seemed ready for that rocking chair.

She took a sip and grimaced into the cup. "How's the leg?"

He hooked a thumb in his wide belt. "Done worse than that in 'Nam. I'm still standing." Crookedly. And he was hobbling and babbling.

Caroline wanted to get back to her classroom. If she didn't soon, she'd either get a history lesson or his resume. It was always one or the other with Hathaway.

"Got me fitty head of cattle and a bunch of pou-lettes," he said.

"Poulettes?"

"Why, little chickies. Just like you." He wiggled his eyebrows at her. And then winked.

OMG. Does he know the word is also French for amour? The wavy hair and eyebrows were not irresistible. It was all she could do not to laugh. She was not embarrassed, and a little sorry.

"Don't think so," she said.

He slapped his knee and winced. He really got a kick out of himself.

She smiled and changed the subject. "Did you talk with the other deputies about Duval? What do you suppose happened yesterday? *Why* did it happen? *If you'd been less into the Bucs and more into Duval, maybe things would have been different for my poetry lesson."*

His eyes opened wide; he shook his head. "Don't know. It happens. I know you got your mission. We got ours, and never the twain shall meet, I'm afraid. Duval's a bad apple. Got plenty of hatred in that young soul." He swirled the coffee, almost white with flecks of cream. "Always buckin' for whatever reason."

For a second, Caroline sensed compassion but it didn't last. It was unlikely he'd have sympathy for Duval who had humiliated one of their own, and then heaped disrespect on all of them.

"Something must have provoked it out of the blue like that," she said. "What do you think? Something new in the wind?"

"A bad wind, if you know what I mean." Hathaway dropped the folksy tone, the leather belt and boots creaking, he sauntered over to master control and turned. "Who knows, Miss McBride. Kids like these, they just not gonna come to a good end. Mark my word. You stand clear. You stick to your books and those nice little stories of yours. This ain't no fantasy world."

His admonition was easier said than done. She was deeply into the care and teaching of the boys, and she was determined to help them. Education was necessary for rehabilitation.

Why can't this staff acknowledge that? Why can't we work together?

Something was going on, despite Hathaway's easy dismissal. She'd been around long enough to sense it, but everywhere she turned, she felt put off.

Poetry had done nothing to help. Sometimes it stirred positive feelings and maybe a little empathy. But she'd been a fool to engage Duval. *Blue butterflies? Really?* Not likely. She'd learned that lesson.

She brushed off Hathaway's silly talk of chickens, but she considered his words about Duval. Maybe he was wrong, maybe not. And maybe it was time the deputy got his own coop and cattle and moved off into the sunset. She'd wish him well. While he was obnoxious at times, at other times he tried to help the boys. She saw him pounding the history text into them, patiently explaining the intricacies of America's wars, she hoped, in favor of diplomacy.

The deputies could help. A lot. Being a deputy was *not* a babysitting job; it required dedication to safety and security, something foreign to most of the boys. Hathaway had done a passable job. At least he didn't appear to be overtly cruel. She wanted to work with empathetic deputies, but she just wasn't feeling the empathy.

Hathaway was old school. He'd worked as a car salesman and banker, and Caroline had once disagreed with his opinion that the inmates were "just dumb young assholes." He ignored her. Pretended to be the worldly, cool guy. But no one could pretend around these boys. Sometimes she heard the murmuring: *Hathaway acts the fool.*

For the most part, the boys loathed the deputies. They belittled and nagged, and in return, the inmates did everything they could to bait authority without getting caught. Most young criminals were just not cool enough to carry it off. They found themselves thrown up against a wall, swallowing the spittle of a red-faced, lathered-up, screaming deputy.

Will tried to persuade the boys to look past the badgering and bullying and beyond the confines of prison. He encouraged them to make changes and dissuaded them from sick thinking that would keep them in the system. They needed to think long-term. Someday they'd get out and have the opportunity to start over, sooner or later. Sooner if they behaved.

The Verdict: Duval's sentence was lengthened by six months with the stipulation it could be reduced for good behavior. No one was betting on that. His disruption was typical of some who angled for transfer to adult population, which had once happened to juveniles who caused excessive trouble. Staff was not about to oblige Duval. He would not go to county and get television and games privileges, be allowed to play basketball in the prison yard daily, and have prison jobs and visits from his girlfriend or his aunt. It would never happen. He didn't listen, except to the rumor mill that was as corrupt as the mentality of those who started it all. The adult population wanted "new beef" over the old drug addicts and drunks who kept coming back. Deputy staff was on to them. Duval would stay put.

Hardwick and Allen were told they would face extended time for their involvement in the classroom melee, but Caroline told administration that the boys had pried Duval off Clemente. Caroline reluctantly put in a good word for Allen even though she was still suspicious of him; he was a good student and helper. Staff checked the videotapes, which revealed mostly a mass of arms and legs and not Duval's initial leap across the room because of the fifteen-second lapse in recording. Caroline was not a lot of help. She had seen it all in one big blur from her corner.

Some of the class had remained in their seats or hit the deck, as instructed to do in case of a riot. It was the rash few who had followed Duval and caused trouble. Separating those few from the fray was next to impossible. Now the cell block was on watch. The deputies were instructed to tighten it up, which meant they'd live with a new strain of tension. And Caroline had learned another lesson. Even though she wasn't found culpable for insisting Hathaway remove the cuffs, she carried extra weight. *Be even more alert. Things can change in a heartbeat. Duval. Definitely a powder keg, that one. And maybe others.*

THE DUST HAD HARDLY SETTLED after the "Blue-Butterfly Day" when Juan Ramirez picked up a chair and tossed it across the computer lab. A reminder of the strength anger could add to muscle, and a further reminder to be alert. The chair crashed in the middle of the room between the rows, missing Youth Ramon Ofasio by a hair. Caroline had just walked into the lab; she thought the ceiling was falling in, but then saw that it was only the furniture-throwing activity. An infrequent, though regular occurrence. Caroline waited, held her breath. She pressed against the concrete block wall.

Deputy Angus Brown's gruff voice sounded from the corner of the lab. "Ramirez!" he roared. The boys turned to him as Ramirez clutched another chair. The deputy had been leaning against the wall. He pushed himself off quickly, smoothly, and set a hand on Ramirez's back. The uproar died, and the hard look on the youth's face softened. It was over before it started.

Brown's hand continued to rest on Ramirez. Not a vice grip, but a calming gesture. "Pick up the chair and the papers and folders and put everything back exactly where it was." He spoke precisely, softly, leaning into the boy's face. Caroline swore she was lip reading to get what he said.

Ramirez didn't hesitate. He even hurried to complete the task. He patted the final stack of papers and looked at Brown.

What they won't do for attention. What they won't do for Deputy Brown. Caroline sighed, still holding back near the door. *Why can't we have more Deputy Browns?*

The boys turned back to their computer screens while the deputy's gaze roved the lab. He didn't read the newspaper and spit chew. He watched, smiled occasionally, or not at all. Sometimes he chided gently, or joked a little, but not much. Not today.

Their respect for Brown was clear in comparison to the hate directed at Haver and some of the other deputies. Brown had five kids of his own. He seemed to understand the inmates. While they had done bad things, Brown told her, "Deep down, they aren't bad kids. Something's been broken in them, and we have to fix it."

He often pulled one aside. He was firm and quick and consistent. He was careful not to embarrass them. And, best of all, Caroline had heard, he listened. They knew what to expect from Deputy Brown. No surprises. But Brown didn't play. They learned that about him, too. They also learned there was only one Deputy Brown.

Alpha Juvenile Correctional Center was a place of singular personalities.

CHAPTER ELEVEN

Song with No Sound

TARVIS HEARD DOORS SLAMMING, deputies yelling. The sound of boot steps in the corridor, somewhere out near the day room? He was getting used to it. Each day brought a new conflict and another reason for ragged commands and shouting. And each day, he asked himself, *What new torture we got?*

He hoped it wasn't coming for him. He was still sore and wrung out from intake, both in his muscles and in his brain, and he wanted out of this cell. He longed for rec privileges, and he wanted to go to class. If he lay low, and shut up, it might be soon. He'd overheard in the showers that class was the place to be. With Miss Caroline. Word was, she looked after the boys and fought for them.

A lot of good it did. They were stuck in here, most of them, for years for doing really stupid stuff they couldn't take back.

He sat on the metal stool and leaned on a small table, both bolted to the floor. Solid and fixed. Like time. His hands opened wide and pressed down on his head. The blue cotton shirt, stiff as a board, smeared with black marker across the back, scratched against the scrapes he'd taken when he hit the concrete floor.

I have to get out of here.

How'd I get in here to begin with? Me, Tarvis Philip James. How the hell did it ever come to this? It didn't start out badly. It even started out kinda good. But now look at where I am. And how am I going to end up?

I had a Dad and a Mom, and a family. A crazy family in a beat-down house, but it was mine. A place I could hang and eat and laugh. And play the guitar. Uncle Tendris and Auntie Millie just down the street. Near the Withlacoochee and them trees like down in the Delta. We was all together there with my daddy. But then he was gone to work in the mills in Chicago, they said, but I knew he was dead. Nobody wanted to say it. My mama was out most of the time, doin' I don't know what. Crying, a lot. I couldn't do anything about that, except feel sad. We had next to nothin' but Aunt Millie could whip up grits and cheese, frittered chicken and greens with fat bacon like nobody ever cooked. How I miss that. I can still 'magine the salt and fat smell of pork if I try real hard. But now there ain't no fat, I ain't got nothin'. How can anyone live like this? They don't want us to live. That's it.

Now I feel like I'm dyin'. I used to be livin' real good. We sat in that bass boat, and we fished for sheepshead and bream in the shallows. We hung out at the Walton Lodge with the other Black folks, leaning up on that open window to the bar where Uncle Tendris would buy cold beer for himself and orange Nehi for me. We had pretty good luck fishing, and we had time. The time was ours to do whatever the hell we wanted. The stories were good. About the time Tendris ran into the ghost of the blues legend, Robert Johnson, on that back road in Mississippi, not far from where he died for messing with someone else's girl. He'd sold his soul to the devil, but it only got him so far. No one really knows the whole story. But Robert Johnson laid a hand on Tendris and told him, "The devil in you, boy, but the music will save you." I believe it. That's what Tendris believed. The music can save anyone, from anything. But can it save me? I don't know. It didn't save Tendris. The juice got to him, and later, other stuff.

But I gotta say, I gotta shout it, he gave me a gift. He gave me a life. Tendris handed over his soul in that beat-up Martin. He taught me the chords, and that was it. I can feel 'em now if I try. That's all I needed to start, and then there I was, on the side of my cot in the laundry room, a box of Cheez-its and a bottle of Mountain Dew on the floor, and I didn't leave for days. So it seem. Millie called me to dinner but I wouldn't come. I couldn't, too stubborn and too crazy into it. When I get hold of something, you can't pry it from my chops. I listened to the blues and it seeped into me and out my fingers and onto those strings of the guitar. Time had no meaning and my soul seemed to leave my body and that was fine, and I wish it would now. Wish I'd never left.

THE BOYS OF ALPHA BLOCK

I can close my eyes tight. Millie out there, in the next room, clinking the dishes and stirring and cooking. I know she's there, listening. I know 'cause the dishes still, the air is full of nothin' but song. She'd say to whoever listen, "It's a marvel the way that boy play the guitar. Every chord, every lick bring me back to the Delta. Listening to that boy play."

I could not be still. My feet tappin', fingers pluckin' out them chords. That was the best time, moss hanging there, breezes and sand and shade. Cold drinks and salty possum squirrel pork and song.

Miralisa, her hair a black shiny curtain over one beautiful eye, the other smilin' at me.

We played and sang and ate and drank and laughed, and then the songs ended.

Tarvis stood and paced the cell. He knew exactly what it meant now when they said it. *The walls are closing in.* But he didn't want to think about it; it drove him too crazy. He could get out briefly for chow, a shower, and that was it. Something told him it was better that he think about that. For now. Those brief periods of freedom, such as it was. In the meantime, Haver, maybe Pilson, seemed to have it out for him. He couldn't stand the taunting, the yelling. He wanted to stash himself under his cot. For three years.

Out at the chow wagon, he'd caught the eye of a youth named Jesse Allen. Said it on his shirt. And some guy named Rick San Antonio. Allen, with his fingers giving street signs whispered, "Let's get the fuck outta here. Serious."

"Fur-ril?" Tarvis responded but kept a cool eye. San Antonio had nodded, his face turned to the mush on his tray. With the deputies hanging around the meal cart, that was about the extent of the conversation. Tarvis didn't know San Antonio. But Allen seemed a familiar face. Tarvis couldn't place him. Maybe they'd crossed paths in the hood, making a delivery or running a job. They'd run a lot when they were coming up. Mostly from the cops, sometimes from each other when things got too hot. When someone took a little more than was his due. Stepped on someone's dick. Checked out his female.

Tarvis would just have to wait on this one. What little he'd seen he knew Allen was a player. He had the eyes of the other youth on him. They looked to him to lead. But there was nowhere to go. Just a dead end.

He choked on a bitter laugh, but it felt good, like a deep stale breath had escaped from deep inside. It was dark and bottomless down there. He could hardly lift his head, much less his leaden arms and legs.

Tarvis fought to get Allen and San Antonio out of his head. He didn't want to go there now, get entangled in their schemes. Not yet anyway. He'd heard rumors in the shower that Allen was cooking up something, but Tarvis didn't want anything to do with it, or any of them, until he got his head clear and his feet on the ground. Get some idea about how to survive at Alpha. Once that happened, there could be possibilities. Figure this out. He didn't want to get ahead of himself. He'd already done that and look how it had turned out.

Fuck it all.

He stood on his cot and tried to peer out the high small window. Just a patch of light out there. A shaft of green from the palm trees. It was a bright and sunny day. Well, it was Florida. And he was missing it.

Tarvis climbed down, paced some more. The music in his head started up again. That was the saving of him. The music. He'd never played a song and sung it with no sound to it, but now he did. The "prison air guitar." And, of course, now he was completely sober. No weed, no orange and gin. No coffee table to leap over, only invisible strings at hand, which was his cousin Tommy's style on a Saturday night after downing most of a bottle of Hennessy. Even without a guitar, his fingers and his songs and his memory of how the words felt ran through his brain, like rain beating down on fire. Playing music to Tarvis was a blinding, time-eating thing, set to the key of his mood, and it calmed him. He could get lost in making the chords in his head. It put him to sleep, and it woke him up, playing over and over, bringing up new feelings and words each time he played.

He tried to make it happen, to coax out the chords and crackly sounds of Robert Johnson and Lead Belly, king of the twelve-string. He plucked away in that cell until he was there in a smoky, noisy cedar shack hidden among the live oaks in the swamp.

He lost himself in the music. He put Allen and his crazy ideas out of his head for now. He'd survive by inventing new songs. He needed paper and pencils, and he'd get those once they let him go to class. He still had his mind. If he didn't lose that, too. He was going to use the time, pretend he was home and Millie was cooking and humming, and the songs were coming, and Miralisa was swaying next to him. The songs were going to come. He couldn't stand the thought of his world without music. He'd just have to make do.

Until I can get out of here.

He picked at the chords, his long fingers straining the tendons in the back of his hand, and his mind broke out of the cell:

I will not throw my love away,
If I did, I would have to leave you
And I don't want to, still I
Got some things I want to say...
Yes, I love you too, don't you see, you can understand me,
Seems like I understand you too.

He could hear the song coming together, out of his head, and down his arm, and the notes carried him. The words rocked back and forth, not too fast, not too slow but rolling in a sequence that was sad but sure. He could see it nearly finished. The art of it was not like a painting, but more like a sunset with Miralisa standing there. Something beautiful and moving. Tarvis knew that every time he played the song it would glow and twist into something finer and stronger, like the branches of shiny new leaves. That is what he most loved about music. It was alive, and he brought it to life each time. He had to believe it so he didn't feel so dead.

The song was for Miralisa. She waited for him. She'd promised. Someday he'd find her again and play the song. In a new life.

He'd forgotten for a blissful moment or two that he was in this six-by-eight-foot cell, wearing this sorry, scratchy shirt. The aftertaste of soy balls—something they called meatballs—stuck in his mouth, even after he brushed his teeth. He was nauseous. He bent over, rested his elbows on his knees. Maybe they'd poisoned him on top of everything else. He wanted to lie down, but he wasn't supposed to do that. If the deputy caught him, he'd get written up—stroked red in the log. He'd have to endure yet another screaming deputy. He got up and paced, then hunched over on the metal chair bolted to the floor, his fingers covering his face.

With his eyes closed, his mind whirling, he tried to grasp the chords of the new music, but he was back there again at that food wagon with the awful smells and Allen and San Antonio and their sly looks. They wanted something from him, and he couldn't figure out what, and why. He had to give some thought to what they were up to because he knew they would not stop. Allen had a fever about him. He had some vague plan about getting the hell out of there. *What kind of shit is that?*

That's some shit. He lifted his head and looked at the bright light framed in the window. He had to listen to Allen and think on it. He said it out loud: "I have to get out of here." It sounded good, and futile, all at once. And stupid. No one heard him anyway.

CHAPTER TWELVE

A Plan like an Egg

YOUTH JESSE ALLEN SLID THE MOP ALONG the base of the wall under the windows outside Miss McBride's classroom, and he thought back to the day. The beginning of the end of his life. The day he got sent up to Alpha. He'd had a pretty good run on the streets, but it all stopped that fall day. You don't get somethin' for nothin' his Granny had told him. *She sure was right. I did somethin' stupid and got plenty of nothin'.*

The mop went back and forth, and he splashed the acrid water on the wall. He wanted to break the handle in half and run and scream. Jab one of those deputies in the eye. But, instead, he swiped, slow and easy. It would all get done soon enough. The hypnotizing motion calmed him down some, but it didn't erase the frustration. He remembered.

I looked at the clock on the courtroom wall, and time didn't move for me. Someone shouted, "Jesse Allen. Case Number 496-802 for the state of Florida."

"Here I am." I whispered.

Yeah, here, in deep shit and all because of that assault on the dumb security guard at the mall. Me and the boys. If only I hadn't held that blade against his fat gut... but then the knife opened and I was cracked in the head. In two minutes, the guard was dead. We all had knives, Bemby with the gun. Then he shoved it at me, stuck it in my jacket. One huge shit storm. The guard was a nobody. A drug dealer. And now I'm a nobody.

When I heard them shout my name and number in the courtroom, it was like a door slammed. It was something final, something awful. There I was. Just a pitiful human being with some regrets.

"All rise," said the guard. Honorable Judge Delia Adley was back on the bench.

"Be seated," she snapped. She glanced at me and seemed annoyed to see me in her courtroom, another juvenile offender. One after another.

The lawyers and the juvie officials talked about me. I had no parents or guardian to speak for me, though I felt my mother around me, in me. I saw her in the shape of my nose reflected in the window next to me. But I was alone. And then I heard a man I don't know. One of the lawyers warned me, I might get maximum security. He asked if I understood; what's to understand? I understood. I was fucked.

Judge Adley wasn't looking at him or at me. She was leafing rapidly through the papers. I was just another irritation in an otherwise boring day. An interruption she could do without. She fidgeted on the bench. Distracted. The crisp white collar inside her black robe didn't quite fit around her neck, and she pulled at the fabric. Her reddish hair was short and thin, like her. She looked uncomfortable. More than me? That wasn't good.

I heard more talk. Things were going from bad to worse. Words like, gun and knife. "He's a serious risk to public safety," said the state attorney. I wanted to yell, and plead with them, but then I was standing and it was too late.

"Jesse Allen, you are aware of the charges. Involvement in the murder of a known gang member. We have no proof of your personal choice to sell or profit from illicit materials. But, the fact remains, you were in possession of weapons deemed to be associated with the crime," said the judge. "I'm sending you to the level ten juvenile facility in Pokatoy for five years, or until your twenty-second birthday. Whichever comes first. The case will be reviewed, but I have no doubt you'll spend the next five years at the Alpha correctional center." Her voice was remarkably soft, and she hardly looked down at me, and still, her words hammered away.

Couldn't she see the remorse I felt?

What the fuck good would that do?

I couldn't help repeating the words I'd overheard. Over and over again in my head. "The worst of the worst." That would be me, Jesse Allen of Capo

THE BOYS OF ALPHA BLOCK

Verde, Florida. Some they call, "the best of the worst," but not me. I knew better. I always have. Yet, the system must see something good in me because I wasn't going to adult. She saw something, even though she wasn't looking at me.

"You are a lucky young man to be adjudicated as a juvenile. God help you." She pounded the bench with one small hand, surprisingly loud, echoing in my brain. I could feel the luck dripping off me. Oceans of it. Swimming in luck.

She was done. She glanced around the room at the lawyers and other suits. She signaled for the next case. I was done, all right; cooked real good. The lawyer walked away without saying a word. I felt like my skin had been stripped away. I was raw meat, ready for the hook, or whatever.

A deputy took me by the arm. I was walking, almost stumbling, out of the courtroom, a nice room I finally noticed, as if in a dream, a room with huge panes of glass framed in gold wood, sun streaming over the cream-colored walls, and long rows of wooden seats with red cushions. I felt warm in that room, the last place I'd see of the civilian world for a long while. I tried to get it all in before the lock-up. I had this cold feeling in my chest and stomach that wouldn't go away, no matter what I said to myself.

Then I was in a room with no windows. Stunned. The other guys were looking at me, up and down. I was sure nothing much to look at, maybe hundred-ten soaking wet, dressed in the faded, ragged denim of the detention center, my filthy feet scuffling along in brown sandals.

They knew what had happened. It'd already happened to them. I was about to go to hell. I turned my head away from them, and I tried not to cry. I could never show how weak I felt inside. I squeezed my eyes shut so it would all go away, but all I could picture was my mom, somewhere, getting the news that her baby was in the system. If she was still around; if she even got the news. She knew the system, where my dad and uncles and cousins have gone. Some of them were still there, and some never came out quite right or never came out at all.

I left them all there and got in the van. It was a nine-hour trip to Alpha Juvenile Correctional Center. Somewhere we stopped and went to the restroom, but I was half asleep. I didn't taste the ham and cheese on stale bread that was like paper in my mouth. I dozed off again. I wished I was on the beach with naked females at night, with a case of beer and a joint, and Tamaya and Raf and Mo. That was the last good time before all this shit happened, so fast, too fast.

The correctional center grew up out of the weeds in front of me. I could see it, not too far away, a grey block in all those green palms and vines. It looked terrible, solid and final. I felt shit upon. But, what the hell, I shit on myself, so who have I got to blame? I was staring at the razor wire that bordered the top of the high security fence at the Alpha. I wouldn't be getting out of there.

I wasn't even in there yet, and I knew I had to get out.

I shuddered and worried about what I'd done to myself, and about what they were going to do to me.

Then I was tossed out of the van. I landed on burning asphalt. A huge hand clamped down on me. Another deputy was there—like a large green animal with a gap in its teeth. He cleared his throat constantly and spit his brown juice on my foot. A heavy-set deputy gave me a look that meant he wanted to kill me, and every time he yelled, so did the other ones.

"This is hell," I said to myself, and it was really a useless thing to say because everybody already knew it.

Jesse Allen didn't give a damn about the floor, but he mopped anyway. He had some serious maneuvering to do, and the time had to be right. He had information to gather, a goal in mind—he had to pull this crew together. Didn't know when they were going to do it exactly, but it would be one day soon.

It was after six o'clock. The clean-up detail would be back in their cells soon, taking showers, lights out at nine. Allen's mind raced, his gaze darting around for the likes of Haver or another deputy.

Haver was making the rounds in the cell block. Allen couldn't see the deputy but he could hear him. He banged on the cell doors yelling stuff that made no sense at all. Just fucking yelling. Allen raised the mop head occasionally and deliberately to the wringer.

It was Haver's bedtime story. "Get those jammies on and keep your hands off your dicks." Haver pounded the metal doors until Allen's teeth were grinding. Allen imagined the deputy jackbooting down the walkway between the cells past his homies. What Allen usually did—what they all did—was peer out into the walkway, and for answer, Haver would bang the small window in their faces. Allen knew this ritual. Their nighty-night.

The deputy yelled, "What are you supposed to be doing, fuck-up? Staring out here? Go scrape your filthy mouth with that toothbrush or I'll have you use it around the toilet bowl."

Sometimes the words ran together in an unintelligible, mean stream of words from his loud mouth, his red face rock hard. Allen almost felt good that the deputy felt so bad, which was pretty clear from the miserable way he acted.

Allen listened to Haver all the while he kept mopping, hoping he could avoid running into him. Especially now. He gripped the mop handle until his fingers were numb. Allen wanted to take the mop and shove it down Haver's throat, but now was not the time, nor the place for that. Not quite yet. A smile crept over his face, as he dreamed of the day it might be possible to get back at Haver. Allen lived and breathed for it. During Allen's two years so far at Alpha, Haver had been relentless. He'd slammed Allen's hand in the locker, shoved him naked out of the shower and into the hallway, screamed in his face and in his ears so many times he swore he'd be deaf. Haver usually made sure there were no witnesses when he played, and he made sure bruises were not visible on faces and arms.

Things seemed to get worse every day. Always some new reg or irritation. They'd been wearing denim shirts and jeans, but now some were wearing stripes. It was a damn fashion show. They said the stripes would be better in "the prison setting" than the denim. They decided to phase in the switch in uniform. Most of the "wardrobe" was a mess of faded blue shirts and pants or dingy black and white pajamas, all of it embedded with the scum of bad washers and years of misery.

This was going to make the plan a bit more difficult if one day soon they were all wearing stripes. All the more reason to get on with this thing. Do it quick. Once on the outs, it would be hard to blend in, running down the highway, looking like a bunch of escaped zebras. Allen laughed out loud. *Maybe I send Miller a memo and tell him to stick with the denim.* Anyway, he had to tell cousin

Mo. They were going to need clothes.

Allen yanked at the ill-fitting black and white striped shirt that scratched and bunched in front. *One time we all looked like we fix washing machines. Now we look like the road gang from Alcatraz.*

The change of uniform didn't make the plan impossible. "All things are possible," Miss McBride said, and often. But she wouldn't be on the same track as Allen for this thing. Sure, she hated the stripes as much as the boys did, but she wouldn't approve of what Allen was cooking up.

She'd caught him coming out of the kitchen. Allen had seen her in the hallway coming into work, but it was too late to get out of the way. Duck back into the kitchen. He'd been sneaking around, all right. Checking the electric control panel near the sink. He'd almost blown it, but he was good at thinking on his feet. Or so he thought. Paper towels, yeah. He'd told her he was looking for the towels over the sink. Right next to the electrics set in the wall.

Problem ended up, he didn't have any towels. He was hoping she didn't pick up on that, but what the fuck? He couldn't think of *everything*.

Yeah, he had to think of everything. It was up to him, and the boys.

They had a lot to do if they were going to bust out of there. He needed Mo and the guys. It was going to be a real team effort.

He worried about the team. Just that morning, Haver had tripped Duval. Allen watched as Duval took a dive against the metal desk in the day room. Allen hadn't seen the whole thing, exactly, but he'd seen enough. He saw the look on Duval's face, and that hateful expression was a good thing. He'd be plenty pissed and ready and willing to do his job. He wouldn't complain. No one would listen anyway. Not a one. They had an abuse hot line, but there was a failure to communicate. Most of the time it took forever to get a response and when it came, the deputies ended up with the last laugh.

Yeah, they laugh. But they won't be laughin' soon 'nuff. They liked to laugh. One boy claimed he was a Muslim and couldn't eat pork and some of the other prison food. He ended up being a source of much razzing, and he got a new nickname—Al. Short for Al Qaeda.

Allen cracked his neck, tried to shake off the anxiety, and he swished a wave of dirty water over the concrete. *How much more we gonna take?* San Antonio, Tarvis, and Duval all felt the same way, and they were waiting for him. Now they were all going to do something about it, sure as shit. They each had a job. It had to get done or die.

They hadn't been able to *say* much to each other. Mumbling in the chow line and in the showers. Hand signals. Notes passed in line, under doors, and in books. The inmates of Alpha didn't know about the plan except for the four. But Allen couldn't count on it. This was another reason to get on with it. The *element of surprise* was numero uno. That old bag of shit Hathaway was right about that. They had to move fast, catch them off guard.

Thank you, Deputy Hathaway, for the history lesson.

Passing notes was harder since Duval busted up that English class. The deputies were up in their grills more than ever. Swanson had caught San Antonio making hand signals in the chow line. But the food cart was prime time. They were packed in together for meals. Just like the food groups dumped on the trays, they were a mish mash, all jumbled together. (In the case of the food served, all of it was barely edible. The potatoes were passable, and filling, especially with packets of chili pepper and Parmesan donated by a local pizza parlor.) Yet, Allen saw the advantage, and he would grab it. Somewhere in that mix, they had to get the message around to each other. There was plenty of confusion served up with those meals, and the opportunity was there. Even with the risk, this was the best time to exchange information, and timing was everything. San Antonio had gotten caught, but they had to keep trying. Mealtime was the time to *get it done.*

They had to eat. Allen read the distraction. The deputies were busy picking off the cart, anything expired, like the Little Debbies and Twinkies, and the carbs, the biscuits and French fries and fritters. All the stuff that Allen hoped would cause instant heart attacks. At mealtime, predictably, Haver was busy yelling, arguing, and shoving. If he wasn't in the line, he and some of the rest were checking the day room and cell blocks for contraband. Flipping mattresses. Tearing up their poetry and the soles of their shoes. Oddly enough, in the middle of all that chaos, when that meal cart rolled out, some days a sort of loose camaraderie crept along with it. Food sort of drew them together. Rarely and briefly, and strangely. Especially Fridays. Then Allen forced himself to let go of the worst feelings. He put on his most obedient face. The deputies loved to have their butts kissed while they were stuffing their faces with plastic brownies. Sugar was good.

At dinner, Bettinger, the Amazon, had waved a book in front of Allen's nose. "Hey, professor," she said. Allen took it, and then he got a good look at her fat round ass as she jiggled away from him.

"Dude," he mumbled to San Antonio. "Wonder what's in that sack."

San Antonio looked down at the grey dinner of peas and gravy. "Dunno, don't care."

They adapted, and they worked it. Masters of the sneak. And so, they managed. The deputies had ears and eyes, but they were lazy sometimes, no, often they were lazy, and they couldn't catch everything. Especially when they were joking and eating crap in master control, feet on the desks, their noses in magazines.

Allen had few illusions. *We're all dumb asses or we wouldn't be in here.*

But the deputies were the biggest, greenest, fattest dumb asses in the world. They didn't catch it all, they hardly caught any of it.

And thank God for education. Miss Caroline, with her books, you gotta love her. The books are a good way to pass the plan.

Funny thing was, he'd really gotten to like reading. When he told Cousin Mo that he liked books, Mo laughed so hard he almost fell onto the concrete in the day room. "Whaaaaat? You gotta be playin' me, J," he'd said. But it was true. Jesse Allen knew he'd be a reader the rest of his life, however long that lasted, and he was so desperate now, he didn't care how long it lasted.

The books and the classes were going to help them get over. Do some communicating of their own. In fact, the classroom is where he was headed now. He looked through the glass. It was dim in there, but he had to get in before his duty was up, cleaning that floor for the thousandth time. He slammed the mop into the bucket, maybe a bit too hard.

Allen had less than fifteen minutes before he had to be back in his cell. Staff was short, the holiday was coming up. That was another consideration. Staff count. It was the quiet time, except for Haver's occasional outburst.

It gave Allen the damn shivers to think on it. The day of the breakout. So many pieces to put together to make it happen. If they pulled it off, he'd be long gone to Mexico. His cousin, Terrence, already had the passports, fake as shit, but they'd work. Guaranteed to work or Terrence would go back to these counterfeiting goons and have a pointed discussion with them. With something pointy, like the blade Terrence carried for such things. He had to get hold of his other cousin, the magnificent Mo, pronto. He'd promised to help with most of the set up. Freedom, tequila, weed, females. Maybe a little shack in Monterey.

Allen dreamed on, guided the bucket with the mop handle. Checked around again for Haver. Soon the deputy would wrap up his rounds of checking cells.

A door to the cell block slammed. And, suddenly, Haver was there. He walked by Allen, and Allen jumped. "Sir, sir." The required acknowledgment was automatic, but it grated on the youth. "Sir" was a term of respect; Haver deserved a good kick in the ass. But should Allen forget to address him properly, Haver would stroke him, and enough of that would only make trouble. Increase the misery, decrease his ability to get out of his cell for duty. And planning.

The deputy shoved the mop with his boot, sneered at Allen, and moved on. He'd be back around, sure as shit. In the meantime, it was down time. The quiet worked to Allen's advantage. The deputies had their guard down. Goofing off. They were careful to keep records in master control away from prying eyes, but it didn't matter how much they tried. The mop was a perfect vehicle for cruising past the window. Floor had to be clean, and that meant under the windows, too. Allen wanted a quick look.

The ledgers and schedules were often left exposed on the desk in master control, and Allen and the rest of them read the numbers as they passed by the windows on the way to class or back to the cell block or chow line. It didn't seem to matter what lengths the deputies took to keep the books closed to them; someone, at some time, *always* left those books open. The boys cataloged what they saw in their heads, they figured out the numbers, and came up one hundred percent sure of the schedule each day. Allen gathered it all and kept track. The boys picked off information from badges and receipts and identification cards that the teachers and administration left around. Youth Marcus Tolby—who knew Martin Luther King's "I Have a Dream" speech word for word—once memorized the Visa number off paperwork left lying on a table in the day room. He then passed the card number along to his girlfriend, who in turn used it at a big box store to buy herself a new TV, some gas, and a phone card for Tolby. Mr. Fraggert, the visiting special education counselor who had left the number on the table when it fell out of a folder, had been the victim of the fraud. He'd been perplexed at the purchases and had them removed from his bill. But the word went around Alpha: Be careful what you leave under the watchful, photographic eyes of Youth Tolby, and others.

Tonight, Allen noted something else on that desk in master control, besides the ledgers: Bettinger's cigarettes and lighter. That gave him another idea, as if he didn't have enough of them running around in his brain. He also saw the key box high on the wall, and he was sure there were weapons, cuffs, mace in there somewhere. Tarvis had to sweet talk his way in there and check it out. *Well, I have to sweet talk Tarvis into doing it. But he's coming around.*

This was the stuff he could use. The lay of the land in master control. He had to work it all into the plan. That, and the mood of the place. He, and the others, were good at sensing the mood, like cows could sense a storm coming.

CHAPTER THIRTEEN

Crack It

ALLEN WAITED UNTIL SWANSON'S HEAD was turned away from the desk in master control. Allen peeked through the wide windows and saw they were light on deputies. This was a useful piece of information. Anything was useful.

Swanson had it down tight, except the clipboard was in plain sight with few signatures. Paperwork was scarce, most of the manuals were in place, and no coffee cups and donuts were scattered around. Staff was short—short-handed, maybe hungover, whatever. Allen had to figure it in, long term, and short term. Keep his own record and track the trends. Crunch it like a computer. He had to be patient. And once he figured it out, he would convince the others about what to do next. One problem was, they were not patient. In this, they must be or the plan would go bust.

Allen moved like a cat. Careful, easy, sly. The talent wasn't developed at the correctional center. He'd been called The Cat on the outside, for his ability to pour through a crack, melt quietly into a burglary scene. They should have called him "Rat," Mo said. "Yo melts mo like a rat than a cat." A talent developed out of a necessity. If his father, or his uncle, laid eyes on him, it was lights out for Allen. Allen had learned to size up the level of drunkenness, despair, and anxiety that roiled in his father's blood at any given time, and quickly he'd learned when to make himself scarce. Before the blows landed. Allen knew he should be dead, but he wasn't. He only felt like he was withering away, his soul shrinking in the hideous grey world of the prison.

The instinct for survival pushed him, and now he had to get the information around to each of the boys. Every day, he took it one step closer. Out the goddam door.

Tarvis was the guy. Allen was sure Tarvis was coming around just fine. He was miserable enough, and he was cool, smooth. Allen had seen that in Tarvis right off, despite his slouching around. There was more strength there than resignation, and in the two years Allen had been at Alpha, he'd seen a lot. Tarvis also had the latest information from the outside, especially about what he'd learned at the detention center. Had staff increased? What other resources were they using for tracking and record keeping? The more information, the better. What was that Miss McBride said all the time? Knowledge is power. *Oh yeah.* Tarvis had it going on. He was calm, too. They needed a talker, someone who could get into master control and look around. Tarvis was the man. Fresh, yeah, and no track record or pile of grudges with the deputies. Not yet anyway.

San Antonio was good with tools. They needed weapons, shivs, anything to threaten and thrash their way out, if it came to that, and no doubt it would. And Duval was ammunition. Crazy. He'd do anything to get out. He was fire in the hole. Literally. Allen had a special plan for Duval.

It had taken a while to figure this out. No one new had come in for a while. And then Tarvis had come to Alpha. He ignited the whole thing. Seemed he also set off a new round of abuse and tension among the deputies. Maybe it was coincidence, but still, it was happening. He could feel it. Duval went off the rails, but that was Duval.

Two years is enough of this place. Time to go.

The water in the bucket sloshed on to his leg. Out of nowhere, Haver yelled, "Hey, fuck up, watch it. Or I'll stick your damn head in there."

Allen jumped. He had to get out of there. If he didn't kill Haver first.

Allen kept his head down.

It was time.

He sidled closer to the door of the classroom that opened from the day room. The fumes of cleaning fluid were making his eyes water, but he ignored the stinging; wiped his eye with a cuff of his stiff shirt. The deputy in master control would be watching him, and Allen didn't like the scrutiny. He had an aversion to it. He hugged the walls, ducked into the laundry room, presumably for cleaning supplies, and then snuck out. Haver was gone. Allen resumed his mopping along the wall of windows of Miss McBride's classroom.

Allen blended into the dull grey light, difficult but not impossible in the early evening. Nothing but a shadow. The low sun shined through the windows on the west side of the building.

He looked up at the corners of the day room where tiny cameras recorded comings and goings. Allen cursed to himself: He looked down at his new black and white stripes. At least it wasn't permanent, so far. All the uniforms hadn't changed over. Eventually, he would make those stripes un-permanent. But for now, maybe the boys could get hold of enough of the denim. The blue would give them some measure of shade, help them blend in on the outs. They would just have to work at it.

He went for it. Hoping the deputy would bite. Allen signaled to Deputy Swanson in master control and pointed to the mop. He made a sweeping motion toward the classroom. Swanson bit. He buzzed Allen through to the classroom. Allen reached for the handle and in one beat, he was inside. Thankfully, the sun barely lit the room through a tangle of palm trees and vines outside the high narrow windows. The lights outside switched on, and this was another feature that Allen noted. He could see the faint spotlights shining through the trees around the correctional center. Another point to put in the brain; better to have a day-time breakout. But, for now, Allen focused on the mission. The shadows in the classroom gave him cover. He had permission to be in there. He needed to be quick.

Allen glanced up at the cameras. Staff only recorded fifteen seconds of activity at a time. Then the cameras switched off for fifteen seconds. And so the cycle went. He was oh-so happy with that piece of intel from San Antonio, who'd picked it off the gossip vine. Allen hoped he could make his move within the blank space of seconds, or at least cut into it for his detour.

His target was a small office slash storage room that opened off the back of Miss McBride's classroom.

He crouched down along the classroom wall, all the while dragging the mop, and slid close to the office door situated between two bookcases. If he was lucky, he could make it into the small room and out again during the interval that the cameras didn't record. It was a long shot, but the whole plan was a long shot and one that Allen had to take. The door to the office had a small window, and he'd already cased inside. He was smooth, and small, and that is why he had chosen himself for the job. San Antonio, Tarvis, and Duval had other jobs to do, and this was one of his.

Allen pretended to jab at the corners of the classroom with the mop. He opened the door to the little back office and was inside in seconds. It took him one more second to snatch the cordless phone out of the cradle on the desk. He stuck it in the waist band of his briefs. He didn't have a pocket, thanks to the zebra suit; now he felt like he was carrying around a large plastic dick in his shorts. *Just what I need.* He slid out of the office, low to the floor like he was scrubbing, or looking for something. *Keep a low profile,* his dad and uncles had warned. It was a rule.

He grabbed the bucket and the mop and continued his way around the classroom in and out among the desks, past the bookcases. If anyone asked, he was just doing his duty. He bent down to swipe a thin film of chalk dust off the floor.

He'd done it. A dull thrill gripped him, a small thing but a big step. This phone. He had one more piece of the plan, and now the phone jiggling in his pants made him think of the next step. He had to get rid of it. Temporarily. And at some point, he had to use it.

He glanced up at the camera. There was no blinking light or other signal that the thing was recording him. *Am I recorded there? Will they check it?* He might be on the footage, and maybe not. He just hoped he hadn't been caught slipping in and out of the back office.

Allen looked through the windows of the classroom into the day room. No deputy. It was quiet, and empty. He buzzed master control to get out.

He wondered: *Will I have a surprise waiting? Has anyone seen me?*

The silence was scary, shrouding him in fear. It was the calm before the yelling, the dark into which he stumbled. He should take some deep breaths, or just shut the fuck down. He had absolutely no control over his surroundings. He had no way of knowing what might come at him out of the quiet.

Still nice and calm. He'd take it. Allen wasn't sure of anything at Alpha. But, for now, it seemed he was safe.

He mopped his way back around the day room pushing the bucket. He checked around for Haver. He'd heard the deputy yelling at some poor dumb fuck in C wing, but for now it was all clear in his area. Swanson had his head down over the control board, talking on the phone, scratching his ass. Whatever. That was one thing Allen was counting on; the lackadaisical, fucked-up, intermittently careless staff at Alpha. These were the cracks in the system. They needed to be wide enough to slip through. Otherwise, they'd never make it out of there.

He was bent over the mop in the bucket and about to sidle into the laundry closet when he saw the green serge legs. Allen's eyes went from the black leather belt with mace and stick attached to the beefy chest of the deputy and the expression full of mean pleasure. Allen froze. He kept as straight a gaze as he could muster. He prayed, such as it was, that his expression did not give him away.

He sprang back a step. "Sir, sir," he said. Upright, the phone jiggled loose in his pants.

Stay, phone. If you don't, I'm a dead man.

He looked straight ahead. He was determined to absorb whatever abuse Haver wanted to dish but he couldn't afford any physical contact with the deputy. He eyed the door to the laundry. He hoped Haver had other boys to torture so he would spare him, let him pass. Save some for later.

"What-the-fuck-do-you-think-you-are-doing, Allen." It was not a question but a loaded accusation. It was clear from the look on Haver's face that Allen was a major-scumbag-piece of shit. Haver never missed a chance to remind the youth of his place in the classification of all things.

"Sir, I was mopping up, sir."

"Yeah, I see that, but you are dawdling. Taking too much sweet time." Haver rocked back on his boots. "And what the fuck were you doing on the floor?"

"Sir?"

"In the classroom, numbnuts. I saw you on the floor."

"I dropped something, sir."

"What did you drop? Your goddamn brains?"

"Sir, no, sir, a book, sir."

Haver muttered something about the "f-ing books again," and his face took on the hue of a bruised tomato. "Oh, yeah? Poking around in the classroom, Allen? In the dark." Haver glanced through the tall windows into the dusky classroom. "Well, where is it?"

"Sir, what, sir?" Allen was so rattled he forgot the lie he made up.

"The book, goddam-you-jackass, the book."

"Sir, I left the book under the desk, sir. On the rack under the desk, sir, sir."

"I'm gonna stroke you, Allen, and you better finish up that floor detail double time and get to showers before I get ideas about what to do with your ass, do you understand, Allen?"

"Sir, yes, sir."

He kept his eyes down. He wondered if Haver had seen him open the back door inside the classroom. It was hard to tell with all the blustering, but he would have said something. He would have *done* something.

Allen made a point of reading the deputies, but this latest exchange caught him off guard, flustered him more than he wanted to admit. Haver must not have seen what he was up to, or the deputy would have done something *bad*. He was safe on this one. A sigh of relief loosened his constricted chest, and his knees ceased to wobble in fear. Allen would take the reprieve. He had to be more careful, and quicker. There were several maneuvers coming up, and if one of them failed, they could all go down. The sweat beaded his back and forehead just thinking about getting caught.

But Haver was surprised. No doubt about it. That's cool. The element of surprise was crucial. Allen was learning something new every day. The thought of it calmed him down. He steeled himself, relieved at the sound of Haver stomping off.

He picked up the mop and bucket and headed to the laundry closet where he cleaned the equipment and put it away. He peeked out the door into the day room, but the deputy had not come back. The area was deserted. The dinner carts were rolled away, out of the day room and down the hall. Allen took the phone out of his pants and stuck it behind the washing machine as far away as possible from the front of the machine where Youth Ramon—always starving—had stashed several expired packages of Little Debbie fudge brownies. He hoped the mice and roaches didn't carry away the phone with the brownies.

So far, so good. The deputies didn't do laundry, and they certainly wouldn't be searching the closet for a phone. Allen felt he could count on that. At least, this part was done, right under their noses.

Allen grabbed a brownie and stuck it in his mouth. Threw the wrapper in the corner. Fuck it. He chewed on a sweet victory, of sorts. All he had to do was figure out how and when to use the phone. To call the cousins. Mo was coming to visit soon, and Allen had to figure out what to do. He'd dump the phone after the call. Miss McBride and the rest of the staff hardly ever used the office, which was more of a storage closet. He'd made sure of that. She liked to use the classroom where she had a desk and file cabinet and all the books she got so excited about. It was too bad Duval had made such a mess. Bad timing. He was glad Duval was pissed, but he'd told him in the chow line to lay low, shut up. They couldn't afford to stir it up. Just yet. Time for that soon enough.

They wouldn't miss the phone, and if they did, tough shit. It's the chance he'd take. They couldn't trace it to him. He wanted to get it back to the office or get rid of it. Right now, he needed that phone.

They needed a car. Maybe. Either that or they'd just have to run. Or get one of the cousins to ride them out. It was why he'd gotten the phone, to check with Mo on the details. Allen thought about it. He was on the lookout for cars in the staff lot. And he'd had the others on the lookout. A narrow window in the kitchen gave them a view of the lot, another way to see outside was from the nurse's office. They could see the rows and rows of sedans and trucks lined up and only guess who drove what.

They read the license plates with their laser-like eyesight. Mo, who knew someone with good "research" skills, had found out that Miss McBride drove that old Cadillac in the lot.

"Tell me how that baby ride, Miss Caroline... How you like that color, what, that purpley-tan-shiny paint job... You must be stashin' crid to drive a car like that, Miss Caroline." Wembley or Gomez or one of those stupid fucks had piped up.

She just chuckled, but it sounded like a real uncomfortable chuckle. She had that look—*How could they know, how they could see?*

But Allen had his eye on that Cadillac. *How hard would it be to hot wire it?* Probably pretty difficult. Had to be an older model, '93 or '94, maybe seven, eight years old at least. He'd check it out with Mo. Damn, he was glad to have that phone.

ALLEN CLOSED THE LAUNDRY CLOSET. Head down, he shuffled back toward the door to the cell block. He stopped the scurrying. Swanson was blabbing away and stuffing his mouth with crap in master control. Allen's eyes flicked to the corner of the day room, his mind moving at a clip. He hadn't noticed the large industrial waste can outside Miss McBride's classroom. Pushed in the corner. Full to the brim. Books, pages, torn notebooks.

Paper. Lots and lots of it.

Paper burns!

He pressed the intercom to master control. "Sir, the can." He gestured to the corner. "All right if I carry it down to the waste closet, sir?"

"Hurry it up and don't stop at McDonald's on the way."

Allen hopped to it, grabbed the lip of the can, and headed down the hallway toward the waste closet next to the unused kitchen. Tucked it out of the way. Ready for use.

Oh, Mr. Duval, sir, Julius, you dick, you gonna have some work to do. You gonna burn, man.

CHAPTER FOURTEEN

It's All Right, Uh-Huh

IT WAS A COUPLE OF DAYS AFTER THEY'D wrecked the classroom, but Caroline was still taping the pages and picking through the battered remains of *Literature: Flights and Fantasy.*

How appropriate. Flights of flying books.

She'd dragged an industrial-size waste can into the classroom and dumped most of the broken textbooks and the ripped pages.

Now she glanced into the corner in the day room and noticed the can with the torn books and pages was gone. She'd thought of rescuing some of the pages, but it was too late. *So clean around here, always tidying and mopping and throwing out stuff... Ironic. Even I have to throw out books.* It pained her to throw away a book, but what good were they? Without a complete set of texts, she had to invent new lesson plans with stories from various books off the shelves.

Will Bonner sauntered into the day room, put one boot on a metal stool, gestured to Deputy Swanson. As if Will had turned on his Caroline radar, he looked up and saw her watching him through the window of the classroom. He smiled. His whole face lit up. His hands stopped in mid-air. *Beautiful hands,* Caroline noted. Square and smooth. She smiled back and turned to her desk. Swanson walked away.

Not a minute later, she heard the key in the lock and Will was walking toward her. A whiff of limey cologne. Bay rhum? He always looked and smelled like he'd stepped out of a spa.

"Hey." He smiled but he was clearly concerned. "You okay?"

She hunched her shoulders and swept a hand over the leftover books, posters, and papers. "I guess we've seen better days." She fell into her chair but her eyes didn't leave his. "And now I am looking at the best thing all day."

"Thing?"

"Person."

His eyes sparkled, the corners crinkling. She longed to touch him but then glanced up at the cameras.

"Meet you there? Say, thirty minutes?" He nearly whispered although no one could hear them. His eyes shifted to the back of the room. To their private meeting place.

"Uh-huh. I'll be waiting." That's what they did. They looked for, and found, the right time together. As many times as they could. For the fun of it. For the danger.

That familiar thrill shot through her. She never got tired of that husky voice, his hands, his expression that took her in and left the rest of the world out. The longing she had to be with him.

It only seemed to grow more in the years since she met him, soon after she took the job. There was so much paperwork, and Will wanted to help. She'd had to file forms with the new education department at the correctional center, and he was the deliverer of the boring stack of folders and regulations. He'd found his way to her house near the bay, a small ranch hidden behind an overgrown palm tree. She'd bought the house ten years before, after fleeing a bad marriage to a bully in Chicago. Her father had lived with her until recently, until the stroke took him.

That afternoon, she heard the car crunch the shell drive and watched as Will came up the walk, the sun glinting off the buckle at his waist where the front of a white t-shirt was tucked into tight jeans. Very long legs, slightly bowed. His boots pounded the flagstone. Her heart did the same dance. He was handsome as hell but she couldn't even think about it. It would never work between them.

He'd lifted a hand to knock on the door. She was wearing a pareo over her bathing suit, and she'd just slathered herself with coconut oil.

She noticed his cologne, something citrusy like limes or lemons.

He'd sniffed and laughed. "We smell like a fruit salad. Together." His eyes were just about the darkest shiny pools she'd ever seen, and she fell right in.

She asked him in for a beer, and one thing led to another. The day was hot. *Perfect for a swim in the pool.*

He sat down in the lounge chair on the lanai. His eyes didn't leave her as she walked through the glass doors to the kitchen and returned with two Coronas.

She handed him the cold beer, their hands touched. That first time, lasting and electric. His skin was smooth, and hers rough from pulling the incessant weeds around her house that threatened to bury her. They hadn't looked back from that moment, it seemed to her, although there were complications to consider. She was divorced from a bully, he was separated from a whacko wife. He was Black. She was white.

Caroline liked to remember that night, how they'd slipped into the pool, both of them half dressed. Then, nothing at all. From then on, the only thing that ever mattered was him. He was one of the reasons she stayed in prison.

She studied him now, leaning over her classroom desk, and wished they were swimming instead. He had a worried look on his face.

"I'm okay. Really," she said.

"You better be. I'll see you. Soon." He grinned at the camera, gave a thumbs up, and put his arm around her.

"Will!" But she smiled. She couldn't wait until he came back.

Caroline stacked the tattered literature books and scanned the titles in the bookcase. She grabbed a Mark Twain and a Richard Wright. Humor and empathy and truth. *We could use some of that...*

But her mind wasn't on the mess of books. It was hard to concentrate for a variety of reasons, and Will was at the top of that list.

She glanced into the day room. She knew he wouldn't come back around to meet her until the coast was clear. The boys were all back in their cells, the deputies were changing shift.

The day room was empty except for Deputy Brown and Youth Duval hunched over one of the metal tables bolted to the floor. It was rare the room was not occupied, except in the afternoon; each morning, there was always an

IEP (individual education plan) to draw up, a tutoring session, a chaplain visit. Sometimes, Deputy Brown would sit at a table, playing chess with one of the boys. But not today. He and Duval weren't playing games. She could vaguely hear Brown's rumbling voice. Duval wasn't talking. His head was down, almost touching his shackled wrists folded on the table.

The deputy leaned on his massive, folded arms. His head was like a large block, given his choice of haircut, and he fixed a stern expression on Duval whose face was set in a determined state of misery. He didn't move, but Brown became animated, waving his hands, and then slapping them flat on the table.

Caroline heard the muffled order. "Sit up straight, Mr. Duval." The youth twisted on the stool and snapped upright. The deputy reminded Caroline of a bear, large and imposing. But bears had their quiet moments. Brown sat back, hands still planted, and waited. She couldn't hear anything he was saying, but, clearly, they were communicating.

Caroline went back to the papers on her desk, but every minute or so she'd look over at Brown and Duval. And then the deputy hoisted himself off the stool and walked across the day room. He took out his keys and opened the classroom door a crack.

"Miss McBride, sorry to bother you," he said, lowering his head slightly, his manner shy. "Would you have a minute to step out here?"

She popped up. "Of course." She put down her book and followed him out of the classroom.

Caroline stood next to the table. Duval peered up at her and slowly got to his feet. "I didn't tell you you could stand," said Brown. Duval clapped his rear onto the stool.

Brown took a position on the other side of the table. "Stand up now. Pay attention to orders." The deputy's forehead glistened. With effort? Duval fidgeted. Caroline peered at him, but she couldn't see the dark hatred of the butterfly-day flurry. He seemed calmer, and she hoped he would shake off the physical as well as the mental uneasiness. It was cool in the day room, as usual. He avoided her eyes and shivered, but he had to put up with it. Duval's grey, withdrawn appearance was not from the air conditioning but probably from the burden of choices he'd made.

"Youth Duval has something to say," said Brown, nudging Duval. The boy studied Caroline. He had unusual eyes, almond-shaped and slanted upwards. An arresting face, a handsome face when it wasn't emotionally charged with desperation. Did he know how unique he was? What potential such a strong, handsome kid had?

Caroline wished she could make him see it, but only Duval could see it for himself. It was in her stubborn nature to stay at Alpha and try to *make* him see it. To make them all see it. She didn't know where she got some of the notions that shot through her brain. It was a regular ping-pong match in there. She spent too much time deep in her imagination, thinking of ways to repair the past, to make their lives better, but she couldn't do it for them. She tried to lead them to it, not telling them *what* to do but *how* to find better ways inside themselves. She couldn't do it without following Will's lead, and Deputy Brown's.

Leading them to alternatives, to books and writing. To long-term thinking about a better future. Each one different. Each book, each boy. She held on, hoping the boys and books would match up and spark something in each other. Open some doors. She handed them books by Hurston, Hughes, Ellison, Carson, Baldwin, Wright—authors who came from backgrounds similar to theirs. They endured. Inspired. Each was unique, each from a different experience. Whatever each one of them wrote, and thought, reflected their own individuality that no one could take away from them. And the more the boys read about those lives, the stronger they would become. She bet on it.

Duval had further opportunity in the person of Deputy Brown. She had some sway, but she was not delusional. She saw the scope of it for what it was. It was Deputy Brown—and Will—who could really help Duval make some changes and change his way of thinking. They were the real leaders, the mentors, and examples of how to be: firm, strong, principled, and gentle.

The deputy nudged Duval again.

"Sorry," said Duval. It was a sullen whisper.

"I'm sorry WHAT," said Deputy Brown. "WHAT were we talking about?" His voice rose with each word, and his face was close to Duval who had not answered correctly with the proper address. Brown was not so much harsh as insistent.

"Ma'am, Miss McBride, I'm sorry, Ma'am."

"Sorry for WHAT?"

"Ma'am, for jumping Youth Clemente, Ma'am."

"And WHAT ELSE?" The deputy did not usually handle the boys, but this time he shoved Duval, gently, in the chest.

"Ma'am. And for messin' up your classroom, Ma'am."

"That's better." Brown leaned back slowly. She didn't move. There was something in the moment, of connection and civility, that was well worth savoring. The three stood quietly in the day room while the prison ticked around them. A door slammed. The smell of disinfectant made her eyes water, but she focused on the deputy and Duval. The rest of the boys were in their cells studying. The deputies were doing paperwork, and Caroline, Deputy Brown, and Youth Duval were making some kind of progress. At least this was her perception. The boy looked from the deputy to the teacher. Almost hopeful, but he seemed uncomfortable under the scrutiny and at once desperately needful of attention.

Brown was a parent to the inmates. A stiff and unconventional kind of parent at times, but Brown pulled it off. Duval was a kid, and Brown whispered a correction, or put a hand on his shoulder. Some days, sometimes, it worked. Caroline could see the spark, the hint of a smile, a nod of acceptance because Brown took the time and relieved the misery. Now, at least the usual dark, angry expression lightened up. Duval stood up straighter, the cuffs jangling in front of him.

"Thank you, Mr. Duval. I accept your apology," said Caroline. "Of course, I do."

He fixed her with a level gaze. Brown peered at Duval. "Tell Miss McBride why you tore up her class. No bullshit, now. Tell it to her straight."

Duval hesitated. Ambivalence flitted across his face.

"Truth ain't nothing but freedom," said Brown. "It's one way of letting the whole incident go so it be way gone."

Duval didn't look so certain that would be the case. But he pulled his shoulders back and looked at Caroline.

"Ma'am, I hate that youth, ma'am," said Duval softly.

Brown's eyes stayed on Duval with a ferocity. "Yeah, and you hate the devil, too. Now, out with it."

"Ma'am, Youth Clemente. He buy into that white sh… ma'am," said Duval. "He buy into the white *culture* and the words and feelin's and poems. Ma'am." He stopped then and looked straight over Caroline's head. At nothing but a bare concrete wall.

"Culture, huh. Maybe you are learning something, Duval. You comin' out with words like that and all. Keep going," said Brown. "You need to be straight, man. But you need to be fair, and respectful." He shifted from one boot to the other, a smile beginning at the corners of his mouth.

"What do you mean, Mr. Duval?" She wanted to hear more. They were getting through to each other. But it was difficult under the harsh conditions and in such stilted language.

Duval remained calm. Deputy Brown stepped closer into their tight-knit circle. His large arms crossed behind his back, he glowered at the youth. "Yes, Mr. Duval, what do you mean?" asked the deputy.

She said, "Youth Clemente tries hard in class. You have to give him that. He tries."

Caroline searched Duval's for a hint of acceptance.

"Yeah, but he ain't white," blurted Duval.

Brown's expression was intense. "No, of course he's not white. He's Black," he said. "No one's taking his Black away from him, or from you, by putting another idea into that head of yours, Duval. You need more ideas besides the ones you got. You got plenty of ideas that put you in here. Maybe you need some fresh ideas to get you out of here and on to better things. Maybe you could use a poem or two or three. Poems is feeling, man, and you need some new feelings."

"Yes, sir, ma'am. 'Spose so, sir, ma'am."

Caroline looked from Brown to Duval and back again.

That about sums it up. Deputy Brown has found exactly the right words. Leave the whole place to Brown.

Duval's face settled into darkness again, but he seemed resigned to consider the deputy's words. The kid desperately needed a time out. Right now, with Brown, he was in a different place, with different choices to consider. He was safe and secure and off the street, and for the moment Haver wasn't spewing all over him. One step backward and one step forward. It was a regular dance, and Caroline hoped this was one major step forward.

She silently thanked Brown. Youth Duval stared straight ahead, seeming neither angry nor afraid. Neutral. The business of the classroom brawl was behind him. Caroline sighed. Maybe something good would come out of that mess after all. Maybe the idea for a fresh start was planted in Duval's head and it was sitting there, ready to root. She'd find out soon enough.

"We hate what we don't know, son," said Brown. "We fear what we don't know. You have to realize that, and it don't hurt to learn as much as you can. It's the only way to save yourself, to get over the hate, and the fear. Make yourself a better man."

Duval's head snapped around at the deputy. "Sir, yes, sir."

The deputy motioned Duval in the direction of the door to his cell block. "And one more thing. You don't fight hate with hate, you fight it with love. A great man said that once…" He scratched his head. "Martin Luther King, I think. And, of course, Jesus."

Duval was brooding again, sunk into the prison of his own making. But, clearly, he had listened.

Caroline saw Will striding down the hallway toward the day room. He stopped in master control. Her heart skipped. She'd see him soon.

She smiled at Deputy Brown as he unlocked her classroom and held the door open. The deputy turned to escort Duval back to his cell.

"Thank you," she called after him. It seemed inadequate for all he did and said.

"The thanks are mine to give." He opened the door a little wider and nodded at her with a smile.

It was nearing mealtime, a busy break in the daily schedule. Most of the deputies were in the cell block or the hallway, mustering the boys, individually checking each one for infractions, and setting up the food carts down the hall at the side entrance for service later in the day room.

Will would be careful. Slip into Caroline's classroom unnoticed. He was good at that. If he was on camera, it was unlikely anyone would check. And what if they did? He was allowed. She went to the small back office of her classroom and waited there for him.

"How you doin'?" He popped in quietly behind her, moving quickly toward her. "Just fine. Now," she said.

His hands moved up her arms. "I worry about you. And I'm not just talking about the boys. Haver and the lot of them are useless in this shit storm. They seem to stir up more trouble than anything."

She leaned into his chest and pressed her cheek against that fine shirt. She sighed. "We live in a shit storm, Will. We all know that. At least that's something we can agree on."

"Yeah, but when they start throwing books and desks and chairs. I don't know. It's getting bad."

"That's kind of why I wanted to see you. That. And the other." She smiled at him, a secret lighting up her eyes.

"I like the other better."

She laughed, but his lips covered her mouth, and traveled down her neck. She thought she'd fall, her legs growing weak, but he held her fast. "Be careful."

"I am. See how much I care?" She put her hands around the back of his neck and looked him in the eye. His smile warmed her, gave her strength. They gave each other strength. "Besides, if I didn't care, they wouldn't be able to get out of their cells and get all those nice books."

He held her away from him. "You're so strong. And stubborn. Never met anyone like you." He kissed her forehead and then ducked his head to the side. "What about working admin?"

She was mildly irritated now. "What about it? Do you have someone in mind?"

He laughed. "You." He kissed her again, his shoulders folding around her. So tall, so hard, and so *soft*. His lips, his touch. She held on to the moment, a fleeting moment, before they had to go back to grim reality. She forgot all about her fear, the incessant buzzing in her ear that something was wrong because now everything was right.

They stood like that, not moving, and then he held her tighter. Next, their feet were steering them, together, like they were on the dance floor, and then they were in the corner, wedged between a filing cabinet and the wall, and his hand was moving up her thigh. Her head back, loving the feel of him all around her.

"Caroline," he said. "I can't help myself."

"I can't either."

They came apart, finally, and fell against the wall, holding hands. Their heads touched and neither said a word, their breathing and hearts pacing with each other.

Caroline straightened up. She yanked on Will's hand. "Do you see something missing? On the desk?"

Will was staring at the ceiling, a grin plastered on his lips. "Uh-uh. Nothing missing here," He squeezed her hand. He glanced around the small room. "Your antique Buddha and that dusty Victorian tea set. It's all here. Nice decorating." He stuck his face into the soft place below her ear.

"Will!" She tugged at him. "Look. Don't you see?"

He nonchalantly studied the desk. A half-dead dracaena, a can of pencils, a blotter with a five-year-old calendar. "Nope." He said. "Oh!"

He still held her hand. He reached for the empty phone cradle and looked at Caroline. "Somebody gonna call Mommy?"

CHAPTER FIFTEEN

Metal to Whip It

YOUTH RICK SAN ANTONIO SAT ON THE EDGE of his cot in his cell and turned the plastic binder over and over in his hands. He had homework to do, but he was not supposed to be sitting on his bed to do it. He could get caught and written up, so he had to listen carefully for that fuck head, Deputy Haver, who would soon be coming around screaming through the cell block to announce lights out. At least there would be some peace after that, from nine until five the next morning, when the noise and the mayhem of living at Alpha would start all over again. It never seemed to end. But he was going to end it—for himself, Allen, Tarvis, and maybe that poor son of a bitch, Duval. He'd be the weapon when they needed it.

Come on baby light my fire ... that old school music be so right.

One good thing about lights out was that he could think over the plan. Sometimes it stirred a mighty fear in him, the kind that shot through him before he'd pulled off a mugging or a buy or some other job—like the one that got him sent to Alpha. He clenched his fists. *That didn't turn out so well, now, did it?*

The thing about nights, too, was that he had time to relive his whole damn sorry life and the day he got himself caught. His brain ramped up on regret; he stewed in it. He didn't have anyone to talk it through—except Mr. Bonner, who was a straight dude—so, for now, he talked to the bare grey block wall across from his bunk.

But the plan. Yeah, it always got back to that. They had to do it, try it. And if they got caught, so the fuck what? At least they tried. Rick stood up and looked at the aluminum back splash that served as a mirror. He flexed a muscle.

They ain't gonna hold Ricky no full three, four, five years. No sir.

As far back as I can remember, I always lived in a rough neighborhood. Me. Rick J. San Antonio. All the crazy stuff that went on there was part of a normal day in my life—the life I can't forget, the life I don't want to go back to.

When I was six, I lived in North Miami near Six Stump, and don't ask me how it got that name because I don't know. I hear it had something to do with a fight, and all that was left were six stumps—maybe people, maybe trees. Who the fuck cares? No one in Six Stump cares, that's for sure. It's a violent, trashy, loud place to grow up in. I heard gun shots and saw drive-bys and killings all the time, and then there were the drug deals. That's where I really got my education, not in school, and the only diploma was a one-way ticket to the hell hole.

I had two sisters, but I don't know where they went. My mother used to be around. Sometimes. She had "business," she said. Some business. She smelled like an old bar room. I grew up with that smell, cheap whiskey and cigarettes and dirty body. My real dad is currently in prison. I never had any guidance, or rules, as a kid. I really did what I wanted to do all the time. I grew up in what they would call a "mafia" family, because my stepfather was in the Cuban "mafia," along with his father, uncles, brothers and cousins.

But I do got one good memory. For my sixth birthday I got a Batmobile. Me and my hoodlum friends, as my mother called us, took turns driving it around, but the fun went away fast because there was always a fight. My mom and stepdad got into it all the time, and it scared me to death. My stepdad, Emilio, beat my mom until there was blood everywhere. Little red dots all over the white walls. I would stand there and stare at those dots, so terrified, and mostly helpless and in a daze.

I couldn't do anything about it.

One day, Emilio punched my mom in the face and broke her nose. When she threatened to call the cops, he put a knife to her throat. At that instant, I couldn't take any more and I picked up my baseball bat and swung it as hard as I could, right into the back of his head. He never expected that. Bullies don't. They think they got it all covered. But I'm a strong little motherfucker. That head of his split open like a watermelon, but I didn't kill him. Too bad.

After that, the fighting let up for a while, but not for long. Emilio came back to life, meaner than ever. I hid from him, and everyone, in those days. It was just too dangerous to come out and get seen runnin' the streets.

Like I said, Emilio just got worse. He was a big-time drug dealer. One night, Emilio and my Uncle Jerry were sitting on the back porch with the dogs. Jerry stole some crack from Emilio, and Emilio shot up the whole house. I'm surprised no one died that night. I hid out in the shed, as usual. The next day, I came out and found bullet holes all over the place—in the refrigerator door, living room walls, and a straight line of shots through a bunch of dusty old pictures my mom had nailed to the wall years and years ago. Pictures of puppies and flowers. Oh yeah, them dogs, not a pretty sight.

Emilio kept making the drugs, carried them around to his customers. He had every kind of drug you could imagine, cuttin' shit, mixin' shit. He built part of a meth lab on that falling-down back porch and started to sell meth out of the house. Our house stunk so bad, and after a while, I could hardly breathe. Ma was never around. On Saturdays, we took trips into Miami and farther south so Emilio could buy his supplies. I got so I couldn't stand it. I spent a lot of time at my Aunt Roma's, chillin', and that's where everybody went if they weren't at my Uncle Denny's strip club. Also, that's where I mostly found my two cousins, Jebbo and Marsh.

By then, I was about eight.

Right about that time, the three of us really got some action. I started with the drugs, thanks to Emilio, my stepdad. He gave me my first blunt and my first alcoholic beverage—Coke with rum in it. I didn't like the way it all tasted, at first, but I liked the way it made me feel, sort of outside myself.

From as early as I can remember, I wasn't liking me inside myself. So I went outside myself. We had some fun. Me and Jebbo and Marsh ran around all day, drunked up and crazy-like, until we fell down dead asleep about midnight. We didn't get to do that often. Sometimes we got up in the morning and went around and drained all the glasses from the night before, after Emilio and them were *partying. The sticky fruit and syrupy leftovers in the bottom of those glasses gave me a morning buzz. But then there were the drugs, and they were everywhere, all the time. Emilio showed me everything I needed to know about drugs; how to cook them, sell them, and bag them. I met his buddies, the drug dealers, and from that point on, I looked at drugs in a different way. I wasn't a kid bothered by the smell anymore. I was a real drug dealer, in the scene, a regular Action Jackson, so to speak. I was on my own, and I would be my own man.*

I moved on to something extreme. I joined my first gang, the Wreckin' Crew. It was a gang started by NWA in California, and it moved itself to Florida. It was an all-Black gang but for some reason they didn't care about my race. Or my age. I was twelve. Everybody I chilled with was 16 and up. Nobody bothered to ask me my age or treat me any differently because of it.

Then came the time that my cycle of incarceration began. It was a cold Friday night in December, and me and my cousins and some of the homeboys were playing Manhunt around the complex. For some reason we ended up on the playground of a local elementary school where we chilled for a bit. I got up and started walking around. I found this metal pipe. I tossed it around for a few minutes, pretending it was a baseball bat and such. Pretty soon, I was throwing it through a classroom window. That started it. Next minute, my cousin went in through the broken window and tossed out a computer, and then another and another. Then all the rest of the stuff came flying out: headphones, keyboards, books, a chair or two. We vandalized the whole place. We broke light bulbs, windows, cameras, and for the last part, I took all the fire extinguishers and set them off.

When I went back to school Monday, I got arrested, because before I broke the cameras, they got a shot of my face.

I always thought I was smart. Now I'm not so sure.

Rick needed that signal from Allen. He was a cat, that one, and up to the job of chief. He'd managed to work out a map and a code of hand signals and words and smuggled it around to him, Tarvis, and Duval in a textbook in the classroom. And they were doing pretty well communicating in the chow line, except for an occasional bungle or two. It still was the best time to talk, and Allen signaled that it might be the best time of day for the breakout. Rick would just have to wait and see. See what Allen cooked up.

They kept their communication hidden in the textbook, second to the last desk in the second row, in Miss McBride's classroom. Allen updated it from time to time. New words, sketches of doors, and such. He was available; he was the floor cleaner, the librarian, butt kisser. He'd gotten so good at doing his jobs, especially keeping the books in order, to get the word out. It was hard to pull out the map and study it in class, but not impossible. Problem was that dick Duval. The deputies were all over him because he couldn't keep a cap on that hate.

But Allen managed it all. He kept all of them informed. To each other, they signaled: flat, open palms together meant "look in the book." They'd all seen the map. The escape plan was labeled "going to church," the staff was "the saints." The cell block was "hell," all door exits were "heaven—east, west, north, and south." If anyone got caught with a note, it would not refer to an escape; it would detail "going to church."

The map had all the light switches, electrics, gates, etc., drawn carefully. Rick wasn't sure where Allen was going with all these details. He would wait and see. It had to make sense eventually. In the meantime, it would surely rouse suspicion, should the map be found. They had to take care the writing was generic and light, spare in description, and appear to be a bunch of doodling. They were all adept at doodling. The map and key words—everything—were all decorated with vines and roses, tears and eyeballs. Rick got the word about the map. Allen said, "Study it." So, he did. Rick had to let Allen take this one. So far so good. He didn't understand the end of it. He'd just do as he was told—that was a new one for the books.

The key to the plan, and the hardest part, was that they had to sit on it until the right time. There were steps to take before they made it out of there.

Lately, they relied more on whispering.

But the plan was ramping up. Rick could feel it. Allen could hardly hold his shit in.

Allen told him about the phone in Miss Caroline's classroom. Maybe he'd gotten it out already. That would take some cojones. They needed a shitload of those. They all knew Miss McBride wasn't going to use the classroom for a few days. Most of the classes were scheduled for the computer lab.

Miss Caroline. Now, that was a project, in herself. He was setting her up, chances are she wouldn't fall for it. But who knew? Didn't everybody like a little flattery? She might be needed in the plan. To soften things up. Put in a word with the deputy staff, or whatever. She was one cool lady, always willing to help out the scum of Alpha. Not that anyone deserved it.

Rick pried at the binder. He thought of Tarvis. The dude was key, smart and cool. Unflappable in front of the deputies, eyes like a damn hawk. Allen said Tarvis was important. They had to go with that. Tarvis was going to do some real chill talking, and if anyone could do it, Tarvis could. Rick was sure of it. He'd seen him with the staff, real polite, letting them know right away he wasn't a problem. That he had questions, that he was earnest to get along and get out on time. He was new and scared, but he wasn't so scared that he wasn't up for a little adventure, that being, *Get the Fuck Out of Alpha.*

Fact was, they needed bodies for this. Not too many, not too few. Just right. Just the four little bears. *Fuck.*

Rick had some time until lights out. He worked methodically on his project before he'd be forced to lay back in the cold dark. He'd take his time with it—this, his contribution to the plan.

He opened the binder and loosened the fastenings of the three metal rings. What the dumb-ass deputies didn't realize was that the cover of the binder was plastic but the spine had a metal splint. He was going to work it.

One of the rings finally popped off the spine. He cursed that he didn't have more tools, except for his hands, a pencil and his toothbrush, and he had his brothers of Alpha to thank for that. Yet, they still managed. Now he used the metal compass he'd smuggled out of Mr. Muldoon's class and poked at the plastic covering the metal strip. He'd gotten the compass out in his shoe and the gash on the sole of his foot was worth the effort. They had to make do. Work around the new rules. They were not allowed to have much of anything in their cells, for fear they'd use whatever at hand to do themselves in or fashion a weapon or two to do someone else in. They'd once had zippers, footlockers, and shoelaces in their cells. Not anymore. One youth had used a footlocker to lift and tone and build until he turned himself into a regular superhero, so the footlockers had to go. Later, the cots were bolted to the concrete floor, because they, too, had been used for weightlifting, and, occasionally, as very large projectiles. There were no mirrors, clocks, metal edges to the pencils. Or zippers to cut with. Their shoes, Bob Barker canvas high-tops, stood outside their doors, which had windows little more than peepholes so deputies could check on the inmates. The boys padded around their cells in rubber sandals, and when let out, they formed a line to the meal cart and to the showers.

It was a spare existence that gave them plenty of time to think, to cry, to miss the outside. To change beliefs, if they wanted to, so that positive feelings would take the place of negative ones and produce change. What they stored in their heads was a tangle of weaponry against the world, but they needed to shift gears. Strip down to the bare minimum, expose that weaponry and defuse it. From there, the supposition was that they would build themselves up. All the dangerous, provocative, possibly hazardous material had to go.

Rick had a hard time rooting out the bad thoughts. Mr. Bonner was trying to root it out for him. The propaganda to change went through Rick's head, and out his ears. Nobody was going to help Rick San Antonio, in or out. No one gave a shit about Rick San Antonio, except Rick himself. And his first level of concern was immediate—to get the fuck out of Alpha. ASAP.

Rick smiled to himself. They took stuff away, all right. The foot lockers and shoelaces, the metal end of his pencil, his ruler. Rec time and books. But no one had said anything about the binders. How sweet it was. Rick had come up with the idea to use the binders, and Duval had helped him out on honing that shiv. And the handle? Made from all that useless paper. He'd managed to smuggle some tape out of the classroom, and he planned to wrap and tape paper padding at the base of the shiv.

Yes, the binder came in handy for something besides storing endless homework and notebook paper for essays.

He had two of the rings removed already, and he was working off the third.

Each was held in place with pesky grommets that Rick had finally chiseled away with the compass. Mr. Muldoon was a good math teacher, but he wasn't too observant. Rick mused that there was other useful stuff he could pilfer from Mr. Muldoon's classroom—stapler, ruler, electrical cord. He'd have to check with Allen. Miss McBride's room was another story. A little trickier there to get that phone, but Rick was sure Allen could do it.

Rick pried the last of the three rings loose and stowed them in a rip in the seam of his pillow, careful to pack stuffing around them. Short of swallowing them, he didn't know how he was going to dispose of them. He was thinking of putting one at a time down the toilet. The toilet was so useful. All kinds of contraband were reduced to shit size and flushed away before any of the deputies could catch them, even the five-dollar bill that that moron Ferris had somehow stolen from Miss McBride's desk. What was he going to do with a five-dollar bill? He'd managed to get to a vending machine even though Rick had told him it only took change.

Now that the rings were off and put aside, Rick worked at removing the metal spine, wiggling it back and forth patiently until it finally came away in one smooth piece. Even though the edges were curved slightly, it was going to serve perfectly. Duval had given him a tip or two about flattening it. It was amazing the shit they could tell each other in the chow line. If they didn't say it, they signed it, and if a deputy saw or heard any of it, it was lights out. For sure.

Rick ran a finger slowly, thoughtfully, almost lovingly along the fine metal edge of the spine. It had a sharp lip.

Yes, this will do just great.

He got down on the floor next to his cot and began rubbing the spine gingerly against the concrete floor, a perfect stone for grinding the edge. He was making a mark on the floor so he squiggled under the cot out of sight. He rubbed and honed. The spine made a scratchy sound, like nails on the blackboard. His eyes darted to the door, his ears on the lookout for Haver. He ground the metal splint with a vengeance. It was working.

He'd take a minute or two at a time and get back to it later. One move closer to getting the fuck out the door. He imagined grasping the finished, shiny shiv, putting it to good use, one day pressing it against Haver's throat, slowly at first to see the growing fear in the deputy's eyes, until finally cutting with precision, like he was slicing a roast. Anticipation and appetite. It almost made his mouth water. He didn't know where he got such lust for blood, but there it was, and it was so much more satisfying than shooting someone, which was cold, impersonal. Drawing blood, stabbing, twisting, the color of it and warm sticky feel of it. That was satisfying, complete. The real kill.

Rick had to be patient, but the thought of it made him want to hurry. Hurry they couldn't. The plan wouldn't work if they hurried. And the plan had to work.

He heard Deputy Haver's key in the heavy door that opened from the day room. That son of a bitch and his story time. It meant Rick had to stash the goodies, for sure. He arranged the metal spine from the binder in his pillow, along with the rings, and smoothed the blanket on the cot. Rick was seated at his metal desk, reading a short story for language arts class, when Haver banged on his door. All the doors down the line. Haver had a stick and he used it, rarely on the boys, but it was effective intimidation. The thought that he might use it was more terrifying than actual blows. Rick had been there, at the end of a beating, and he'd survived. He'd survive this, too.

Haver passed by and left them in some kind of restless peace.

Quiet tonight.

Rick read this to mean staff was down. He was becoming more adept at deciphering the clues about staff. It would help in the end. Yes, the end.

CHAPTER SIXTEEN

Where There's a Will

CLASSROOM 110 WAS EMPTY, EXCEPT FOR the enormous presence of Will Bonner. He sat at the teacher's desk, bent over scattered papers, passing one pile to the next in neat manila folders as he wrote notes with a black Pilot fine-point gel pen. Thinking of Caroline when he should have been emptying the pen and bottles of fresh Wite-Out on to page after page of reports about the boys. Thoughtful, slow, plodding, and careful at his work, elegant and nonchalant with his documents. He chose to write all his comments long hand in florid cursive instead of using the computer, much to the consternation of head staff.

Will had work to do. Treatment team was due to start later, and he was the team's psyche leader, a job he'd held for ten years. He interviewed each boy once a month, with representatives from the other departments: education, health, deputy staff, spiritual. He also taught classes in Rational Emotive Therapy (RET), helping them turn their negative beliefs into positive ones so they could change their feelings.

This was most difficult. To change feelings. Will knew this. He'd been a young thug himself, going deeper and deeper into the dark life until he was caught. Dead to rights, with the keys to that sweet ride, a black T-bird, leather seats, trunk full of booze.

He often thought back to those days, and he still marveled that he was still alive, much less working to straighten out these kids. He and his thug friends had stolen that T-bird for a joy ride, and then gotten the bright idea to stick up Marty's Grocer, a neighborhood place off the beaten track. Who'd catch 'em? The po-po would, that's who. Will spent three years in a juvie north of Miami, missing a good chunk of teen years, eating rot and listening to rot.

Except for Sister Beth Ann. To that rotting hell, she came. From heaven. What a sign from God she turned out to be! Will would hear her coming down the hall of the cell block. At first, he was terrified. He'd thought Godzilla was on the loose, but here she was. A nun. Wearing combat boots. He almost laughed when he met her, and then he figured right away he better keep a straight face before she swiped him clear across the room. She didn't play. "You got two choices. Change the way you think and change the way you think."

She was right. He could and did. He changed his thinking to a positive, hopeful track, and his feelings followed. It wasn't easy. Especially with his Uncle Cob (short for Cobra) visiting him, laying out plans for the next heist.

Will got tired of that life. He was only eighteen years old, and he didn't want to go out there and do it again. He made change stick. He went to Miami Central College of Therapy and learned the ways he could help other boys. Another thing Sister Beth Ann had said, "What you did to get in here, there's no future in it. Someday you might show others what you learned. And you'll do it the hard way. Nothing easy about any of it."

She had that right and a whole lot more. He left the old ways and learned the new. Will persuaded the young inmates of Alpha who were resistant to working the program that they should give it a try. And how they loved stories about Sister Beth Ann. She loved art? She rode a motorcycle? She dyed her hair red, but few knew it with those ragged ends tucked under her starched cap. Will knew it. She'd sit on the opposite bunk in his cell, hands folded over her knees, and sweat in the Miami heat. Her hair wasn't only red, it was curly as it escaped from the cap, and she tucked it back in with a slim, blunt finger. The boys hung on Will's every word about Sister Beth Ann.

Will built rapport, however he could. He made his mark, and he was invaluable in the rehabilitation of the boys. Especially as an example. They listened to him, at least the successful ones did. He pushed them, but, in the end, they had to do it themselves. And despite the setbacks, he was relentless. He didn't give up. He couldn't let them down. Sometimes he felt alone, but then his thoughts went back to Caroline like they did constantly. He was not alone. She never left his head, nor his heart, it seemed. Now something was bothering her, and the thought of it got to him. Something was on her mind, but they never got around to what it was, what with pleasant distractions.

He thought of her eyes, her mouth. He put the pen down. She gave new definition to being in this prison. They'd figure a way out. Together.

He bent to the work. Today, the cursive was shaky, his brain rattled with thoughts of Caroline. He hoped he was doing the right thing by her. He couldn't stand it if she were hurt, and he didn't ever want to be the cause of it.

They needed to be discreet. Oh, they were so discreet. Not so long ago in that little office of hers. Now this new thing. They'd noticed the phone missing. He had to find out about that. Discreetly, of course. What a place of secrets and lies! If he told the deputy staff, they'd toss the whole damn place. And find nothing, for sure. They'd cause more chaos. Will had to take this on himself, and somehow protect both of them from being dumped on. The phone was missing from the office off her classroom. There would be questions.

He looked at the clock. He shifted the never-ending stack of paperwork on his desk. Pages of misery. The boys. He found himself at odds with the deputy staff whose main method was force, for all things. He wanted them to use their heads and hearts, not their fists.

Twelve boys were due for treatment team each week. Next week, another dozen or so until each one reported about once a month. They had assignments to share when they sat down with Will and staff; essays they had to write on a range of subjects, including peer influence, substance abuse, family issues, education goals, anger management. They wrote their own histories about how these issues had affected them and the people around them and what they were going to do to achieve peace and health. When they got closer to "graduating" from the program, they wrote about returning to society as responsible citizens, achieving healthy social skills, earning a living outside of crime, preventing negative behaviors and lifestyle, making good decisions. In a matter of months some of them matured. Their time at Alpha had helped, and for some of them, nothing helped.

A lot of what they wrote was bullshit. Will saw through it. But, for many, the writing was cathartic and insightful. They told Will they didn't know what to write. They didn't understand how they felt—not until they sat down to write about it. Then the dam broke. Will could see it in their faces, and in the writing. Hear it in their voices when they talked about what they learned about themselves. They didn't like what they saw, what they learned, when they wrote it and read it in black and white. It made many of them want to change.

Lately, Julius Duval was the glaring exception. He didn't like anything, or anybody. He wrote page after page of hate-filled script that didn't make any sense at all, and there seemed to be no stopping the flow.

"This is a waste of time I hate you this is a waste I hate you...."

Something was up with that kid, Will thought. Something not so good. He could see it constantly in Duval's scowl, without let-up, hear it in his one-word dismissive answers, read it in his RET essays. Brown had made inroads, but still, the hate burned, smothering everything, destroying every step forward.

Will liked nothing better than a challenge, and Duval was the challenge of the month. He needed to reach that kid.

He bent over a stack of manila folders for the next meeting, which would probably run over into the next day. The pen looped over page after page. He enjoyed the hands-on touch of writing down each infraction or rare bit of progress the boys were making. The method somehow made the process more formal, more personal, than the clacking away on the computer keys.

The pen-to-paper business drove his boss, Lewis "Deeds" Dedelow, nuts. Like right now. Will didn't see the expensive golf shirt, nor get that whiff of Irish Spring, until Dedelow was practically leaning over his desk. Deeds looked, always, like he'd just run track, panting slightly, his hair wet and slicked back. "Bonner, time you came into the tech age, ma man." He flopped into a desk chair and put his feet up on the seat next to him. A kindly smirk played around the lips.

Will put the pen down and looked up at Dedelow. Weary lines etched around Will's eyes. "What up?" He deflected, but it wouldn't do any good. "You can't read my writing?"

"It's not that so much. I need the files on the hard drive."

"Quit driving me so hard."

"Real fucking funny."

"They have to write their reports by hand. So should I. Sets up better communication."

"The paperwork. It's mounting with astounding speed, in huge piles. At least if it were in the computer, we wouldn't have reams of shit to go through. We'd have neat little *bytes*."

Will looked him right in the eye. He was dying to say, "Bite me." But he didn't. "You have to go through it anyway. At least I hope you're going through it." Sometimes Will had his doubts. He held the pen over the yellow legal pad like it was a loaded gun. *The pen is mightier... etc., etc.* His script looked like something from the Declaration of Independence, so florid and neat and scrolly.

Dedelow mock-squinted at the report, avoiding Will's eyes. "I know, I know. You do a bang-up job, but really. I've got piles to deal with here. Literally. Goddam local, state, and federal rules, the physical and mental health and education permits, the projected plans and follow-up facilities and halfway houses to contact."

"You act like I invented it. Take it a day at a time. That's what I tell the boys and that's what I'm telling you." But he felt a twinge of sympathy for his boss whose job it was to drive all over the state riding herd on psyche team staff in the juvenile correctional centers. The regulations seemed to quintuple, then they sat on desks, mostly ignored, so more regulations seemed to spring from the old ones. It was a system that was drowning in itself.

As a contractor in mental health services, Dedelow, and his funding, teetered precariously. He needed all of his workers to think as a team and shuffle out that paperwork double-time, in triplicate. Deeds complained that most of it came out as the worst, incomprehensible, mind-numbing memo writing of all time. He thanked Will for his service, for well-written, thoughtful reports, while he struggled to make it look like he was running a top-notch business. Will wanted to hide when he knew Deeds was in the area, before he started prattling on and nagging, but he did all he could to accommodate him. In his own way. He still felt like he had a target on his back as far as Dedelow was concerned.

"Thanks for the free session," Deeds said.

Will glanced briefly at his boss. Dedelow jumped up and rocked back and forth on his sturdy black shoes. They looked like gun boats, and they were coming for Will. He looked back at the paperwork. He knew it was coming because Dedelow couldn't shut up for long. He was always dashing around, looking like he was ready to explode, and he probably was.

"Well, if you aren't going to come on board, I'll just have to get an assistant, and funds are tight," he said. "That means I'll have to cut your salary."

Will put the pen down. "You must sit around thinking up ways to bug me." Part taunt. His eyes went back to the stack of paper. "Do what you have to do, Lew. You can't change this old horse." His sympathy ebbed just as swiftly as it rolled over him.

"Old? What are you? Forty-eight?"

"Forty-nine."

"You're not old, and we all have to bend some. Or we won't have a freakin' juvenile justice system."

For a flash, Will reveled in the glow of that thought. No more torture of the young, of sorts. At least not here. But that would mean they'd all go to the adult population. Florida, depending on the judge, adjudicated children as adults.

"I'll try, Lew. I will." They'd have a choice. Juvie or county. He'd try even harder. He knew how to play the lesser of two devils.

Will wished Dedelow would leave. Miller and the rest of the team were due later, and Will liked to be ready for them. He hoped Caroline would be there, her presence at once unsettling and calming, full of questions or intensely absorbing it all. He didn't know which of Caroline's moods would show up, but he loved every minute when she was there. She had something special with each boy. Seemed she knew what to say when sometimes he was at a loss for words. His focus on behavior modification was different than hers although they both had the same goal in mind. Rehabilitation.

"Well, gotta jet," said Dedelow. "It's been nice chatting…"

"Yeah, me, too, D. You take care." With an ever so slight tinge of sarcasm. His eyes stayed on the stack of papers and folders piled on his desk.

Dedelow turned at the door. "Will you think about what I just told you? You he said, ignoring her signal to keep it down. He still had his pen in his hand. He tapped the end of it a couple of times on the desktop. "You've made me lose my train of thought." Those perfect white teeth in that handsome square jaw of his. He had a crescent scar over his right eye that Caroline wanted to touch. Will wore dreds, another statement that drove Dedelow nuts, but he kept his hair neat, tied in a thin strip of leather.

"Let's get back on that train. What are you thinking?" He glanced toward the door. A reflex they'd both developed. Be careful. Caroline was sick of being careful, caring what other people thought, watching each step that might stir up trouble. Yet, she was in prison. She had to remember that and watch all of her movements, with or without Will around.

She studied his intense expression. "Something is definitely brewing. Think I told you I caught Allen in the kitchen, and then this Duval business. Deputy Brown calmed him down, but these boys—secretive. Their eyes, furtive, and the whispering."

"It's getting to you."

She sighed. "Maybe. I'm trying. I went to Harvey, but you know education is a political football around here. He's got to play the game. I hardly blame him. Harv fights, but he has to choose his battles if he'd going to win anything."

Will sat back, folded his hands. "I know what you mean, but I think it's more of the same. These kids are desperate. Just keep that in mind. They'll try anything, and we have to keep a certain amount of emotional distance from that. You know that."

"I do," she said. "But now, I think I'm being set up."

"You got some good radar on you, girl. But it wouldn't be the first time they tried that crap. Remember Youth Poole last year? You shut him down nice and tight."

"I remember, of course I remember. But there's more, and this is different. It's Rick San Antonio and Jesse Allen. Something funny's going on. They're testing me," she said. "I think I'm being cultivated. Not sure why, but it seems they have something in mind."

Will reached for her hand. Caroline tensed; she hated when the deputies teased them. She'd signaled him to keep the conversation private, but here they were charging ahead, and that was how they were. She told him everything, knowing he would be open. If he believed anything, it was that "the truth shall set you free." All of it. It's how he got himself out of the jail years earlier—he'd been used, and instead of blaming others, he pushed for the truth. The wheels of justice hardly budged, until Will pushed them hard.

But cultivation—that sneaky series of precise steps inmates took to achieve some end—was part of prison life. Caroline knew she was being set up. She'd been in the system long enough to smell it.

"Will, I'm getting in deep, not too far into it yet, but enough to know," she said. "I'm starting to feel like a victim."

"How."

"The compliments and pleas for help and sympathy."

Caroline studied his face, and she could see it. They both knew some things never changed, and for all their wiles and smarts, the inmates of Alpha were just as predictable as most kids who got themselves into a corner, for whatever reason. They were going to manipulate their surroundings until they got what they wanted, and they would go through a series of fairly predictable machinations to get there. And, oh, were they good at manipulation. "Am I being paranoid?"

Will threw back his head and laughed. "Paranoid? In prison? Now how could that ever happen?"

"Seriously," she said. She loved him and had no patience with him at the same time. His laugh irritated her all the while she delighted in it.

He put a hand on her arm. She relaxed. "Paranoia. It's in the very nature of this place. It's in the mortar and concrete block," he said. "But it's all right. We'll find out, you know we'll find it. And we'll do something about it. What, I don't know, but we'll handle it."

"I think you're right about 'emotional distance.' I've got to be objective about this."

He stood up and walked toward the door, looked out and turned. "You got it. You certainly have that. What else?"

"I'm sure San Antonio and Allen are the runners. They ask for favors. They keep trying to get closer. I didn't notice at first, but now they're right in my face."

"And?"

"They allude to sex. Will, they leave these bizarre poems on my desk." She thrust one of them at Will. "Read this. From San Antonio."

Will took the poem and read it out loud:

The grace of a single dove,
Is the essence of a teacher's love.
Flowing with the juices of a heroine's appeal,
A teacher's love is so real.
She'll never call you dumb or stupid
Because, in her eyes,
You are one of God's qupids.

"Well, you should be flattered. It's lovely," Will said. "Especially the part about the flowing juices."

"Will!" She blushed then.

He laughed. "Well, yeah."

"It's unnerving, to say the least. And this isn't the only one. He also told me, straight up, he likes my hair and my eyes. And things. He says it's sad admin doesn't recognize my outstanding talents and achievements."

"I can't argue."

"Come on. I told him to knock it off, in so many words. And I'm saving all the little notes. They—Allen and San Antonio—both said they'd act as my guards against anything that happened bad around here. And, God forbid, Allen said the word. 'Attacks.' What's that supposed to mean?"

"Attacks?"

"Yeah, attacks."

"Sounds like trouble."

"That's what I'm saying."

Something definitely was up. Not in all the years had she faced such an organized onslaught of paranoia. And bullshit.

CHAPTER SEVENTEEN

Funny Little Game

CAROLINE HAD MANAGED TO MAINTAIN A neutral expression when Rick San Antonio gave her the note of burning love. Jesse Allen stood next to him, watching her. She'd studied their eager faces. Butter would melt on this toasty duo. The deputies had allowed them time to work on arranging the bookshelves, and they could hardly contain themselves.

She read the poem, and they waited for her reaction. She remained impassive, bland even. "Impressive writing," she said, walking over to the bookcase. She drew out a volume of E.E. Cummings and another of Yeats and handed one to each boy. "Here's something for you two poets. Read the poems, pick one from the volume I'm giving you, and write an analysis. At least three paragraphs. Due tomorrow."

She walked back to her desk, without a backward glance. They were already paging through the books she'd given them.

Might as well steer these two toward a Pulitzer. Funny thing was, she looked forward to their perspectives. Their creepy sentiment aside, she appreciated their ardor for expressing themselves. She'd welcome it. Their assessments were rough and raw, and unique. They had plenty of time to think, and many of them had started to love words. Caroline always learned something new about old authors.

Allen piped up. He had that perpetually fresh look of the young, like he'd just woken up from a nap. "Thank you so much, Miss McBride, ma'am. I'll get right on it." He backed away, holding the volume of Yeats like it was a platter of caviar.

She nodded coolly and returned to shuffling papers on her desk. She didn't know what they were up to, but she'd play the little game. Maybe get a glimpse of what they were planning. She was getting close, and she couldn't look away. She couldn't shake the feeling—that they were headed for disaster.

San Antonio had been silent, a quizzical look on his face as he paged through the poems of Cummings. He looked from the book to Caroline and flashed a smile. "Great, this is great. Looka this dude. No caps, whoda thought? Genius." He held the book with two hands and shook it a bit. "And, have to say, I've never seen such a great teacher in all my life. You are the best! You're not like some instructors who don't es-plain things the right way."

Apropos of nothing. Where did that come from?

Deputy Brown had been standing just inside the door. "San Antonio, shut your pie hole." The boy folded like the sun had gone down. "Clean it up. And get back to your cell." Brown looked over at Allen. "And, you, you got about a minute there to wrap it up. Let's go." He lifted an arm toward San Antonio in a mock gesture as the youth put the last book on the shelf. He flinched, but Caroline couldn't imagine Brown hitting him or any of them. It wasn't his style; he didn't have to resort to it.

San Antonio stood at attention with a look of relief. Haver wasn't around. When Deputy Brown signaled, the youth shuffled out of the classroom in his plastic sandals, whispering, "Sir, yes, sir." With Deputy Brown on duty, they had a respite of sorts. They'd stay in line and like it. "Hope they got those books in order, Miss Caroline. Do some good around here," he said, glancing at Allen who was finishing with the reference section.

Caroline walked to the door and whispered to Deputy Brown. "Really appreciate it. The books. And the time you give them. Especially Duval lately. I think it helps."

Brown folded his huge arms, shrugged. "It's the job."

Caroline sighed. "Don't I wish."

She smiled at Brown and went back over to her desk. She even thought of turning back, confiding in Deputy Brown about her latest fears, but then thought again. She should keep her suspicions under wraps until she, and Will, had more information.

Whatever was happening behind her back, the boys hadn't reached the point of the classic set-up. If that's what they were planning. One of them might attempt to make physical contact with her, but she was not afraid they would hurt her. Instead, they might use it.

When the boys were around, she'd never let a deputy out of her sight. It was part of the territory. It just made good sense.

She needed to be careful. They'd do anything to get what they wanted. She thought of how the inmates at the correctional center in Orange County had used physical contact with her friend, Kathleen Danfrey. She'd been the victim of blackmail after getting set up. "He only wanted a hug," she'd told Caroline. That one hug had been caught on camera. It resulted in a series of payoffs to the young scumbag until Kathleen finally ended it, but not after damage was done to her reputation and to the correctional center—and she lost her job.

Setting up the victim usually took a good six months, depending on the prison and the population. The victim, with luck, was able to get out of the cycle, but then suffered backlash from prison staff for tripping into a set up. In the first place, Caroline would be damned if she'd pay anyone off. She wanted no part of it.

She glanced at Allen. She went round and round in her head trying to make sense of it. The missing phone, Allen and his kitchen detour, his book chatter, the poetry… The other day, Youth San Antonio had requested an extra binder and more notebook paper, and Caroline obliged. He was a prolific writer of essays and poetry, a good student. He'd earned that binder. Caroline was the last one to stifle creativity, and order. She was all for it. And yet. The love notes. She didn't react when one landed on her desk from time to time. Lately, there had been elaborate pencil sketches of Caroline with wings and a halo, roses framing her face, hearts with thorns and banners and a passable rendition of the Virgin of Guadalupe. Enough was enough. She had to get to the bottom of it, and she wanted Will on board.

At least the boys were progressing in class. Reading more, asking for help with Spanish lessons and social studies. All of it would help with the GED testing. Maybe they'd have their high school diplomas when they got out of Alpha. Going from second/third grade reading levels to high school graduate? It happened all the time.

So—what? So they could work at Best Buy, stocking televisions and electronics? If Best Buy would have them. They'd have to weigh a future selling television sets against one of boosting them and selling them for drugs on the street corner.

Caroline shook her head. *Again, why am I here?*

Deputy Stinson crossed the day room and signaled to Deputy Brown. The two deputies stood in the doorway chatting. Allen glanced their way, then approached Caroline, again pushing it, taking brazen advantage of initiating talk with a staff member. She remembered the episode in the hallway with the meal cart and the non-existent paper towels. Her radar switched on.

Allen smiled, his teeth flashing in that smooth young face. "Ma'am, would you have an extra pencil, ma'am?" She was still leery, but the teacher in her produced a pencil. He'd been showing an avid interest in writing essays and not so much in love notes. "I hope this is not a burden on you." His English ever so precise for the English teacher.

"Burden?" She snapped off the metal end of the pencil. She'd do whatever she could to encourage writing. She kept an eye on the deputies who were sharing a laugh. Allen stood perfectly still; his hands braced at his sides. The perfect young model prisoner.

He accepted the pencil and headed toward the door. Brown was waiting to scoop him up.

"What's that you got there, Allen?" It was Stinson. His white-blond face and hair faded together, hiding his bland expression.

"Sir, a pencil, sir."

"Well, give it back. What you need a pencil for?"

"Sir, for writing, sir."

"Oh, yeah, the great American novel. I forgot. Get over here and drop the pencil. Now." It clicked on the desktop.

Caroline let this one go. She'd get the pencil to Allen. Later.

"Sir, yes, sir." He didn't dare turn his head. If he wanted to keep it.

IN CLASS, ALLEN AND SAN ANTONIO WERE as enthusiastic as ever. They finished their silent reading and essays and then offered to return and straighten books that were stored on racks under the seats. Allen fussed around the desks. He seemed obsessed with the task.

Allen and a bunch of them had devised a filing system for the different genres. They'd labeled the shelves, with roses and tears sketched over the novels, and placed a roadrunner over nonfiction.

Allen glanced up every now and then, from the deputy in the corner to Caroline. "Ma'am, sorry, ma'am, for what Youth Duval did to your classroom, ma'am. Just not good, ma'am."

She studied him. *What would Shakespeare say? He "doth protest too much, methinks."*

"This is *your* classroom, Mr. Allen. I appreciate the care you take with the books."

"Ma'am, yes, ma'am." He spoke softly so the deputy and the rest of the class would not pick up the conversation. "Thanks for giving me that pencil, Miss McBride, and sorry for the confusion."

Is that what it was? Confusion when the deputy made him drop it?

He kept his head down. "Maybe I can get it back soon?"

She wasn't going to play that game. She pursed her lips.

Quickly, he added under his breath, "I don't know why you care so much about us, Miss McBride. We're failures. I'm still having trouble with those thesis statements... I really need help. Maybe you could tutor me? Youth San Antonio needs some time, too." The deputy eyed him from where he had his feet propped on a garbage can. He crunched a bag of potato chips.

"Cut the chit-chat, Allen, and get back over to those bookcases."

"Sir, yes, sir."

Caroline felt he deserved an answer. "We'll see about that, Mr. Allen. You're doing well though." She picked up Fowler's text on writing and handed it to him. "I think you can have this in your cell." The deputy was watching. Allen took the book from her and smiled. If she did do any tutoring, it would be in the day room under the watchful eye of a deputy.

Enough of making nice. I'm in prison.

THAT AFTERNOON CAROLINE FOUND the drawing. She was picking up around the classroom after language arts when she saw the raw edge of art paper sticking out of a book tucked neatly under one of the desks on the metal rack. She pulled it out and held the paper first one way and then the other.

It looked like a map. But the heading at the top amid a bunch of thorns and tears said, "Church."

Church?

A bell went off in her head. She wondered who'd drawn the map. It was hard to say. Some had distinctive style, but this one was pretty cut and dry. The print was light and generic. She couldn't be sure, but she had the strong feeling it was the work of San Antonio. He was an accomplished artist. His subjects were usually cartoon characters, popular tattoo designs with helmets and shields, swords and dripping blood. Or, dream houses and office buildings, even bridges and theme parks. He'd once re-drawn the correctional center to include a McDonald's, a video game room, and a basketball court that didn't have torn nets and cracked concrete where weeds thrived. The swimming pool was also a nice touch.

This drawing was different. On closer inspection, it was a realistic rendering to the last frightening detail of Alpha, including locks and door handles, measurements door to door and window to window. *A sketch of the kitchen off the main hallway.* A complete overview of the cell blocks, with exits marked, and of several of the classrooms—hers included—with a landscape of master control and the front gate. She hoped it was idle sketching, but Caroline's gut reaction was sharper than that.

Will was in the adjacent classroom planning a rational emotive therapy class and writing reports for treatment team. He had to see this.

Caroline buzzed master control and left her classroom, signaling admittance to Will's classroom. He looked up; gel pen poised. He smiled. She smoothed the drawing on top of the papers on his desk. He put the pen down, and his eyes ran over the sketch. He knew the boys' handwriting. He turned the paper one way, then another.

She put a hand on one hip. "Studying for clues?"

"Stick around," he said. "Duval's coming in soon for treatment. He's cogitating in his cell, but he'll be here. Kid needs help. Bad."

CHAPTER EIGHTEEN

It Eats a Hole

I always had a problem with authority. I just don't like being told what to do on the streets or anywhere. It's always gotta be their rules. But whose rules rule? Mine do. Julius Duval's rules, and I break all of them whenever I want to.

Nothin' can make me do what they want me to do, on the streets or in prison. I never had no rules at home. Well, I never had no real home. What happened in that home, if you call it that, isn't what a home should be anyway. I don't think you could call El Paradiso Motel in Vaca Palms, Florida, a home, exactly, but that's where I spent a lot of time in a closet while my mom was in the bed with some trick. I got to know that goddam closet. I should have paid rent space on it. My blood's all over the inside of that closet from the pimp who beat me up, for watching out the crack one night, for crying to be let out.

He came back again and again. I can still hear my mama's screams but it wasn't any use. That's how I spent my time growing up. And that's no lie.

What's school or authority got to do with me?

I stopped going to school because my mom didn't make me go. She got sick, and now she's dead. I love my mom, but she was no authority in my life and I don't know authority. I hate rules and any kind of authority. I hate cops, always will. People tell me to do things and they talk a lot. They can talk to the wall. I'm not getting anything out of it, and it's not stopping me. I know that if I don't do what they say, they are going to try me with some bull junk. But that's okay because I have a lot of bull junk to say.

Authority is stupid. I hate them and I wish they were dead, and I want their families dead. I talk back to authority because I have no respect for authority.

Authority is just a game, and you have to know how to play your cards. Authority never meant nothin' to me. Authority tries to trap us up in the system, but that don't work either. The system keeps the strong down and the weak from holding on. Authority won't change this broke-down hopeless life. I'm a nothing young Black and I don't give a rat's ass. Authority, I just don't see y'all. I just can't make it. My life is the sky with no stars and the world with no trees and a plant with no leaves, so how can I have a dream?

What does authority have to do with that? Nothin', and that's my point. Nothin'.

IT WAS DUVAL'S TURN. Treatment team began mornings once a week around ten with one representative, at least, from each department of juvenile justice: medical, administration, education, and, of course, God, in the person of the Reverend Robert Temley. The reverend had been a hard-core alcoholic and heroin addict, but he'd given all that up and found his calling in Miami Glades Correctional Center. After a nine-year sentence, he went on to get married, raise six children, and take a fancy to RV's and motorcycles. Caroline knew he had a special affection for Duval, mostly because the preacher had divulged they were from the same backwoods patch of Florida palm scrub. It was something they could talk about. Before Duval would clam up and set his features in that brooding stare of his.

Temley came to work at the correctional center on his black Harley. He was a most untypical biker of barely five foot three, bald and proud of a beer belly—that he insisted was the result of a diet of Hot Pockets and Sprite. After prison and finding God, he'd sworn off Jim Beam, straight from the bottle, and all *usquebaugh*. (The Gaelic word for whiskey translated to "water of life," but Temley preferred to call whiskey "water of death" for the path to hell it had led him down.) As for all the other substances he'd tried, the thought of doing that again made him gag, he said. "If I go back there, I might as well shoot myself in the head."

Duval hung on his every word, not only because he could get a piece of candy out of the preacher but also because he made phone calls to his distraught girlfriend, and to his aunt. His tiny office was lined with pencil drawings of hearts and tears, Jesus Christ and the crown of thorns, blood dripping, and the Virgin of Guadalupe in blue with her signature sun rays shooting out around her. Temley drove everyone crazy with his political opinions—which fell far right of the most conservative— and the Bible. He took a dim view of Caroline's presence, to begin with, and he told her so, often, with a smile. She was a woman in a male world. But he had warmed to her. "A do-gooder with heart," he'd say.

Despite their differences, Caroline felt an attachment to the reverend. Most people did. The tension in the correctional center was stifling, and Caroline's nerves had been pulled taut. Temley was positive in a negative world, and he often added a bit of levity to meetings with the boys, which could heat up, and even explode. The igniter-in-chief of most explosions was Sergeant Miller. The man had no patience.

She felt they needed Temley's presence more than ever today.

The reverend had his own key, and he let himself into treatment. His ruddy face and haystack hair indicated he'd just gotten off his Harley. "What's up, Top?" He directed his question at Miller, but he smiled all around the room. "Ah, my favorite English teacher. Ain't you lookin' swell today?"

Caroline grinned at the preacher. He meant well, but sometimes he was as clueless as a first grader. He greeted staff like he was inviting them to sit down to Christmas dinner. He'd have his turn at Duval, and Caroline knew it would be some high-sounding cheerleading "to stay on the right path" and "avoid the snares of the devil." Temley took a seat in a desk near the door.

Caroline sat down, ready for treatment team. Duval was seated front and center at a desk. He hadn't moved one muscle, his hands, in chains, folded on the desktop. Caroline could cut the tension with a knife.

Miller nodded, smiled, but then resumed his sour look. He thrummed his fingers on the long metal table next to Will and then folded his small hands, wracked with savagely bitten fingernails. He stuck out his chin, adjusted his neck in the tight collar of the green serge. The short sleeves of his military-style shirt were tapered to fit the pronounced muscles in his upper forearms. Other than that, Miller looked like a human version of a Rottweiler. Much to his own dismay, he was short, hence, Caroline assumed much of the way he acted could be traced to a severe case of the Napoleon complex. He compensated for his short stature with warlike bravado. Most of the time, Miller's performance was laughable. But if one dared to laugh, one paid dearly.

"Well, Duval," said the sergeant. He cocked his head and waited. Duval clinked his cuffs on the desktop and folded his hands in the exact same fashion as the sergeant. The youth's head was bowed, now he lifted it, turned it to one side and nodded at the deputy.

Caroline could see the blood start to boil under the closely shaved jowls of Miller. The skin turned an unhealthy red, and he abruptly stopped nodding. "That will be, sir, yes, sir."

Duval nodded again, and Caroline knew that things were not going to go well for Youth Duval that morning.

Miller shifted in his seat, both arms on the table now. He shoved the folders aside and stared down Duval. "You had your little play in school. Nice job in Miss McBride's classroom," he said. "You'll do more time for that. Though I hate to think we have to put up with you any more time than necessary." The sergeant bit off and spat out each word. Duval slowly sat upright in the desk and stared back at the sergeant.

"We'll get to your classroom performance later, after we review all the damage and talk to staff," the sergeant finished. He had jumped the gun in the treatment process. Couldn't wait to get to the part about punishment.

Will's mouth was set in a tight line, but he kept his eye on the paperwork. It was clear Miller was on a tear this morning, setting a tone of fear. If history were any indication, he surely intended to send a message to Duval about bad behavior. Word would get around to the rest of them. Nothing grew faster than the grape vine in a prison.

Duval was on fire. Will was determined. "Has anyone ever sat down and listened to you and talked with you one on one, Mr. Duval?"

Duval straightened up. "Sir, no, sir. I don't think so."

Jeez, does he even know what talking one on one, positively, means?

But Caroline knew what Will was getting at: He'd often said the worst ones could make the sharpest change. Or maybe it seemed like that, in contrast. It was as if Will was staring into a blazing fire, and he was armed with a powerful fire hose. She hoped it worked with Duval because he was one kid on fire if she'd ever seen one. Will was responsible; he knew how they felt. The years he'd spent *being* them were far away, but he'd said each day he spent at Alpha brought back his days in a cell.

"Let's have those essays," said Will. "You were to write about authority issues, right, Youth Duval?"

Miller sat back in the chair, crossed his arms, and scowled.

Duval handed over a sheaf of papers, and Will looked them over. His face was impassable. But Caroline knew, sitting next to Duval, that his writing had been six pages without punctuation, capitalization, or decent spelling, full of the venom he felt for authority. She knew it without even looking, but she would keep her focus as an educator. Oddly enough, in class, Duval followed the rules of grammar as much as he could to his ability, but not so for treatment team. It was no aspersion cast on Will. It was an in-your-face to Miller.

She read Will's expression. She tried to think of something positive and came up with nothing. But Duval did have that seemingly productive conference with Deputy Brown… Didn't that count for something?

Caroline sighed. Duval was the darkest cloud on the rainiest day of all prison days put together. It would take time with him, lots of time, and that was something they didn't have a lot of as far as Duval was concerned.

Will passed the papers to the sergeant without even looking at him. He stared a hole through Duval. "Son," he said. Duval knew that Will could feel his thoughts; he'd tried to read his papers. "Son, that anger's eating a hole right through you. You got to put that wasted energy to better use, and you know it."

And then Will said it again because it always bore repeating, "Mr. Duval, you need to change the way you think, or you will never change the miserable way you feel."

The shift in the youth's face was subtle. He still looked ragged, but he stuck his chin out slightly and looked up at Will.

"What you say?" Will said each word softly, but firmly.

"Sir, I got nothin' to say. Sir."

"You got nothing to say? That isn't what I heard," said Miller. His voice had the screeching tone of nails on a blackboard. "And. You had plenty to *do* in that classroom."

Will sat back and opened a folder.

Miller wouldn't get to square one with Duval. The sergeant was hated throughout the cell block. Why he ever was put in charge of Alpha Juvenile Correctional Center was a mystery. It must have been his reputation as a tough guy that made him a stand-out for the job, but Caroline thought that anyone so miserable could not possibly like what he was doing. Miller didn't seem to enjoy his bursts of rage and the torment he set aflame in the boys. Still, he scratched that itch. He tried over and over again to demonstrate satisfaction as the leading authority at Alpha, but he missed. Sometimes power—like money—missed hitting the mark altogether.

"Miss McBride?" Miller turned to her, barely able to contain his rage at Duval. "Please say something half-way decent about this half-ass before I get up and knock him silly. Maybe that would do some good."

"Well, Mr. Duval is not an essayist. But he does seem to like to read. That true?" She directed her question to Duval who didn't move a muscle. He clinked the cuffs on the desktop again and stared back at Miller.

"I like books," Duval said. Clink, clink. "Especially horror stories. Like this one."

"Sir. Ma'am," said Miller, leaning forward.

Caroline broke in quickly. "…And he does his assignments although, I'd have to say, his grammar skills leave something to be desired. Also, his reading score…"

"Enough. Thank you, Miss McBride. I don't get how you'd find anything positive there, but we'll take it for now. Right, Mr. Duval?"

She felt a heat rising up her neck all the way to her forehead. She sat back in the desk chair and folded her hands.

Duval stared straight ahead, the line of his jaw clenched. Clink, clink went the cuffs. She looked from Miller to Duval, and a new fear crept through her.

He couldn't leap up again. This time his ankles were shackled. But he needed to stop this defiant tone, and the looks that could kill. He was racking up the red marks in his record book—every time he looked cross-eyed—faster than the deputies could write them. In the book of hate, he had volumes written. Even with good behavior, he was weeks away from having book privileges in his cell. Caroline was on the march to end the restriction against reading, but so far she'd been highly unsuccessful, to the point that resistance to her requests was spurring the deputies to toss books into the trash barrel. Just to make a point.

Miller's arms remained folded on the table, his biceps bouncing. His face was a mask of hard hate. "You been talkin' shit about how you gonna keep bucking authority. We'll see how much you buck, we'll see." Miller leaned back, clearly satisfied he'd gotten in another lick. A chuckle barely made it past his thin, tight lips.

Duval stared straight ahead at a patch of blue sky in a high rectangular classroom window. Will measured the sergeant. He'd had his show.

Will turned to Duval. "I got a call from your aunty. She's coming out here for a visit, and we're going to sit down together and talk some things out. What do you think of that, Mr. Duval? You willing?"

As soon as Will mentioned Duval's aunt, the youth's miserable young face softened. She was the one person in his life, the only person anyone at the correctional center had talked with, who had a possibly healthy and loving link to Duval and his rehabilitation. Temley looked up from his Bible and chimed in. "Hear, hear." He'd been calling her from Alpha for Duval, and staff supported it. Duval was one of the lucky inmates. Some of them had a friend or relative who cared about them, usually a grandmother, or an aunt or godmother. It was rarely a parent. Family was needed in the process of rehabilitation, and it was hard to find them, contact them, involve them. Most of the youth were in prison because they had no close relatives who were willing to get involved. Ever.

"I guess," Duval said. "Sir." His head down, hands folded.

"You guess? What does that mean? You like it here? You want to stay 'til you're twenty-two? That's what, about six or seven more years, Mr. Duval. And you're buckin' for it to happen. Mark me."

"No." He whispered. "No, thank you. Sir."

Will cocked his head and didn't take his eyes off Duval. The thing about Will was that he'd sit like that and give the boy his attention all day. If that's what it took. Unfortunately, they didn't have all day.

"Look. You got to be willing to try. To believe in yourself, to start making an effort here," said Will.

Duval lifted his head. "Believe in myself? There's nothing there. I be empty. Sir."

"You're not empty, Duval. And if you *is*, we can just fill up that space with some good shit. But you got to try."

Caroline saw a glimmer, maybe because she wanted to, maybe because she believed in the power of Will. Maybe she believed in Duval. The glimmer might just glow into a full-on change.

Duval sat, silent, slumping in his chair. Miller shouted, "Sit up straight, you! Put those hands where I can see them and plant those feet squarely."

Duval's face resumed the hard-bitten look of the beaten, and he stared straight ahead, inching up.

Miller had jumped into the attack mode at the first sighting of Duval. Now he sat fidgeting with papers and binders. The missing phone and the discovered map haunted Will and Caroline, but they were both loath to tell Miller. They needed to report it. They had decided to wait and pick the right time. Sadly, Caroline had found the map in a book, which Miller would surely use as ammunition against the evils of books. He would seize upon any opportunity to do away with the privilege.

Will's focus in treatment was always to get young prisoners to believe that changing the way they were *thinking* would change the way they *felt*. He told them, "The brain is a powerful tool, but you have to work it, or it gets rusty." The practice to an elemental shift in thinking and feeling was the whole basis of Rational Emotive Therapy. And it worked. If given half a chance.

"Well, what do you have to say?" Miller barked, ruining whatever communication bridge Will might have built with the youth. "Are you going to start working the program around here, or do we have to start working you over?" His threat was not an idle one, but threats and abuse wouldn't work. Anyone with half an ounce of sense on the subject of rehabilitation and therapy knew that. Caroline felt so rigid in that chair she thought she'd crack. Nothing good was coming. She'd learned a thing or two in her years at Alpha, and this was not working. It certainly wasn't Will's way of reaching the inmates, and it wasn't hers either.

Duval looked up at Miller with such ingrained hate, it startled Caroline. "I'm down, whenever, for whatever's in play."

Miller sneered. "What's that supposed to mean? And you address me as 'sir'."

"Sir Whatever," said Duval, softy, with venom and a level gaze.

Miller didn't hesitate. Caroline watched, incredibly, as the sergeant stood up, knocked his chair over, and bounded around the table. Papers and binders and one coffee mug landed on the floor. He grabbed Duval by the neck of his shirt. Caroline heard the rip.

Temley stood halfway out of his chair, and fell back, shaking his head. His mouth formed an O.

Caroline looked from Will to the reverend. A beseeching look. Will was on his feet.

The youth landed on the floor with a thud, and the sergeant spread-eagled on top of him, arms and legs going at once, beating Duval around the back and legs while the youth rolled himself into a ball. Duval didn't move at first, probably out of shock, and then he made an effort to sit up. Miller knocked him back down. He held the youth against the linoleum, and Duval strained to get loose, a look of terror on his face. Caroline feared for him. She took a step forward. Spittle, with blood in it, leaked from a corner of the boy's mouth.

She stood there, hands on hips. "What the hell... Stop!" But no one was listening. It was dizzying to think how fast it happened. Again.

Will moved around the table, fists clenched. "That's enough." His voice seemed to echo in the room. Miller let go. An insistent buzzing at the classroom door, and Pilson sprang into the classroom. He sprayed Duval with mace while Miller retreated to a corner with the radio to his lips. Duval let out a scream. Caroline froze to the spot with rage. She looked at Miller's smug expression and felt the urge to find a lethal use for the heavy textbook on the desk.

What's it come to? I'm gonna kill that mf-er with a textbook?

The mace seemed to be unnecessary since Duval was on the ground, cuffed and shackled, and he wasn't moving. But no one asked her opinion. Pilson had his foot on Duval's back.

Her eyes started to burn. The faint peppery odor lingered in the room. Through a watery gaze, she saw Will grab Duval's arm and then he came for her. He withdrew his key and in one motion they were all headed out of the classroom and over to a basin in the laundry room off the day room. Will didn't seem affected.

"We need cold water," said Will, soberly. "We need lots of cold water. And soap." Caroline blinked and rubbed her eyes. She felt all right, except for this bizarre experience—standing at a wash tub with Duval and Will—all splashing themselves with soap and water. Will held out wads of scratchy brown paper towels.

"You okay?" He blotted her forehead.

"Fine." She took the towels from him and started in on Duval—stock still, stunned and confused.

Duval's face and shirt were soaked. As they all headed out of the laundry and over to a metal table in the day room, he held on to Will's shirt. His head was down, and red-hot rage had not cooled with a dousing of pepper spray, soap, and water.

Miller stood in the day room, feet wide apart, tensing his fists.

Is this supposed to make him look terrifying? Powerful?

He was pitiful, a small man with a smug expression. The radio crackled in his hand. "Roger that." He clicked off. Caroline shot him a look. But the sergeant didn't seem to notice. He was busy hooking the radio to his belt, re-blousing his shirt, and lining up his gig line, seeming to put the dust up behind him.

"All right, then," he said. "That did not go well, but it went. Let's go back to work, and you, Duval, back to your cell." Pilson grabbed Duval's shirt and steered the youth toward the cell block. He dragged his feet unwillingly. Stubborn to the end.

Miller opened the classroom, and Caroline and Will followed him in, silently.

Caroline didn't trust herself to talk, so she fumed instead.

Miller righted the chair, picked up a coffee mug, and slammed it on the table. He sat down and began shuffling papers again. His movements now level and modulated. But the attack had done it. Apparently, it had taken the edge off, smoothed him out. Pilson's voice, berating Duval, carried from the day room. Then the cell block door slammed, like an exclamation point to the whole incident.

Caroline shivered.

"You just attacked that boy. Defenseless. In *chains*." Her tone was as even as she could make it. She didn't expect much of a response, and she didn't get one. She stood next to her desk, feeling remarkably calm, but for reasons different than those of the sergeant. She was right, and Miller was wrong.

He didn't look up. "Defenseless," he sneered. "Isn't that what that cop was, defenseless, when Duval shot him in the leg? That punk doesn't know the meaning of defenseless, but maybe he does now." He brushed a speck off his upper sleeve.

It hit her again. Miller was a vengeful bully of the first order. "The old eye for an eye?" She looked around for a biblical backup from the reverend, but he'd escaped.

"Maybe I am saying just that. Doesn't it come right out of one of your books?"

"Yeah, the Big Book," said Caroline. "Which also says, do unto others as you would have them do unto you."

He grunted at her, like he'd crawled out of a cave. He looked at Will. "What asshole we got next?"

They still had eleven boys to review for treatment. Now, they'd surely hold the sessions into the next day. She put the Kleenex to her nose. The pepper spray had wafted around the room, but it was dissipating, thankfully. She kept her head down. She didn't want Miller to see the anger and disgust that threatened to twist her expression. She'd keep it to herself for now. Nothing was to be gained from taking it up with Miller now. The mace was annoying, burning, but nothing like the mean dose aimed at Duval. And nothing like the irritation she felt for Miller.

Will looked grave. He held a pen, his head down, studying Miller. She was sorry that he was subjected to sitting it out with Miller, week after week, and, at once, she was glad. The boys needed him. They didn't need Miller's demonstrations of power and hate.

Caroline could not sit there and carry on. Not today. Maybe not anymore. She was fed up. She backed out of the room quickly. She needed to find Harvey. She had to tell someone. She had to put this on record before she exploded.

CHAPTER NINETEEN

Let's Have a Party

"IT'S THEIR FACILITY," SAID HARVEY, WEARILY, almost whining. He half turned from his desk littered with dog-eared manuals and piles of paper. The sun streamed into the small office overlooking the parking lot, and despite the air conditioning, Harv was sweating.

Carolyn sighed and slumped onto a chair next to a heap of folders. Harv's thankless job sent him bolting around the correctional center campus with documents and directives on futile errands; his position as director of the Alpha charter school was hardly of great importance to Sergeant Miller even though they pretended at being buddies. Harvey Sanders tried. His heart was in the right place. He was continually forced to go to battle for education and make excuses and promises to Caroline and Art.

"The thing is…"

Caroline frowned. She knew how this would go. Education was the pawn in a power trip. The department received state funding for rehabilitation through education, but the deputy staff resented their mission. Instead, the administration pushed containment and punishment. Yet Harvey played the game. He understood both sides of the coin, and he was good at playing. Everybody liked him. They couldn't help it. He was generous, ready with a joke, and he had an infectious laugh.

Well, she wasn't laughing now, and neither was Harv.

While she waited for him to think up an excuse, the fax machine pumped out more regs for Harvey to carry out, or most likely, file away. Caroline looked at the round filing cabinet next to his desk on the floor. He had five stacks of papers lined up and each day he moved one closer to the wastebasket as the week progressed. If the pile closest to the basket didn't get taken care of, it got "filed." But that didn't mean the matter went away; a follow-up was sure to appear within the week, in triplicate.

Caroline could tell from the tedious single spacing, letterhead, and bullets on the faxed pages popping out of the machine that more directive was coming from the Great Colonel or Sheriff the Almighty, or whoever thought up correctional center garble. It was a place of "no's": no talking, eating, drinking, littering, loitering, singing, large bags, yoga pants, shorts, tank tops, glitter and sequins, zippers, jewelry (excluding some rings and watches), music of any sort, phones and other devices and materials that the deputy on duty objected to. The list was tweaked depending on the season, and whim. On every wall, it seemed, there was the list. In the Alpha lobby, someone had drawn an extra "o" on each "no," put a dot in the middle of each of the two "o's," and created a list of eyeballs. "Were watching U" was scrawled underneath in orange marker.

Harv pulled a sheaf of papers out of the machine and looked over at Caroline. "More shit," he said, shaking his head.

"Don't divert, Harv."

"I'm not. It's just that…"

"It's just that you're snowed." She tried to smile, glancing at the scorcher outside behind Harvey's head.

"I'm snowed, but you're right. This is not right."

"We have to report it," she said. "Miller can't just go around beating up kids. Duval was in handcuffs and ankle bracelets, and then to top it all, Pilson maced him."

Harvey wiped his forehead and swiveled in his chair. He was simmering with irritation. "I'll report it, but I didn't see it happen. You'll have to fill out the paperwork, Caro."

She stood up and thought of moving toward the doorway. Just getting the hell out of there. She needed a break. She felt weighed down, suddenly, like she was wading through Vaseline. But stubborn as could be, she was not about to let this go. Even though it would make Harv even wearier.

"I will, I'll do it. You'll have it on your desk. Soon." She managed a smile. "It's the thugs leading the thugs around here. We could use a little civility."

"Well, I couldn't agree with you more. But enforcing it is another matter."

A fist lightly pounded the arm of his chair. "I don't like to hear this happening with Miller. He's supposed to set a good example of authority. What are the kids supposed to think?"

"That's the point, Harv." She rapped her knuckles on his desk. "What the hell's *anyone* supposed to think?"

The phone rang and Harvey waggled a finger at her.

She'd go.

She could write up it up all she wanted, but would it do any good? Harvey had too many battles, and he had to pick the ones he had a chance of winning. His was a strategic effort to keep the peace between deputy staff and education, and to get space, money, time, and material inside the correctional center for his department.

Caroline waved, started for the door. She had an ace left but she'd keep it close, for now. She could play the game, too.

She'd stopped short of telling Harvey about the sketch she'd found in the book—the detailed map of Alpha that one of the boys had drawn. And the phone. *And* the kitchen. Was it part of a plan for a set-up, or worse? It wasn't time for her reveal. She was too angry to go into it, and she wanted to work out something with Will. She could trust him, and he would fight for the boys. He'd sort it out. Harvey meant well, but he'd use the information for more game playing with Miller. The sergeant would go ballistic, toss the place. No good would come of it. It drove Caroline crazy, but she was going crazy anyway.

She clomped down the hallway, arms swinging. It seemed to help. She'd let off steam to Harvey and at once felt a measure of guilt. He was doing as much as he could even in the face of all the obstacles. She wished she could be more supportive.

Two things: I have to talk to Will, and we can't lose what's left of the tenuous connection to deputy staff.

A foreboding swept over her. They were all in for it. Each step toward her classroom brought her closer to that realization.

TARVIS WAS ABOUT TO HAVE A RARE moment in the sun. He and the rest of the cell block were allowed to spend one hour outside playing basketball—at least three times a week. It was near ninety degrees on a late afternoon, but Tarvis did not care. He was about to get out under the blue sky, among the birds and crackling palms. The sounds alone were music.

He stood in line at the back of the cell block. A door opened to the basketball court. It was hardly an ideal spot, but much of Alpha was anything but ideal. The state had allocated millions for the construction of the correctional center in the late 90's, and this is what they had for rec? Someone had cut corners. Especially here. The buckled concrete, weeds growing in the cracks. Tarvis knew they didn't even have a decent basketball. He was already aware that whoever put this dump together hadn't planned the heating and cooling systems with any degree of success because they either roasted or froze half to death.

The air conditioning was stuck on overdrive, especially when Haver was on duty, and that was often, because the deputy worked overtime. The youth froze. They were not allowed to wear jackets to class unless it was officially winter, and therefore, the prescribed time of the year for jackets to be worn in Florida. It was the rule—one among many in a rigid system housed in an inefficient building.

Tarvis thought of the useless kitchen and lack of training in the trades. *Rehabilitation? What a joke.* The inmates couldn't use hammers and screwdrivers any more than they could use knives and other utensils for culinary arts. They were stuck with tattered textbooks (thanks, Duval), limited computer use—no internet—and their brains. Tarvis was certain that his would rot or freeze before he got out of there. The routine was mind-numbing.

Some vocational classes were offered in the computer lab. Tarvis wanted one of those "construction" certificates. But without ever touching a hammer or a screwdriver? There was some talk of computer-based culinary arts training, and that turned out to be a dud.

They certainly were not going to chop up tomatoes—and each other and the deputies—with kitchen tools. Baking? Bread? Cookies? It was never going to happen. Especially after word went around that a few geniuses at a North Miami juvie found a way to make explosives out of baking soda, powder, and flour. They even came up with thumb tacks and paper clips to put in their bombs.

Tarvis spotted Allen. Apparently, Allen had found a use for the kitchen. It was part of this so-called plan. He'd communicated as much to Tarvis, San Antonio, and even Duval. Something about the "electrics," he'd said. "We may have to cut 'em off at the right time." Mo was going to find out more, he told them. *Soon.* Tarvis couldn't wait to hear more about this crazy shit. It was getting complicated, and Tarvis was frustrated, but he'd keep an ear out.

TARVIS WAS GOING TO ENJOY THIS hour outside. He'd been on a mandatory lockdown since his intake, except for chow and shower, and now he was getting a taste of "freedom." The word was bitter in his mouth.

This place of freedom to let off steam was a broken-down basketball court out behind the correctional center—a leftover parking pad from the old county jail. The stubs of gas pumps and other equipment poked out of the scrub beyond the fence. The concrete was a sorry, uneven stretch. Still, it was outside, and outside in Florida was often glorious. Even in the heat. The vapid humidity was redolent of green growth and the hint of salt air; the sun shined almost every day, year-round; the birds twittered and cawed happily.

Tarvis marched out the back door with the rest of the "team" of seventeen or so (a couple of the boys were in the sick bay). He stopped abruptly against the concrete block wall and breathed, his face turned up toward the sun.

Even this was not allowed.

"What the fuck, Tarvis. You gettin' a suntan?" It was Haver with a welcome taunt.

Tarvis got a move on. They had less than an hour out there, and he wanted to run. Oh, did he want to run.

He'd have to contain it to sport, but even that hit a snag. The ball got stuck in the razor wire surrounding the courtyard, giving new meaning to, *"Wilson, you're really in trouble now. Come back!"* Pilson retrieved the ball with a broom handle, but not before threatening Youth Roberts with it. The ball was a loss, a sorry, flat blob. The bouncing game was over. Now it was a throwing game until they got a new ball.

Deputy Brown brought out another, and Tarvis hoped it survived the afternoon—that he would survive without running afoul of Haver or some other deputy. He'd been to the point of exploding in that cell. He ran the length of the concrete pad and back again, not even keeping his eye on the ball. It just felt good to work up a sweat in the sun. He ran for his life. He'd been having border-line anxiety attacks at night, and who could he tell about that? Who would care? He didn't want to draw attention to himself. He could only guess what sort of interrogation and paperwork would go into such a complaint. He knew what was going on inside his head and heart, and while it wasn't good, he was determined to live with it.

He'd seen his aunt have an anxiety attack, and it wasn't funny, with the sweating, heart palpitations, swooning. She'd thought it was a heart attack, but Auntie Foona drank bottles of Coca-Cola Classic and coffee with loads of cream and sugar like it was going out of style. She weighed 300 pounds. The doctor said her problem was her weight, a combination of caffeine and sweets, and "a proclivity to anxiety in the genes," he said. "Nerves." Tarvis liked repeating that: proclivity in the genes. He'd been in the doctor's office when the nurse gave the news to his auntie, and the words just stuck, because words always stuck to Tarvis like honey to the toast, and then they went right to the strings on his guitar. If the words didn't stick, he looked them up. He guessed he was kind of a mixed-up poet. As for his auntie's type of anxiety, Tarvis wasn't sure it was his actual type. Tarvis wasn't allowed caffeine of any sort at Alpha, but he knew anxiety when he felt it, and the feeling wasn't going anywhere soon. He didn't really have words to describe it, but his air guitar helped get rid of it whatever it was.

The metal doors to the cell blocks slammed behind two more deputies. They leaned against the concrete block in the shade, one eating chips, another jawing on the radio. The boys wore baggy shorts and tanks that constituted athletic gear at Alpha. The only other time they wore the gear was when they left their cells to do push-ups in the hallway. Tarvis had thought gym class in elementary was bad, but this was unbelievable. Some unlucky one always got a deputy boot in the ribs, a kick to the shins.

The hot sun hit Tarvis full in the face and on his shoulders, and for just an instant, hardly a second's worth, he felt free. He squeezed his eyes shut and soaked in the heat, the air. It was hotter than hell, and he forced himself to like it. He let the Florida humidity wrap around him like a wet, warm, loving blanket. Oh, what he would do to be in St. Joe, on the beach, under the pines, breaking open a nice cold forty.

"What the hell are you doing? You actin' like a damn lizard out here. Why you keep standin' there?" Tarvis knew the remark was for him, but he played innocent. It wasn't a question, it was a bark, and Deputy Swanson came after him, not with a basketball, but with a clipboard. Tarvis was going to get written up, again, surely, but for what? For enjoying a few minutes of sunshine? It was possible the deputy would write that on his record of gigs for the month.

"Sir, yes, sir,"

"Get your ass over there."

Tarvis was suddenly embarrassed that the deputy had seen the pleasure on his face, his sheer enjoyment of getting the fuck out of that cell and into the sun. Pleasure of any kind was absolutely forbidden to inmates of Alpha. Some of them didn't like to go out for ball. They weren't any freer out there, and it was too hot, they said. They had sunk into the lethargy of prison life. Tarvis didn't want to let that happen to him.

Deputy Pilson stood against the chain line on the other side of the court. He was sweating bullets, his red face getting redder and swelling up to the size of a basketball in the heat.

Tarvis looked up at the razor wire surrounding the basketball court. He ran along the edge, dodging here and there for a way into the game. He tripped on the weeds growing out of the cracks, stopped, and looked down. A yellow lantana, its petals smaller than apple seeds, its struggle to meet up with a butterfly doomed. Tarvis plucked the flower out of the crack and stuck it in his waist band. He looked around. No one saw him bend over and pick the flower.

No one saw me? With their cameras and beady eyes? This was a bit of information to file away. No telling how he could use that.

"Heads up!" Allen tossed him the ball. It was soft as a rotten melon, but it felt good in his grip. He bounced it. It still had some life. He checked out the court and met Haver's stare. He quickly looked away for fear of attracting any further attention. Tarvis shook off a wave a misery and almost collided with Allen when he passed the ball.

"Hey," Allen hissed. "Watch for a note. Soon. Like in a minute."

Tarvis caught himself before surprise gave him away. He put on a poker face. He didn't know what Allen was talking about, but he had a strong feeling it would be better if he never knew. Tarvis ran after Allen, faked a move and pivoted. He was near enough to Allen's ear to hiss back. "Wha...."

But Allen was gone. Tarvis ran after him and glanced at the deputy. Pilson saw Allen pass Tarvis twice. The deputy pushed himself off the fence and took his thumbs out of the pockets of his trousers. He took one step toward the end of the court where Allen and Tarvis were handing the ball off to each other, putting out what appeared to be a pretty good fight for the ball.

It was just about then that San Antonio made a loop around the court, right before Pilson decided to move into ball territory with Allen and Tarvis. San Antonio dove, or tripped, and landed on top of the deputy's highly polished boots. The youth would pay for it, but the move was worth it. Pilson kicked at San Antonio, like he'd stepped in a doggie pile. San Antonio rolled around on the concrete, moaning and apologizing. "Sir, sorry, sir," he said. "I'm really sorry, sir."

"Get the fuck up you asshole."

"Sir, yes, sir," said San Antonio, who looked up in supplication.

Diversion in progress.

The maneuver took just enough time for Allen to complete his mission. He circled Tarvis again, and this time, he palmed off the note. Tarvis took it, rather than have it flutter to the court. He coughed and bent over and stuck the piece of paper in his shoe. He would deal with it later. He didn't want any more trouble than he already had, and he had plenty, facing three years in this place. He didn't want to stay any longer. He could always flush the paper down the toilet, after he read it. In the meantime, the note burned a hole in his shoe.

Pilson looked over at him. But he was still dealing with San Antonio, who was sprawled on the concrete, doubled over, his knee clasped in two hands.

Tarvis ran another lap, showing he was in the game. He was definitely in a sweat now, but so far so good. *I should get an award... Did dick head see the hand off? Well, I'd know soon enough if he did.*

Pilson walked off. Swanson and Hathaway jabbered away near the entrance to the cell block.

Wesley ran by and yelled, "Man down, man down! Sir!"

THE BOYS OF ALPHA BLOCK

"What the fuck. Shut up, Wesley," said Pilson, and kept walking.

The deputies at the door looked up casually. San Antonio was still on the concrete. Swanson smirked and went back to talking about fishing and girls. The ball was still bouncing around the court in a fashion that had no purpose, no game.

Hathaway blew the whistle and the action stopped, each player panting and sweating. The boys fell into line, San Antonio was running in place, shrugging off his pratfall. Hathaway took the ball and threw it to the end of the court behind them where it stuck, once again, in the razor wire.

Tarvis caught the look that passed between San Antonio and Allen. A slight nod. San Antonio couldn't hold off the smile. Tarvis pretended he didn't see any of it, his feet shifting nervously.

It was too late. The play was a successful fake, so far. He had the damn note in his shoe, and one thought in his brain. *Why me? Now I'm in it whether I want it or not. All in for sure.*

CHAPTER TWENTY

Pipe Up

TARVIS PUT THE LANTANA IN A PAPER CUP of water and stashed it high up on the window ledge, the squashed yellow petals opening up to the sun. He marveled over the hardy little plant. It gave him hope, and in it he found music. He was sketching another line of a song when a loud bang sounded on his metal door. The pencil snapped in his fingers and Tarvis bolted to his feet.

"I'm gonna stroke you for that. Sittin' on the bed, dumb ass." It was Grappler, peering at Tarvis through the high small window of the door.

Tarvis didn't look back at him. He stood at military attention, waiting.

"And that may be only the start of it." Grappler had his keys out and Haver was right behind him. "We're here to toss you, boy."

A tossing was to be avoided. At all costs. But Tarvis, of course, had little to say about it, and not one idea why this was happening to *him*. Then his stomach froze into an icy knot. The note. The fucking note.

They'd never find it.

Grappler was a lazy green thing. He looked like an enormous fire hydrant, but, well, he was green. Even his face was on the green side of sallow yellow. His hair was cut in the usual uncomplimentary style of a cactus caught in a blender. That is to say, it was short but uneven and bristly on all sides. Deputy Grappler fancied himself a tough guy, having played, momentarily, second string corner back for Florida State. Tarvis hadn't been in prison long, but he knew he would get a weird send-up of football references in any face-to-face with Grappler.

"Grab him by the laces, or the cojones, or whatever," said Grappler. "Wish he had a face mask; I'd rattle his cage."

Haver shoved Tarvis against the wall. His knees knocked so loudly he was sure he'd get written up for "making unnecessary noise." Tarvis kept his eyes straight ahead, and braced himself, endured it.

The mattress went into the air. Of course, the sparse furnishings were bolted down, including the bed base, the chair, and a small metal desk. Whatever was left over in the room was shredded, ripped, stomped, and finally spat upon by Haver.

"Foul," said Grappler.

"Where's the fucking note," said Haver. "We're going to start ripping up what's left of you if you don't come up with it."

"Sir, deputy, sir, I got no idea what you sayin'. Sir." He was afraid of what they'd do to him. Fear of the unknown. It was a bitch. But all he could think of was Uncle Tendris. *They can beat you to a pulp but they just gonna find the inside sweeter.*

"Deputy Pilson seen it."

"Sir, seen what, sir?"

"The paper, the note, goddam it. You passing contraband on the b-ball court. He seen it."

Tarvis managed to keep himself upright in military posture. *They never gonna find that fuckin' note.*

"Sir, no, sir."

Grappler ripped the pillow apart, started on the extra uniform until Haver stopped him. "No. That'll cost us. Let him keep his Gucci designer duds." Grappler grunted but didn't stop going through the folds and cuffs and pockets. He threw the pants and shirt in a pile on the cement. Tarvis still looked straight ahead. At nothing.

"One of you assholes better fess up or it's curtains."

"Sir, yes, sir."

The deputies filed out, the cell door clanged behind them, and Tarvis collapsed. He felt like a wrung-out, wet dog, and the smell of sweat and heat nearly made him faint. The meaty hatred of the two deputies hung in his cell. He went to the sink and ran the cold water and rinsed his face. *Fuckers never find it. Unless they go diggin' in the pipes. It down the sewers of good old Alpha.*

The note hadn't said much, and just enough. *We gonna do it. You on board? We need info bout the outs. See you in chow line.*

Tarvis was conflicted. His religion was that he keep to himself. He knew this instinctively, and his whole crew of friends and family had lived by it. Nothing good would happen from spreading himself around and "blabbing all ya know." That was Grannie. She'd also said, "An empty barrel makes the most noise," and she'd been dead right about that.

He'd just come to the correctional center, and they wanted him in on their escape plan? What the hell? Tarvis was more curious than anything else to find out what they were up to. He already had a good idea about what Allen was up to. No question, Allen and that crew wanted out. He wanted out. His hatred of the system, and especially of the deputies, was tipping him in Allen's direction. He wanted to hear what he had to say.

Have to keep an open mind, 'cause I'm already in the game.

Oh, yeah.

CHAPTER TWENTY-ONE

Welcome to the Jungle

DEPUTY BETTINGER MADE HERSELF AT HOME in Sergeant Miller's office. He was busy, but he always had time for the "Amazon," his old drinking buddy. They'd started out at the Bradley Detention Center together and "graduated" to prison when the colonel decided to open the juvenile facility. They were both good at ass kissing, and at one time, had kissed each other's asses. Literally. That time had passed, mostly because the Amazon had called it off. Miller still tweaked, just a gnat's wing, over the thought of it. But bygones were bygones. He wasn't all that sorry now that he looked at Bettinger.

She still smoked, in fact, reeked of it. He glanced at the Bic and Marlboro Reds she casually placed on the corner of his desk, like she owned that little square of him. And she'd gained at least twenty pounds. That tight green uniform had once revealed an enticing crack in her butt and nice cleavage. Now it pulled across her thighs and chest. And she was sweating. What was that his grandma said? *A lady don't sweat, she glistens.*

The Amazon was in a sweat.

"What's up, lady?"

"Don't call me lady, you asshole."

"Hey." But he laughed. So did she.

"Just joshin' with you, sarge." She propped her boots on the rim of a waste basket and then swung them off and planted both on the linoleum. She leaned forward, her hands clenched. "Got some news. Maybe a problem. Maybe just news. I don't know."

"Oh, yeah? Since when you got a problem you can't handle by yo little ol' self?"

"This is a little bigger than that."

"You don't say."

"I say." Bettinger was all business. Miller was all ears. "Well, actually, I don't know how to say this, but I might as well say straight out. I think these little motherfuckers are up to something. Big."

"What the hell's so new about that." The sergeant casually flipped a pencil end over end. "If they ain't hiding the Little Debbies and shit, or lipping off, they're sneaking books out of McBride's room. So what."

"No, this is something bigger," she said. "Way bigger. You know that kid, Wesley? He saw a plan. Stuck in one of the books in McBride's classroom."

"They're always drawing shit. Glass houses and castles with roses dripping blood and such. Jesus. They're all a bunch of creeps."

"Wesley's a snitch. He says they got a plan. An escape plan." Bettinger's curly wisps stuck to the beads of sweat on her forehead. Her green eyes were like go lights.

Miller snapped back in the swivel chair and laughed out loud. Just about tipped himself out the window.

"What the fuck? What's so damn funny?"

"How do you think these little fuckers could *possibly* escape this place? If we didn't taze them out the door, or beat the shit out of them, the razor wire would get them," said Miller. He was still chuckling.

"I know, I know. That's true. But listen. I didn't see it, but Wesley did. He's not sure who did it but said it looked like San Antonio's work. Who the fuck knows? They're all a bunch of Picassos around here."

"Jesus. A plan of *what*." He wasn't in the mood for questions. He wanted answers.

"It was an elaborate map of Alpha, right down to the light switches. It had a detailed sketch of master control. The key locker. Every damn buzzer in the place."

"Oh for fuck's sake. OK. Let's suppose they are planning something. We'll put everyone on alert. I just hope they try something. We'll have a damn field day." Miller leaned over his desk and pounded it so hard the coffee jumped out of his cup. "Lights out."

BETTINGER TROMPED DOWN THE HALL toward the sally port for a cig and a read. She had one of Hiaasen's books under her arm, and she was going to see what all the fuss was about. She'd heard McBride loved the author, and Miller hated him. She'd make up her own damn mind about it.

She didn't feel any relief from sharing the information about this supposed plan with Miller. No, not at all. She wouldn't put anything past these felons. She'd always thought they were dumb asses, but, lately, she'd come around to thinking they weren't so dumb. Staff would be the dumbest to think otherwise. Maybe McBride was right after all.

CHAPTER TWENTY-TWO

Big Ears, Little Brains

"WHERE'D YOU HEAR THAT, ART?" Caroline was flabbergasted. She'd thought her discovery of the map of the correctional center was a secret. She'd only shared it with Will. Did he talk? Nothing seemed to stay underground in the prison. Rumors flew like a virus.

"Harvey. He heard it from Miller. Apparently, Bettinger told him about the map from none other than our sterling pupil, Youth Wesley."

"Jesus. How'd *he* find out? What are they gonna do with that info? Besides roast Wesley," she said.

"I don't know. But like you said, just a week ago, something's going on with these boys. Something's definitely up."

"Will's got to know something. And he might know what Miller is planning now that the cat's out. What'd Miller do?"

"Nothing. Laughed."

"Art, this isn't funny."

"You telling me? When was the last time you had a good laugh around here?"

She didn't think long on that one. The answer: never.

THE EVENING "CRASH" CART WAS COMING around, so named because the food often caused such stomach cramps, they thought they would crash and die. Jesse Allen led the complaints. A lot of good that did. The so-called food kept rolling out of the jail cafeteria, and God only knew what ingredients were added.

Staff got the goodies in the county cafeteria; the inmates ate shit.

Allen was back on duty, pushing some kind of grey slime over oblongs of reprehensible "meat." He poked it with a spatula. *At least, they say it's meat. No one can tell for sure.*

He was nervous as hell. They'd tossed Tarvis's cell but had skipped him. A miracle. Or maybe they'd get to him later. He had no way of knowing, and the fear of not knowing was more nerve wracking than the actual act of getting tossed. No telling what they were up to. Still, Allen was determined to stay focused on the mission. He had to get the word around. Fortunately, there was too much confusion at mealtime for anyone to notice his attempt to communicate.

Duval was at the end of the line. They'd sprung him for chow, which was amazing given his recent track record. But there weren't enough deputies to give him "room service." So, he lined up with the rest of them. Duval stood behind San Antonio. He whispered without moving his lips, without moving at all. "What the fuck happened to Wesley?"

Wesley Pautz was in the opposite line, a black eye and long red bruise etched along one side of his face and down his neck. San Antonio answered, "Slipped on soap."

Rumor was the kid had snitched. On someone, about something. The deputies usually left bruises that weren't so obvious; these were more than obvious.

"We have to move things up," said San Antonio. "Allen'll let you know." Not a muscle gave away the message. If San Antonio were auditioning to be a ventriloquist, he'd have gotten the job on the spot.

Duval looked up just then to see Allen almost in his face. He dipped the ladle and slopped gravy on to a plate while he leaned in. "Gonna talk to cousin Maurice about a day to go to church. We gonna need you. Get fired up."

"Yeah," Duval said. He looked down at the mess on his plate. "Thanks." A rare grin.

"What the fuck, Duval." It was Haver, passing out heartburn to everyone in line. "This ain't cocktail hour. Get your ass back to your cell and finish that filet mignon afore I kick ya here to kingdom come."

Duval stifled a sneer and let a smile play around his eyes. He looked up at

Allen but the youth ducked his head, got busy serving the dinner down the line. Duval kept smiling. It was well known amongst Allen, San Antonio, and Tarvis that Duval wanted nothing more than to bust out of there and beat the shit out of Haver and Swanson and a couple of the others on the way out the door.

"Yeah," Duval turned away from Haver, his lips barely moving when Allen looked up. They were all equally adept at messaging without moving. "I be right there, and ready."

Duval moved closer to the rice, but still close enough to Allen. "I mean fire up," Allen said. "You gonna make it real hot 'round here. Let ya know more later."

Duval seemed unconcerned, absorbed in the grey shit on his tray. He picked at a biscuit as hard as a rock. He was still smiling despite the hovering, swaggering Haver.

Allen plopped another slab of meat on the tray, grabbed a rag, and rubbed out some spilled gravy. His wheels kept turning. San Antonio had the shivs. And Tarvis, well, he was going to do some talking. None of it could be done without a little communication.

He had to figure a way to get the master key out of the locker in master control. *Oh, snap. Not gonna be easy but what is?*

The thought of it made his insides pucker, and his brain click like a time bomb, and all at once he enjoyed it. He felt alive when his mind was whizzing with the details of the escape. It was going to happen, or he'd die trying. It wouldn't be easy, no way, but it could be done. It had to be done.

Duval was going to set the fire. With Bettinger's lighter. Allen stifled a laugh thinking how the fat deputy would be an unwitting participant in the escape.

Allen had all kinds of ideas about how to make this happen. He just didn't think about the alternative. There couldn't be an alternative, and if there were, it was too dark a place to think about. A deep soundless hole of nothingness. He'd be *dead*.

Allen glanced in the direction of the laundry. He was happy they didn't lock it up. The youth had to have ready access to washer and dryer, mops, and rags. The phone was still under that machine, and he had to use it to call Cousin Mo. *Fast.* He needed his new phone number—Mo had business, and that required a lot of phones.

He'd get a number from Aunt Dorcas who was scheduled to visit Saturday.

Hey, better yet, maybe the chaplain would make a call. Get her to bring Maurice with her. That would be real nice.

He had to use the phone soon. Sooner the better, before it was missed, before it lost its charge, before they all lost their minds and nerve to do this. He wouldn't, but he wasn't so sure about the others. His experience with loyalty was spotty at best. He'd just have to speed this up and go with the best plan. What was it he read? *Plans are useless, planning is indispensable.*

They can take their daily plans and stick them where the Florida sun don't shine 'cause me and the boys have our own planning.

There was some organization to reckon with, some plans he could count on to *plan* around. The more he thought about it, he began to think it best that they rush master control, get the key, and blow. But, still, he had some more thinking to do on the matter.

Allen just wished Duval could keep it in for a while longer. He hated the place so much he just couldn't calm down. They needed him, and his determination and hate. It was fuel for the fire. And that's exactly what Allen had in mind. He'd been on the lookout for a good way to get it started. Bettinger smoked. He could smell it on her. The square outline of the pack in the pocket of her blouse. He'd seen her set the cigs and lighter down on the desk in master control. Right under the key locker. Allen had been an adept pick pocket on the outs, and now he had a challenge. He'd be swift, but he had to be sure. He had to zero in on the places and times he might get hold of that lighter. Take advantage of the laziness of the deputies. Seize the opportunity. But one slip up and they were dead.

Haver saw Allen and Duval eyeing each other in the chow line again. Duval had pulled away from Allen. "That does it, Duval." The deputy stood planted, feet wide apart, thumbs in his belt. "I thought I told you to get a move on."

The boy looked up into the deputy's face, and something switched. Duval's expression went blank and hard; Allen could feel the tension from behind the cart, a ladle suspended and dripping.

Duval dropped the tray on the linoleum. The clatter of plates and forks and spoons, along with the splash of dinner on the youth's sandals—and Haver's green serge legs and shiny boots. Twenty boys and three deputies in the hallway froze in place.

"You done that on purpose, Duval. I seen it." Haver sputtered, the poison in his tone ramping up the disaster. He reached around the back of his belt where he kept his stick. Duval's eyes got wider. He stood still, blazing with hate. He didn't move. He looked like a dog about to be kicked, except Duval didn't cower.

"You fixin' to use that on me?" Duval asked. *"Sir."*

"I'd like to beat your brains in with it. Make you get down and lick the crap off my boots."

Duval lifted his foot and brought it down hard on a pile of meat and gravy congealing on the floor. The grease made a new splotch right above Haver's knee and a few droplets landed just under his chin. He wiped it away, slowly. Too slowly. The tension thickened to a blinding fog. Haver clenched his jaw. Whipped the club off his waist and cracked Duval right in the thigh. "You're buckin', you buckin'." He dropped the club and braced himself. They all waited for the inevitable, their trays clutched in their fingers. Some of them stepped back.

Allen didn't see him coming. But he heard. Everyone around that cart turned as Deputy Brown sauntered into the day room toward the line. He was whistling. Lumbering along, swinging his arms. He stepped right between Duval and Haver, like he'd slipped. Or fallen into place. Like he was just out for a walk in the breeze and happened to drop in.

Like hell. Allen was smiling. The move worked. Haver hesitated, Brown deflected. Diffused the bomb. Most of the youth didn't see it that way, but Allen did. Haver most likely didn't, but his shoulders let down. He stepped aside and got busy brushing off his pants. Allen took it all in. Not much escaped him. He stared at the smiling Deputy Brown. He was one straight dude.

Right then, it struck Allen. Deputy Brown had to be off duty when they went to "church." The deputy would put a stop to it somehow. He had a way of calming troubled waters, and Allen didn't want calm on the day of the escape. He had to plan on chaos.

"Hey, what's going on? You puke, Duval?" Brown was the master. Playing it off real good with a whole lot of common sense thrown into that gravy. He hadn't cut into the Haver show and embarrassed the deputy. In fact, Brown had given the enraged deputy a second or two to shut it the fuck down.

Haver looked up, threw a towel on to the pile of mashed dinner. "Yeah, he puked all right. He don't have any idea what a stink he made."

Brown's voice was low. It rumbled around the day room and leveled the confusion. "Can we talk about it? Youth Duval?"

Duval had his head down. Haver piped up. "He got nothin' to say." Haver grabbed the boy's arm and dragged him toward the cell block. "Ought to strip you and haul you out back and hose you off, you piece of shit." Duval seemed to go limp, a rag in the grip of the deputy, the sandals slipping and sliding on the grease.

The boys, their trays held tightly in their fists, still hadn't moved. They watched Haver and Duval disappear into the cell block.

Brown snapped straight up. The boys stood at attention. "Okay, party over. You, San Antonio. Get the mop."

The incident happened in less than two minutes. Allen still clutched the ladle, not sure what the hell to do with it. He thought of Duval's pain. Of all their pain. Duval was a big old pile of it. He'd do anything to get out of Alpha, for sure, and Allen was betting on it. He smiled to himself, blew off some steam. *Wow. Guy stepped in it. He ready to step out.*

BACK IN HIS CELL, OUT OF THE SHOWER, a fresh bruise on his upper thigh where the deputy had given him a swift kick, Duval sat on the metal stool bolted to the floor. His arms were crossed tightly over his chest. He rocked back and forth. The deputy was gone but his words hammered around in Duval's brain. "You're in the shit now. For real. Just wait. It's going to be a tough morning and a whole lot of tough mornings for you." Duval couldn't wait to see what that meant. What new hell there was in store, the not knowing, the fear, the absolute loss of all freedom to move, live, even breathe.

He thought of Allen's promise. He'd be ready, all right. Couldn't take it anymore. He had to get out, and anything was worth a try.

CHAPTER TWENTY-THREE

Simmer

THE NEXT MORNING, CAROLINE MADE HER way through a couple of doors, down the dim hallway toward her classroom, and as she drew closer to master control, she saw a shape on the floor against the wall. Her eyes adjusted from the bright Florida morning to the dark, and she thought she was hallucinating. The hall was usually swept clean, except for a moving food cart or mop. But she was not mistaken. It was a person at the end of the hallway. A lump of curled human. In a chair on the floor. Duval was in a seat of some kind, almost like a child's car seat, and he was strapped into it, his legs drawn up, feet flat on the floor, and his arms held down with wide brown canvas straps. Caroline turned away, the fury building in the pit of her stomach. She was on the verge of screaming. Instead, she whispered, "What the hell…"

Bettinger came out of master control and leaned against the wall, boots crossed at the ankle. She didn't look up, nor did she greet Caroline. "Boy needs a bit of counseling," she said. "Acting up in his cell. A dinner and after-dinner performance."

Caroline stood about ten feet away from the deputy. If she got any closer, she was afraid of what she might do. Maybe take those hefty green shoulders and shake them until some sense shook loose. She drew closer and hissed, in a low voice. "What are you *doing*?"

"*We* didn't do it. He did. And until he learns that acting out doesn't work, he's gonna be reminded. One way or another."

Duval stared straight ahead in a trance of sorts, which Caroline hoped was the case. Maybe he could transport himself from these moments of hell to another state of mind and place. Duval seemed to be good at it. He could call up that blank look and drift off.

"How long?" Caroline pointed to the restraints.

"Don't know." Bettinger was studying her stubby nails in a curled fist. "Depends on him, I guess."

Caroline had the urge to yank Duval out of the chair and kick Bettinger in the ass, all in one fell swoop. Instead, she turned on her heel and stomped down the hall to Harvey's office. She knocked. Nothing. Education was out.

Miller. She had to get to him. He must know this was happening, and he had to put a stop to it.

And with each determined step, she knew she was headed toward a dead end.

The sergeant was in his office, a large space with a fig tree thriving in the corner, the sun streaming in over his shoulder and on to his neat desk with hardly a spec of paper in sight. Miller had his boots up on the desk, and he was jawing on the phone. He saw Caroline, swung around. The chair bounced him toward the desktop. He smiled up at her and signaled: one minute. He indicated to a chair across from his desk.

That one minute would save her from starting a rant she couldn't win. She was fuming, lips drawn tight, blood pressure on the rise.

He put the phone back in the cradle. "What can I do you for, Miss Caroline?" His hands neatly folded. The muscles in his upper arms flexing.

She sat down opposite him and took a breath. *Let's appear nice and calm and casual... before I fucking flip out!*

"Duval," she said, her tone as even as she could manage.

"Yes, our star pupil." His expression didn't change. She could have been mentioning the weather or the price of beans.

"Well, he's restrained. In the hall. In a child car seat of some sort."

"Yes, we do that from time to time."

"Why?"

"For our good, and his own. He's the kind who'll hurt himself and others if he's not stopped."

"It won't work. Humiliation and physical abuse don't work, sir. They just don't."

"Well, we have to give it a try. We're within the regs on this one."

"What regs? Torture regs? Ridiculous."

Miller stood up. He wasn't tall, but he was wide. Somehow, he must have thought he was an intimidating presence. Caroline stayed right where she sat, in fact, leaned back in her chair and stared a hole right through him.

But that sinking feeling hit her.

My protest is futile. Duval's situation doesn't belong to education, and we're just not gonna win this one.

She hung on. "You have to let him out of that thing. Now."

Miller sat back down. "Look, we'll let him out. Soon enough. Although I think we ought to keep him in that seat, and diapers, for the rest of his visit. He's a danger, real or not. He needs to be held down. Held to correctional center standards. I'm telling you, the boy's a curse on humanity."

"I'd say he's a curse we need to deal with. And this is not the way, sergeant. Trust me." The last of her words were barely audible. Her eyes wide, glaring at the sergeant. What she lacked in authority, she always made up for in longevity and determination. She'd demonstrated that many times. Miller had the whiff of defeat in his expression, but not by much. No one could deny she knew what she was talking about when she was talking about the boys. She treated them like human beings.

She pushed him. "You can't treat people like this."

He laughed, but there was no humor in it. His face was an unhealthy red, the veins in his neck, tense, stretched and pulsing. "If I trusted you, they'd all be out dancing around the palm tree. Beer and dogs on the beach. What the hell," he said. "These kids are felons." Both hands—large, square, fat pink pads—slapped the desktop. "Now, enough's enough. I got work to do. Don't you?"

"Yes, I've got work to do. And so do you. You have to make things better because if you don't they're only going to get worse." Again, the nagging tickle in her brain. Something was up with these boys.

"What's that supposed to mean?"

"Something's going on around here. There's an unusual amount of tension.

And mischief."

"Miss McBride. This is a prison. Tension and mischief come with the territory."

"Yes, but this acting out. Duval's actions. It's symptomatic…"

"Yes, symptoms of a lot of young fools," he said, standing, fingers tented on the desktop. "Now, will you leave the door open when you go? Thank you."

She took a parting shot. "Will you at least think about it? Please. Will you let him out of that chair? Not soon. Now."

Miller fiddled in a drawer, slammed it, opened another. *Looking for something?* To Caroline, it was doubtful he'd ever find what he was looking for.

She stood in the doorway. "When's Deputy Brown on duty?"

"Who wants to know?"

She sighed, hand on hip.

"I do. I want to know. He's good with the boy."

A snarl curled at his lip. He had a scraggly mustache that no amount of grooming seemed to improve. "Why do you always have to be acting the mother? They don't deserve it."

"That's not fair. What about Brown?"

"Brown won't be in today, or tomorrow, and Brown ain't the ticket. Just let it alone, Miss McBride. Let it alone."

Caroline headed back down the hall toward her classroom. There was language arts to deal with. What a crock. Not much art around here.

Duval was still in the chair, and Bettinger hadn't moved from her place against the wall outside master control. She smiled when she saw Caroline. A secret sort of smile that said I'm in and you're out. Caroline ignored it. She looked down at Duval. "Mr. Duval."

He looked up her, straining his neck, his eyes glazed over. She didn't know what to say. "It won't be long now." What the hell else could she say?

"No, Miss McBride, it won't be long now," he said. "Ma'am."

"Duval, shut the fuck up," said Bettinger. "You got no say. You got nothin'."

Caroline looked at the deputy. The futility again washed over her like a dirty wave. *Be careful what you say, what you wish for, deputy, ma'am.*

Caroline hit the buzzer to gain admittance to the day room. She walked around to Art's classroom and signaled to enter. The math teacher was bent over his desk. He looked up and smiled at her. "Well, Miss English Teacher, Ma'am. What's up?"

"Nothing good." She threw herself into a student desk facing Art. "What the hell we gonna do? Did you see Duval out there?"

"Now what? I got here early. Did hear a lot of commotion in the block but that's hardly new."

"They got him in a restraint chair. Out in the hallway."

"What the f…"

"If anyone lit a match near him, I bet he'd explode. And it might not take that."

"What happened?"

"I'm not getting much from anyone. He's bucking, and that's not unusual. I just don't like the look of it, Art."

He pushed the folder of papers away, his lips tight, a deep furrow between the bushy brows. He walked over to the window in the door. All was quiet in the day room, master control, the hallway, dark and empty.

"I heard something," he said. "They're trying to keep it quiet but Harvey got some intel. These kids are definitely trying to get out of here. Like, out the front door. Maybe this week. Wonder if this Duval situation has anything to do with it."

"*What?*"

"Yeah, and Miller thinks it's a big joke. But he's getting pressure. He told the staff, and we'll get the word later today from Harvey, to be on alert. They're just shy of tossing the place. Well, I think they've already done some of that."

"Oh lord. Tossing's to be avoided. Like I have any say." The deputies had a way of ripping when tossing, and kicking, screaming, and generally treating it like a field day of horror. All stops out. It terrified the boys. Besides the intimidation of wrecking their cells, they didn't know what was behind it, or what would come next. The not knowing drove everybody crazy. What would the deputies find? Or worse, what would they *plant*? The latter was most fearsome of all.

The boys were at the mercy of a certain knot of renegade, power-struck haters in green. Not many but enough of them spread terror. The boys were prolific writers, and they wrote about their fears. And while most did not give it all away, it came out. They had so many fears, some on the surface, some dormant, but fear ran wild.

CHAPTER TWENTY-FOUR

Last of the Mo-hooligans

COUSIN MAURICE "MO" DANIEL WAS DRESSED in his Saturday night best: red velvet bomber jacket and black satin sweats, Gucci high-tops, and a black baseball cap with a fuzzy M stitched on the front, all the labels hangin' in full view. He'd topped off the outfit with a gold chain that looked like it could tow a boat.

Jesse Allen sat across from his cousin Mo and feasted his eyes on his good friend, close relative, and lucky son-of-a-bitch for never getting caught like Jesse did. He'd managed to get a word with the chaplain, who asked Aunt Dorcas to bring Mo for the Sunday visit. His auntie's famous chocolate-frosted peanut brownies helped convince the Reverent Temley and Sergeant Miller to allow "the extended family visit." So, while Allen cooled it with Mo in the day room, Dorcas was catching up with the chaplain, who couldn't resist talking up his favorite parts of the Gospel. His aunt could match Temley's God-pounding quotes, word for word; the two were a match made on earth with an eye toward heaven.

"Mo, you lookin' fly."

"You like? It's my persona con grata."

"You mean persona non grata? That means not acceptive, man."

"What you talkin'? I got plenty of grata. I'm down with the grata, ya know?" He laughed at his little joke, his voice rising just a tinch. Swanson, standing over in the corner, gave him a sideways look. Mo folded his hands on the metal tabletop and leaned closer to Jesse. "Ya know?"

"Yeah, okay," said Jesse, who was happy to change the subject. "What's that M you got there on the lid?"

"The M? Dunno. Think it's the Mets or some shit. But I just like it. M for Mo da Man." He looked around the day room like someone was going to ask for his autograph.

"Fuck sake, Mo. You gotta be careful with colors and all. Some crew be out to cross you."

"Don't worry, Jesse. You just worry 'bout yo little ol' self. Looks like ya got plenty to worry 'bout." Most visitors were antsy a few minutes into sitting in the cold day room, a cross between utility and cell. But Mo was just plain cool. Allen could see him chillin' in hell when the time came. But before they went to that hell, Mo would be the one to come through to help him get out of Alpha.

"Listen, I ain't got much time here. You gotta hook me up."

"Yeah? Watcha need, J? You lookin' to bust out of the pen?" He put his head back and laughed again. He almost lost his hat. Mo had a deep, rumbly kind of laugh and Jesse loved hearing it again, but not right now.

"Shut the fuck up, Mo!" Allen hissed, lowered his head. "That's e-zactly what I'm talkin' about."

Mo looked across the day room at Haver and Swanson. "Fuck, no, J. Don't be messin' with me." The deputies were carrying on about the Dolphins who were just about as sorry ass as they were. Mo leaned in real close. "Lookee, ya gotta cool it, J. Ya got yo real good friends in here and all, and you'd hate to leave 'em. I think ya should just take a pass on that idea. Get in line, do the time. We're waitin' on the outside, bro."

"Not for long, bro, not for long. Listen to me. You gotta look up the electrics in this place. How master control is hooked to the exits and fire alarm and all that shit. Capiche?"

Maurice looked like he had Fruity Pebbles for brains, but nobody knew the real Mo. His ears pricked up when Jesse mentioned "electrics." Mo's looks fooled everyone; it was part of his jam. He had a first-rate, high-tech math brain that mostly had been wasted on the street corners of Pokatoy. But that brain was never wasted when it came to the interests of Mo Daniel and his hooligan friends. That's when he went to work. When the call came in, he was sharp as the point of your super-sharp Spyderco.

Mo's expression changed from bland to bright, a regular cross between Arnold Schwarzenegger and Albert Schweitzer. He'd always been fascinated with electricity, in particular, electrical engineering, which dealt with the intangible—not regular engineering of mechanics, water, bridges, other stuff. He'd become obsessed with "the electrics," as he called them during a brief stint in a high school vo-tec class. And his talents bloomed from there, over into the tech field and computers. He was self-taught; he had no patience for class training. And Mo was a marvel to watch. Jesse'd seen him apply his plug-in wisdom to hack into banks and real estate, schools and grocery stores, all for various and nefarious reasons. And the authorities never thought to look into the small business operations of little old Pokatoy.

Mo was good at getting in where he had to go, getting out, and then covering up. He needed a steady source of revenue to outfit himself, his three girlfriends, and four kids. Mo was only twenty-three. He'd been busy. And he was very, very careful and not too greedy. That was key with Mo. He had just enough cash to bounce around a bit, get himself some nice wheels and rims and such. He was the man, as far as Jesse was concerned. When he grew up, he wanted to be Mo.

Mo studied Jesse's face. No two ways, the dude was *on*. He looked around the day room one more time. "Got it." All fire and concentration. "Mind tellin' me your plan?"

Jesse relaxed but not a whole lot. "I'll lay it out. I got a phone," he said. "I'm gonna call you soon, maybe tomorrow, so be ready. I'll only have a few minutes, but I'm tellin' ya, we got it together. Four of us. We gonna bust out of here, probably end of next week. Friday, maybe. Dunno yet. Ya gotta help me line shit up, Mo. I talk to you tomorrow night. First, just find out how the electrical system works around here."

Mo looked skeptical. "That's just fine and good and all. But a jail break? Are ya crazy, J? Ya never gonna make it. Not with all this po po."

"Don't worry 'bout it. I'm not gonna get you involved. Well, not too much. But we gonna do it. Element of surprise and all that shit. Mo, I need them electrics real soon." He smiled, a wry grin from ear to ear. "One thing at a time, just like they says in the good book. One day at a time."

Mo still looked doubtful, but he'd been hanging with Jesse for as long as either could remember. School, and up. But not too far up. They'd always figured a way to bust out of every place that had held them down. They were closer than brothers; they'd been through the worst and come out the other side, except for Jesse, and now Mo knew he'd do anything to spring his cousin and best friend. Jesse knew it, too.

They didn't dare go for a crew handshake or any of that other stuff, not in front of the deputies. Instead, Mo put his fist on his heart. Jesse looked around first, and sneaked one in.

It would get done.

They both kept a straight face. Not a drop of sweat. Lips clamped, brows fierce. Just chillin'. Planning the average jail break.

CHAPTER TWENTY-FIVE

Feed Your Head

RICK SAN ANTONIO WANTED TO KILL THAT fucking Wesley Pautz. Telling about the map he'd found. He didn't know shit, but he knew something, and now he'd blabbed. *What a goodie goodie asshole.* What was he thinking—that he'd get a year or two shaved off? That was never going to happen to any of this Central Florida riffraff. He was in good, and deep. He'd gotten in over his head when he helped kidnap the mayor's daughter. It was bad; she didn't die, but she'd pretty much lost her mind. They'd tied her up and stuck her in hog shed where she nearly roasted to death over a weekend in August. He and his boys went down hard for it. The older guys to adult population, and Wes, light-haired as a lab rat (which is what he was) and the only juvenile in the bunch, went to Alpha for a minimum of six years.

San Antonio had seen Wesley pick up the book in the classroom and open it, and he'd watched his eyes get rounder and rounder, the Adam's apple jump, as he looked over the schematic of his home sweet home, Alpha Juvenile Correctional Center. Rick kept a straight face and an eye out for what Wes did with the map. He didn't do a damn thing. Simply put it back in the book, closed it, and stuck it on the rack under the desk.

Problem was that the map wasn't there when San Antonio went looking for it. It had been meant for Allen, their fearless leader, but Allen never got it. San Antonio did some mild detective work on the thing, but he had to be careful. The map had to be in the hands of a deputy or Miss McBride. He couldn't think where else it could be. He'd spent a shit load of hours on it, and he'd have to do it again.

He still had notes and sketches, and a damn good memory. He told Allen he'd get him another map. He was going to pass it to him in the chow line. It was risky, but Allen needed it for Tarvis and Duval. He needed to do it, make sure they had a copy of their route out of the correctional center. Allen had been cruising around on that food cart so he was pretty well-versed in the layout. So was San Antonio who'd been swinging a mop up and down the halls.

"Staff know who wrote it?" Allen mumbled to San Antonio in the breakfast line. Allen dropped a glob of oatmeal on San Antonio's tray.

"No way. Not much writing. Lines were real short and neat, in pencil, like everybody's got. No way they could know."

"Make sure you do it up good. I gotta give some particulars to Duval, once they stop fuckin' with him, and Tarvis. And make sure them two are solid, good to go."

San Antonio kept thinking. If it weren't for the awful food and the necessity to keep the slop coming, they never would have gotten their little plan off the ground. As it was, the chow line had turned into the pipeline. And so far, the deputies were too busy and too lazy to notice. They thought the boys were asking for gravy; in fact, they were asking each other, *Which way out the door?* They were all on board with that.

AT FIRST, TARVIS HAD BEEN LUKEWARM to the plan but he'd opened his yapper to Allen and said he was in. They'd exchanged preliminaries in the showers. Every night. After all, they had to be clean. The showers, though dicey, was a good place to pass a message or two back and forth.

They were all standing around, soaping, rubbing it up. Allen got himself within mumbling distance of Tarvis. "Who don't go to 'church,' T? Gotta go to church. Come on, now." Allen looked around for the deputy, held the towel up around his ears and pretended to be drying the stubble on top of his head while he carried on with Tarvis. In the meantime, Tarvis pretended to adjust his rubber sandals, a necessity on the treacherous tile surface of the open shower room. If he didn't fall down on the gummy surface, it was likely he could catch his death of athlete's foot. The deputies usually let the boys alone to do their business of nose picking and ear cleaning. Tarvis didn't like to linger in the showers. *Shit, shave, shower. Get out.* It was freezing cold and the water tepid on the best days.

"What I gotta do?" Tarvis looked around nervously.

"Let you know. You pretty smooth. Maybe you can sing 'em a song."

"What you talkin' about. You want me to sing to Haver?"

"Not zactly. What I'm thinkin' is you can talk them into an extra rec time, say Saturday or Sunday. Church, you know? We need a little chaos and ball passin' to firm things up. Gonna talk to Mo soon. He's lining up stuff outside."

Allen hadn't sprung the whole plan. Tarvis had the feeling Allen was boiling him like a frog, so to speak. Had him on the edge of the pot, then he'd tip him in before he realized what was happening. Allen's plan was pretty bold, and Tarvis wasn't dumb. He didn't want to think of what could happen. Allen was smart to keep some of the details to himself, else the whole crew would head back to their bunks and cover their heads. And pray. Probably for the first time.

Tarvis dried his feet, slowly, working up the ankles, behind the knees. "Okay on the rec time."

"What about on the outs?" Allen whispered.

"Once you get outside the razor wire, there ain't no gate around here. Just open palm and scrub and swamp. Staff at the main jail, and all over, is down. That's what I heard them complainin' about at detention."

"That's what I wanted to know."

Haver lingered outside the wide-open door to the showers. He picked at his fingernails with a pen knife. He stuck his head into the vaporous soapy air and yelled. "All right, all yous. Get in line and back to the rack. Enough with the bubble bath. And you, Tarvis, and Allen, enough of the jawin'. Drop your dicks."

Allen lifted his towel over his face, rubbed and whispered. "T, got to be on the nose. It's comin' up, for sure. Goin' to church. I'll let you know."

Tarvis gave Allen a look and shuffled out of the showers toward his cell. He was more reticent than ever to get involved in this harebrained scheme. But, no denying, he was already in the pot. Boiling, for sure.

The door slammed behind him with a reverberating smack to the brain.

It was nine o'clock. Lights out.

He hit the bunk with the scratchy blanket, buried his face in the flat, grey lump of a pillow, and screamed. He lay like that for an eternity. Every minute, every day was an eternity. He wiped his face with the rough fabric of his sleeve and stood up on his cot in the dark. He could barely make out the concrete walls closing in around him. The moon through the high window said there was a world out there. The lantana rested, slivers of sun under a moon.

He had to go for it.

CHAPTER TWENTY-SIX

The Juggler

IT WAS ENTIRELY, AND ORIGINALLY, ALLEN'S idea to get out of there, so, by default, he'd become the ringleader. Now Tarvis was looking to Allen to juggle all the parts, firm up the plan, and tie it tight with Mo and the boys. It was fortunate Allen had the job on the meal cart. It was their master control.

Allen shuffled back and forth at his usual station, dishing up lunch, which once again smelled of overcooked vegetation and grease.

"T, did you get that extra rec?"

Tarvis nodded without looking up. "Workin' it. More later." His gaze scoped the area. Haver was leaning against a wall, yelling into a radio. Tarvis stared into the macaroni and cheese on his tray, which was an odd shade of puke yellow. He felt sick and hoped he didn't let loose right there in the chow line. "Details later." He moved on, eyed Swanson and Miller talking in master control. Maybe he'd ask one of them tonight, or tomorrow during mandated cell-block check. Deputies were supposed to come around every ten minutes to check that the boys weren't hanging themselves or slitting their wrists. They didn't look for poison per se; they said the food was doing that already. But they would be around to search for drugs, pills, powders, things of that nature. Candy bars, weapons, photos, cards with glitter, string, rubber bands, glue, tacks, pins. Anything forbidden that had gotten to the boys through a visitor or contractor or by way of light fingers. One inmate had made friends with a driver from the jail who managed to get LSD tabs smuggled into Alpha, stashed among the paper napkins, soy balls, and buns. In the weeks after that delivery (paid for by a generous relative on the outside), the prison walls were multi-colored paisley and the deputies fire-breathing dragons—until Braulio Trevor raced across the day room into the window of master control and bashed his head in. When he came to, he asked if he was on Mars yet.

These various attempts at self-destruction had not been successful so far, but not for lack of motivation or opportunity. They tried, and they were caught. Cell-block checks were fairly efficient in catching a suicide attempt here and there. But it was common knowledge that someone who wanted to do himself in would find a way.

In the meantime, Tarvis would talk with Deputy Friendly, whoever, on watch.

Tarvis felt the sweat along his hairline, prickles on the back of his neck. He couldn't eat the dinner, if that's what they called it. They were really going to do this. *He* was really going to do this. It didn't look like they were turning back. He wasn't sure why Allen wanted another rec period, but he could guess. More opportunity to meet up and firm things up. Tarvis planned to oblige.

Something deep inside pulled him forward into the plan. Much as he was slow to go along, he couldn't help the pull toward freedom. He had to try. The alternative was to sit around in this sewer and rot. He knew an escape meant they'd have to run like hell and keep running. *But where would he go?* Miralisa, if he could find her. He couldn't head to Aunt Millie's and his guitar on the back porch. Not just yet anyway. He'd wait on that salt pork and greens and grits, and lazy days by the river. That was for sure. Mo was setting up a route to Mexico, and Tarvis wasn't so sure about that. He didn't speak Spanish and had no desire to learn. He had to think on it. Anything was better than sitting in Alpha for three years, if he was "lucky." He could be here six years, given the situation with the deputies and the opportunity to buck. He could be stuck at Alpha until he was twenty-two. After all, he'd been complicit in the murder. They hadn't planned it that way, but that's the way it went down. And now the only way out was with Allen and this crazy plan of his. He'd take the chance. The fear that they could keep him, the fear of the unknown stretching ahead for years, the constant abuse. It was torture.

He had to roll out with the boys.

CHAPTER TWENTY-SEVEN

The Electric Door

"MO, YA GOT THEM ELECTRICS?"

"What the fuck, J. How'd ya do it?"

"Do what? Ain't done nothin' yet."

"Callin' and all."

"Quit jawin'. I got me a phone but I only got a minute. What y'all find out about the electrics in this place?"

"Man, you're gonna need keys, unless you can walk through a three-inch-thick, three-hundred-pound door."

"Mo, I ain't Jesus. We got to get out the door and then out the gate."

"The key, J. Ya gotta get the master. It'll open all them doors, but, I don't know, man."

"'Bout the electrics. What if I turn off the power? What you find out?"

"All hell sure to bust loose, and the doors will lock down. Them's slam doors, J."

"No shit. Doncha' think I been hearin' 'em slam on me for too long now?"

"Yeah, well, maybe ya ought to think this over. Like I says, you're gonna need the master key, and I don't see any of them deputies handing one over."

"I hear ya. We get it." Allen's breath came fast, the adrenalin running away with him at the thought of how he was going to get the key. "You in, or not?"

"What kinda question is that? When ain't I been in witch ya?"

"I know, I know. You gotta get a car, some clothes and cash and meet us. I'll call again with more. Soon."

"Yeah, man."

"Ya still got them phony passports?"

"Got 'em. Ya know I do."

"Be back in touch. Over and out from goddam Alpha shit hole."

Allen crouched next to the washing machine in the dark. He slipped the phone back under the washer, glad as hell it had kept its charge. He stood up, flipped the light on, and dunked the mop up and down in the bucket for deputy entertainment. He had to sound busy.

"What you doin' in there, Allen. Get out here on the double." It was Deputy Swanson. Allen could hear the boots, practically smell him. Burned coffee and grease, like he'd just pounded ten hamburgers and a ton of fries.

Allen banged the door open, snapped to. "Sir, yes, sir."

Swanson looked him over. "Watcha' doin' in there? Talkin' to your girlfriend?"

Allen felt the heat rise up his neck. *Had the mf-er heard him?* "Sir, don't I wish, sir. No, sir."

Swanson sneered. "What's all that mumbling going on in there?"

"Sir, I talk to myself. Calms me."

"I'll calm you one. Get back to the cell."

"Sir, yes, sir."

The buzzer sounded and the door to the cell block, and to his cell beyond, opened at once and Jesse Allen went home. For tonight.

TARVIS STOOD INSIDE THE DOOR AT master control, a rare appearance for a youth, but Swanson was smiling at the tall, quiet boy. He'd toed the line since arriving at the correctional center and hadn't caused any trouble for deputy staff. Miller had even agreed to let him in class earlier than usual. Tarvis was well-spoken and knew a lot about music, especially the blues, which was one of Swanson's favorite subjects.

"So, ya play the blues?" Swanson leaned back in the chair, one finger stuck in his cheek. He looked up at Tarvis.

"Sir, yes, sir. Lives it, too."

"I bet. Why'd you get yourself in this mess, Tarvis? Seems you could have skated past all this somehow."

"Sir, bad choice. Real bad choices, sir."

"What ya gonna do when ya get out of here?"

"Right back to the Martin, sir. I got a bunch of dudes, strings, drums, and such, and we play in some of them raggedy shacks up north of Tampa."

"Oh, yeah? Up there 'round the Withlacoochee? I been up there. Real swampy, sort of Delta-like."

"Sir, yes, sir."

"Well, maybe one day I'll come and hear ya play."

Tarvis thought it time to take his leave. He'd done his duty and softened the deputy up some, even more than the dough-like lump of his deputy-ness already was. "Sir." Tarvis spoke so softly the deputy leaned forward. "Do ya think we could have an extra rec? Maybe play a little b-ball after class? Been kinda nice out, it looks like. Sometimes Deputy Brown even throws the ball 'round, sir."

At the mention of Brown, Swanson sat back, consideration written all over his face. "Now, that so? I hear he used to play semi-pro. Bet ya can't get past him."

"Sir, yes, sir, no, sir."

"Well, what the hell is it?" Swanson lobbed a ball of paper into a waste basket across the room and missed. "Go on, Tarvis. I'll see what I can do." The control board beeped, and he whipped around in his chair to answer the call.

Tarvis looked around quickly. He saw what he'd come to see. The master key hanging above the desk. High in the corner near the entrance. It was in a lock box, but the door to the box was open. He checked the clock over the window. One just like it on the outside in the hall, just like Allen said. That door had to be open when they busted out, or they were sunk. They were probably sunk anyway. But an escape would pivot on access to that key.

Allen had been watching through the window to master control for weeks. He'd told Tarvis the key box was open around shift change. Bingo.

Tarvis stood perfectly still and waited for the deputy to finish with the call. In the meantime, he scoped the desk, the floor. Up and under. Extra cuffs hung on hooks under the long ledge that ran under the window; sticks, mace, cuffs on shelves and hooks. A treasure trove!

Tarvis was surprised he was standing in master control, but Allen was genius that way, delegating, figuring out who best could do what. Allen, big ears, knew Swanson was a music buff. The way they all gossiped in the day room, and in class, it was no wonder the boys picked up all kinds of intel. They'd played Swanson big time. *And it worked.* Tarvis had gotten in. Deputy was so lazy he didn't even get out of his chair. Every little piece helped.

Tarvis made his way back to his cell, busy as a fuckin' bee. Buzzing out of master control, through the day room and into the block.

Shit, this might even work.

TARVIS PASSED ALLEN IN THE DAY room on the way to class. "Key in corner, man, next to door, just like you said." He whispered the location. "And right on time, about shift change."

Allen got it. He'd had a good idea already but he wanted confirmation, and now he was sure. Check that one off. But he hesitated. He still needed to keep vigilant, see things didn't change up.

Tarvis said, "Other stuff, too, cuffs, mace, shit like that under the long desk on the east wall, that's to the right when you walk in."

Allen's eyes lit up while he glanced at Haver opening the classroom door.

"Damn, T. That's good. Yeah, we can use it."

Allen's head was spinning. Mace? Sticks? Tarvis turned out to be gold.

Allen's gaze flicked toward master control. Through the window, he could just make out the lock box up in the corner. Location was all-important—the where. He was still working on the how. How were they going to get the key out of that box? He had a real good idea how, and it sent shivers right through him. The deputy would not give it up easy.

For now, he'd dwell on the positive.

Nice goin', T. Very nice.

CHAPTER TWENTY-EIGHT

The Games They Be Playin'

SAN ANTONIO TOOK THE SHIV OUT OF HIS PILLOW and got down on the floor next to his cot. He honed away. The concrete proved to be a good sharpener, and now he was working on his second metal-binder weapon. He needed one, and he was going to pass another to Allen before they pulled this one off. He was confident and determined. Allen hadn't let up on planning. They just needed a day, a time, the final details.

Light filtered in through the high window over his bunk, but it didn't do anything to lighten the grey cell. He looked up at the palm tree, whipping back and forth. The wind blew fiercely like a tropical depression was moving through, but how would he know? He didn't exactly get the weather report. They didn't tell the boys anything, except to get in line, eat up, clean up, and shut up. Fucking depressing.

He was hoping to get an extra rec this week. Now it looked like they wouldn't get it with all the rain. He wanted to pass the shiv to Allen. Do his part. Be ready, be prepared. Like a good scout.

ALLEN HAD THE BRIGHT IDEA TO GET an earache. A cold wouldn't work. His nose wasn't running, and he wasn't coughing. Didn't have a temp either. He thought of all the ailments that would get him into the nurse's office. He thought he could fake a good earache.

He buzzed master control from his cell and spoke into the intercom. "Sir, can I go see the nurse?"

Grappler, deputy at the board said, "I don't know, Allen. Can you?"

"Sir, yes, sir. I think so, sir." His disembodied voice came over the speaker into master control.

"What the fuck for, Allen? You got an owie?"

"Sir, don't know what I got, sir. But my head and ear hurtin' somethin' awful."

"Don't know if she's back there. It's early Saturday, Allen."

Allen could hear the chair squeaking. He imagined the fat deputy reading a *Hustler*, eating donuts, feet up. Working hard and checking the clock to see how many more minutes he had left in prison. "I know, sir. Sorry, sir. But will you try. Sir?"

"Shit. Ten four. I'll see what I can do."

ALLEN WAITED IN HIS CELL. NOTHING. Grappler didn't give a shit. He could be dead for all the deputy cared. That was pretty clear. Allen would have to wait until the next shift, or cell check, and hope Nurse Rainer would still be in her office. He needed to get in there. It would be way tricky, but what wasn't? He needed a bottle of isopropyl alcohol. If he couldn't get it today, he'd follow up this week and try again. The earache might be a stubborn one that called for more than one visit to the nurse. It had to be done this week.

He was planning the bust-out for Friday—if everything fell into place. He'd firm it up with Mo.

Line it up. Fur-ril.

Allen went over the "supplies" in his mind. So far, San Antonio had the shivs, Tarvis nailed down the key, mace, cuffs, sticks. Allen needed one bottle of isopropyl alcohol. And the lighter. Also tricky.

He was tracking Bettinger for that lighter. She had duty coming up. Another piece of intel he'd gotten off the ledger in master control. He thought of enlisting Tarvis to get it. Dude had gotten himself into master control to schmooze Swanson. Maybe he could get to Bettinger and her lighter. But, in the end, Allen decided to do it himself. He had an idea for that, too. Ideas were just busting out of his head.

He sat on the edge of his cot and rubbed his bristly dome. They let him shave it off and now the hair was sprouting. He was nervous, but it felt good to rub his head—rub some calm into it. Being the boss was a bitch. He was good at delegating, but he suffered his doubts. Shit had to work out. All of these plans balanced on the head of a pin, and it all fell to him. *It's gotta be my way or the highway.* That's what cousin Mo would say. He was going to run all this by Mo. But, for now, he had to get that lighter and the alcohol. He'd wanted Duval more involved but the guy was always in trouble. Deputies all over his ass. But Duval was still in. He would definitely be the muscle when they needed that.

The key. That was another thing, the last thing. The final move on master control. To get the key and get out the door. Allen was thinking the four of them would rush the deputy—there would only be one in there. Cuff him, maybe mace him real good. Tarvis had confirmed where the key was and all that other shit under the desk. T had to get in there one more time, scope it out again. Allen wanted to know *exactly* where the cuffs were, the mace. Check out that locker, just one more go-round.

The locker had been left open at least a dozen times. Mostly at change of shifts. If it wasn't open when they made their move, they'd have to shut down plan and take it up later. Or threaten a deputy to open it. That would be real fun. But Allen had watched, kept track, and now he was counting on routine. Damn locker was open at shift change.

Seemed four o'clock might be the best time. Cart coming out. Deputies tired, some of them leaving. All day to plan, watch the weather, gauge the temp. In any event, they'd get the key out, and then they'd get the hell out. Together. Allen and Duval, that strong son of a bitch, would be all over it. Duval hadn't actually been a linebacker but he was going to have some tackling. Game time. Friday night lights. On. Guys had to be ready, all lined up. It would be quiet, staff down at that time. All the shit in place. Had to do it then. Allen got off the bunk and paced the cell. The fucking deputy still ignored him. If he buzzed again, he'd get cut off. He needed to get back there and see the nurse. *Now.*

He looked up at the window. Didn't look like they'd have rec any time soon with the rain, but it was Florida. Wait a minute and it would blow through. He had to keep that in the back of his mind. He could use the time on the court. He needed that shiv from San Antonio, and opportunity to get it. They needed to talk. But for now, he couldn't count on doing this any time soon.

Think, gotta think. Got plenty of time for that and so I use it.

He sat down again, clenched his hands into fists, arms resting on his knees. He wasn't a big kid but he was strong. Fast and quick. And his main talent was his ability to melt in and out of places and take what he wanted in plain sight. It amazed him that he pulled this off so many times right under the noses of clerks, store managers, teachers, cops. Almost anyone. Preferably someone puffed up with self-importance and, therefore, less aware. Someone busy or taller, which was an easy one because it seemed Allen had stopped growing. He was stuck at five feet four, for now anyway.

He'd learned to steal in plain sight almost by accident. When he was about five, his uncle had taken him to a convenience store to buy cigs and milk. Allen stood next to his uncle in line, eye height to a rack of candy, all too tempting to a five-year-old. He looked up and pleaded for a Snickers.

"Naaaaaa, gonna eat yo dinner. None of that shit now," his uncle said.

Jesse Allen did not understand the concept of waiting. He didn't then and he didn't now. He simply reached up in one fluid movement, swiped the candy bar off the rack, and stashed it in his waistband. No one noticed, no one cared. His uncle was jawing with the clerk and the quick, bold move had been a lesson to Allen. He practiced later, and often, moving quickly through sporting goods, big box stores, convenience stores. He once rode a bicycle right out of a K-Mart in Lakeland and never looked back. His specialty later was "dine and dash," which for Allen meant he'd drive an hour or two out of town to a busy, popular restaurant, order the biggest steak on the menu, and then leave by the back door or bathroom window.

He had eliminated a significant number of restaurants he could return to throughout central Florida. But he was small, quick, non-descript. He had options. He made all of them work in his favor. He took what he wanted and moved on. Quick and smooth. Right under their noses. Trick was to be bold and not hesitate. Allen often laughed at his exploits, it had come so easy. "I could write a damn book."

If only he'd stuck to his talent without the knives and guns and drug dealers, he wouldn't be in this damn hell hole. But he learned the hard way. For future exploits, he'd be careful how he picked his crimes, and how he carried them off. GED and books were good and all, but he had to stick to what he knew best. It was the life. Get in, get it, and get out. He'd do it again, he had to. What else was he going to do? Be CEO of Kroger or Home Depot? He was smart enough, but he preferred to be his own man in the wide, wild universe of employment opportunity. Once he got out of there, no one was going to tell Jesse Allen what to do.

Swanson busted into Allen's thoughts. "Hey, scuzz, hear you need to go see nurse."

"Sir, yes, sir."

"Get up. Be ready. Pilson'll walk you down."

"Sir, yes, sir."

Me, Jesse Allen, always be ready. Party on.

CHAPTER TWENTY-NINE

One for the Money

"HERE'S THIS BAG O BONES, NURSE RAINER. See if you can do some brain surgery on him while you're at it." Pilson was real funny. Allen stood inside the door to meds, face impassive, with a severe case of wanting to kick Pilson in the ass. But that wasn't in the plan. Not yet anyway. Pilson turned and swaggered away, like a fat ballerina in combat boots.

Allen stifled a laugh at the green meanie, pants sagging below his belt. For all his macho bullshit, Pilson's walk was kind of dainty.

Allen remembered he was supposed to be suffering, and so he adjusted his expression accordingly.

The nurse and Miss McBride stood in the middle of the office, heads together, chatting at once. Miss McBride looked worried, the lines in her forehead traced a distress signal. He couldn't figure why she stuck around this awful place. But he was glad she did. He even liked reading, but he didn't think it would save his soul like Miss McBride kept saying it would.

"Youth Allen," the nurse said. "What can we do for you?"

Miss McBride smiled at Jesse and headed for the door. He'd been hoping she'd stick around so he could slather her with more bullshit. "I'll let you go, Carmen," she said. "Thanks for lending an ear."

Speaking of ears... now I have to get to it.

He ducked his head, humbly, while she passed him. "Ma'am, yes, ma'am." Then to Nurse: "Nurse-Mo—" He looked around for a deputy. Pilson was out in the hall. "Miss Carmen, I got a bad earache."

"Let's have a look. One sec."

She bent over into a drawer and fiddled with a blood pressure cuff. Her large round butt both revolted and intrigued Allen. She was like a large glob of cookie dough, this woman. Not sexy. But sweet. He had a rush of feeling for her but forced himself to get back to the mission. His eyes darted around the office. Glass-front cabinets lined one wall, a metal cabinet floor to ceiling on another, a sort of gurney examining table for the ailing.

The cabinet door was open and he saw what he wanted. Had to be quick about it. He scooted around, his back to the cabinet shelves, and while Nurse Carmen fussed with the ear thing and the fabric cuff that somehow got Velcroed to her sleeve, he reached behind and grabbed the bottle of alcohol. *In ya go*. Into the back of his pants, it snuggled down into his tighty-whities. He felt like he had a load in his pants. He needed to be careful how he walked, like a baby with a diaper problem.

"Now, Mr. Allen, why don't you sit over here. Let's have a look."

"Ah, Miss Carmen, ma'am, if you don't mind, I'll stand. Been at my desk all day studying. I like to stretch them legs."

She hardly acknowledged the remark. Was she humming something Elvis?

"Well, you never killed a rabbit..."

"Ma'am, you have a right good voice."

She smiled. "Why, thank you, Mr. Allen." She eyed him over her glasses. "Shame he died of the drugs. You know, Mr. Allen?"

"Ma'am, yes, ma'am."

She adjusted the cuff, pumped up the pressure. "Think you'll live, Mr. Allen, do you?"

"Ma'am, yes, ma'am."

She peered in his eyes, stuck the point of the device into his ear. "Hmmm. No evidence of infection but sometimes it's hard to tell." She studied him. He shifted from one foot to the other.

"What's really going on, Mr. Allen? You act like a rabbit being chased by a hound dog."

"Ma'am, nurse-mom, I got nothin' but this here earache, ma'am." He put on his best, sick face.

She patted him on the arm. "I'll give you a bit of Tylenol, maybe do a blood test later if the pain persists. But your temp and other signs look good. You let me know now."

"Oh, I will for sure, ma'am."

She went back to the cabinet again, withdrew the pills. She handed two to Allen and a cup of water. "Deputy Pilson!" She yelled and the deputy appeared instantly.

"Got Mr. Allen here for you. We done." And to Allen, "You keep your nose clean as well as those ears."

"Thank you, ma'am, yes, ma'am." He put on his best little-boy face, one that had gotten him a candy bar or two and out of trouble with Aunt Dorcas on occasion.

Allen shuffled down the hallway with Pilson, aware that if he made the wrong move, he was dead, and it wouldn't be the earache that killed him. That bottle had to stay put. He was out-of-his-fucking-mind-happy that he'd gotten the alcohol so easily, but he wasn't surprised. He was good at hiding in plain sight. Now he had to make sure that bottle would do the same.

They were another step closer out the door.

CHAPTER THIRTY

Two for the Show

ALLEN HAD A MINISCULE RIP IN THE SEAM of his mattress and into the opening he deposited the bottle, careful not to tear at the cover further. If he got tossed, the bottle had to stay in place, tucked into the lumpy batting. He thought of putting it in the toilet tank, but that was the first place the deputies checked for contraband. He wanted to stash it in the laundry room, eventually. There were more places to hide things, and more inmates to blame if it were found. For now, this would do.

Now he had to think about another item on his agenda: the lighter. Somehow, he had to find his way into Bettinger's space. There were a couple of places to consider.

She liked to hang out in master control where she'd unload her gear, including her Marlboros and the lighter. A little dicey there.

Or she lounged in the sally port and smoked. Waiting for the jail birds to drop off chow. There was a picnic table out there and she'd sit in the breeze, reading her book, like a big old green chimney.

After much study on the matter, he decided the best time and place to get that lighter was when the men from the jail delivered the food.

He'd kept watch. Considered the possibilities.

LATER THAT MORNING, A LARGE HAIRY guy wearing a white beanie unloaded huge metal serving pans from the back of a van onto the meal cart. Allen stood in the doorway and breathed some humid freedom before he had to wheel the cart back down the hall and into the day room. Pennington had caught the duty day before, but that was rare. The deputies didn't bother training a cadre of cart pushers, so Allen kept his job. He was fast, efficient, good at it, trying not to gag at the smell of the slightly-acrid, greyish food. He'd only ever smelled such a thing when he visited his old grannie in the nursing home. Slop you gave people who were almost dead, like us.

Bettinger was out there at the back door. Supposedly keeping watch, but there she was, puffing away, nose in her book. The cigs and lighter were on the picnic table. He'd be quicker than time it took for her to turn a page. But not this morning. Later. And when the lighter went missing, she could blame herself or the jail birds. Or him.

His problem was storage. Always the storage. He still had the bottle of alcohol in his mattress, which occasionally shifted in the night and poked him awake. He'd be glad when this shit was done and he could sleep in a hammock on some Mexican beach. He could almost taste the grilled fish tacos with slaw, his favorite, and the Tecate.

He was psyched, dousing himself in "the power of positive thinking." Just like in that book he'd pulled out of the nonfiction section. Dude had a point.

Once he got hold of that lighter, he'd slip it into his pants. He was ever so grateful for the issue of tighty-whities. He always made sure he picked up those that were nice and extra tight. Had to be ready. The phone had gone in there easy, then the bottle. Next, the lighter.

Planning consumed him. Now he just had to get 'er done.

CAROLINE MASHED THE AVOCADO, but not too much. He liked it chunky, with lots of lime juice. Will came in from the lanai, an apron tied around his middle. "Kiss the cook" was stitched in red on the white canvas. He had a large fork in one hand, a spatula in the other.

"Can't you read?" He stood in the middle of the kitchen, waiting.

She laughed. "Yeah, I can read." She licked avocado off her fingers. "And I can do other things."

She put her hands around his neck, a place she especially loved, under the dreds. The knotted hair was surprisingly soft there, and she twisted it in her fingers.

The kiss was long and leisurely. They had all day. No prison, no deputies, no misery. Just the two of them together.

He only wore the apron, which came down below his knees, covered his chest, and left his smooth dark behind exposed to the elements. Her elements. The glass sliders were open, and out on the screened lanai the grill was smoking. The turquoise water of the pool shimmered. Ground doves scuttled and cooed in the thick growth of hibiscus and oleander around the pool.

"You gonna eat like that? Nekked as a jay bird?"

"Why not?" He pretended to wipe sweat off his forehead, his eyes shining, happy. "Awful humid out today."

"You know you like it."

"I do. I was raised on the dew of splendid palms and green grasses, the sea baptizing me in its spray…

"Oh really."

"Where're the steaks?"

She produced a ceramic dish, two tenderloins prepped with olive oil, salt, and pepper. "Just what the doctor ordered."

"Gonna be good tonight." He leaned into her neck. "Roses. You always smell like roses. And peaches, and plums, and apples…"

She poked him and her fingers wandered the front of his apron. He leaned into her neck again, took the platter, and turned to the lanai with the steaks and utensils, his backside gleaming in the dim light of the kitchen. She wanted to throw her arms around him, but he'd drop the steaks and then they'd starve. They could live on love, for all she cared, blissfully happy.

She followed him out on the lanai with the bowls of chips and guacamole. "Guac." She was dressed in a thin coral shift, trimmed at the edge, the beads clicking softly, like a wind chime.

"If you aren't a sight. Don't know whether to take a bite of you or that guac. Guess I'll have both."

She put the bowl down. Her thoughts were not on dinner. His arms were strong and she could feel all of him through the apron. She wished they could stay like that. Eyes, lips, fingers locked on each other, the world locked out.

The steaks were delicious, the dishes were piled in the sink, and Will and Caroline were naked in the pool facing each other. They bobbed in the flickering turquoise light, the evening descending around them like a blanket. A slash of fluorescent pink streaked the lapis blue sky.

"Things okay with you and class? Any more suspicions and worries?" Will put his hands on her shoulders and then gently dunked her.

She came up, hair plastered down, and spit a stream of water at his forehead. "Thought we weren't going to talk business."

"You're my business, my love, my concern. I'm doing RET on you."

"You can do other things on me." She splashed him.

He ducked and came up under her, his arms wrapped around her middle.

"That's all the therapy I need," she said.

"Maybe. I can't help but worry about you. We need to stick together, stay alert. What other choice do we have? We need to watch out."

"You mean us?"

"No, that's not what I mean. We're fine. We are always going to be fine, Caroline. I mean, *we* have to watch *them*."

"Seems like things have settled down last day or two."

"Don't count on it," he said. "If you think it's calm, that's all the more reason to keep an eye out."

"What're you thinking?"

"I'll tell you what I'm thinking—that you have to promise me something." Now they were swimming around the edges of the pool like two dolphins in their own private ocean. "If it gets really bad—you feel like it's blowing up—that you'll just get the hell out of there. Tell them you're leaving and *leave*. Lock yourself in the car, drive away. You gotta promise me." They stopped and looked at each other. Water ran down his face, dripped from his chin. His earnest plea mixed her insides like he'd taken an eggbeater to her. She loved him all the more for his concern. She didn't want him to worry, and she didn't want to hear it. She was sick of the condescending, patronizing, overly sexist deputy staff, but he wasn't like that. She didn't want a hint of it from him. She could take care of herself.

"Don't you trust me?"

"Trust you?" He took her hands and kissed them. "What a thing to say."

"I can make the right choices. I can take care of myself. I got this far, I'll go the distance."

"I know you can. But you know me. I care about you."

"And you care about the boys, and your job. It's a *job*. Remember that. And don't worry." She squeezed his fingers, put them to her lips.

"Promise you'll do it? You'll just get out?"

She flipped around and swam to the end of the pool. It was a thirty-five-footer, just long enough for a stretch away and back into his arms. "I will, Will."

CHAPTER THIRTY-ONE

Three to Get Ready

ALLEN HAD ALL THE BOYS TOGETHER within whisper-range. He had details to tie down.

"Friday gonna be the day, T. Four o'clock, chow time," said Allen. He was back behind the cart with something they called chicken fried steak, and the boys called roadkill. He slopped a greasy rectangle on to Tarvis's plate. "They be all TGIF-in' it and shit." He looked around for a deputy. All clear.

"You sure, man? Think about it."

Allen squinted at Tarvis and slapped down a ball of rice. A little too hard. "We gonna rush 'em in master control and get the key. You, me, and San Antonio. No other way. Workin' on Duval."

Tarvis had a tightness around the mouth and eyes. He looked stressed, keyed up. "We got some time to iron it out, man, if you need to."

"I been ironin'. You know it."

San Antonio was behind Tarvis and heard every word. He nodded at Allen. "Got the map, got the shivs."

"Don't need no map." He was thinking "simplicity," and thanking Deputy Hathaway and Von Clausewitz. "Simplicity in planning fosters energy in execution." Although the Prussian general probably would have used a map.

Allen glanced around. "We streamlinin' now. We know the way out of here. We be tight, stick together, and out the door... But the shiv," said Allen. "I need that shiv. Maybe at rec."

San Antonio kept his head down. "We gonna rock. I'll pass it to you on the court. Be ready."

Tarvis's ears were burning. Allen smiled. He took his time ladling gravy onto rice that stuck together like a huge colony of maggots.

Allen, eyes on the peas, said, "Far corner. Watch for me when you round the court and keep a look out for when the deputies be jawin'. Far corner, west, next to the net. Pass it to me then."

They were ready as they'd ever be, but ready was a relative term. Allen didn't try to figure out his state of his mind; he'd go with his body, and his body was saying, *Move it*, even while his insides were roiling. He had to keep moving forward, and the steps he was taking were getting further and further into dangerous territory. He had to get that shiv from San Antonio. They had to pass that weapon. *Right in front of the deputies.*

Duval was last in the chow line. "Listen," said Allen. "Gonna get a lighter and pass it to you. Maybe at rec. Maybe on your tray end of week. We gonna bust out Friday, four o'clock. You gonna set fire to that barrel of paper in the closet next to the old kitchen." He spoke fast while he carefully and slowly measured out Duval's food. Duval hovered over the tray, blocking Allen from Haver's view. He didn't talk; he listened.

"Gonna douse it real good with alcohol I got from Nursie," Allen continued. "Just be ready. Light that fire. Three of us gonna rush master control and get the key. Then we team up in the hallway and out the door. That's all for now."

"You make it easy," said Duval. A smile crept across his face. He slowly picked up the tray of greasy food, all of it shit brown. His face said it all. He wanted to throw it against the wall, just for the hell of it.

"Don't," said Allen. "Keep it together. You gonna have plenty opportunity to jam that thing up Haver's ass. But, for now, keep it tight, you feel me?"

Duval looked at Allen, steady and hard. "Get me that lighter."

PILSON UNLOCKED THE SIDE DOOR in the hallway and Allen pushed the cart toward the loading dock. It was light weight and rattled without the food on it, the drawers jangling and the utensils loose on the shelf underneath. He'd thought of lifting a utility spoon or two to use as weapons, but the damn things were too big to hide. Not short and lethal like San Antonio's shiv. Which reminded him. He had to find an accessible place for it. Had to be able to grab it quick when he needed it.

Bettinger lounged on the picnic bench, her back against the tabletop, swinging that boot. She didn't look up when Allen and Pilson came through the door. The chow wagon from the jail was just rounding the curve in the road. The van made a circle and backed up toward the loading doors. She stuck her finger in the book and cocked her head.

"Hey, Pill. How's it hangin'?"

He snickered. "It's hangin' real good, boss lady."

They all stood together. Bettinger put her hands on her back and stretched. Didn't pay a bit of attention to Allen, which was good. She walked closer to the loading station, left the cigs and lighter on the table and chatted up the deputy.

Allen had seconds to do it. He sidled out from behind the cart and reached for the lighter.

And dropped it.

Bettinger whipped around, caught the look on Allen's face.

"What the fuck," she said.

But in the second he'd taken to fuck it up, he also made a split decision. He threw himself down on the lighter, tripping over a brick next to the table. It was an award-worthy performance.

"Ma'am. Sorry, ma'am." He rubbed his shin dramatically, winced as best he could. He'd really fucked up now. Maybe they'd swallow his cover-up, maybe not.

"What are you doin', Allen?" said Pilson. "Get the hell up and load this chow."

Bettinger's gaze darted from the table, to the lighter, to Allen—all three within close proximity. She bent over and picked up the lighter. She tossed it up in the air all the while staring at Allen who was brushing himself off.

"You takin' up *smo*-king, Allen?" The tone of her voice shifted from the light banter with Pilson to venom with Allen.

"Ma'am, no, ma'am. Never touch them things."

"But you want my lighter?"

"Ma'am, no, ma'am."

"What you need a lighter for, Allen?"

He found a thin rib of steel deep down inside himself. He bolted upright. "Ma'am, I tripped. I'm a dumb shit."

"You got that right," said Pilson.

Bettinger smirked at him, a finger stuck in her chin, head cocked. "Ya know, Allen, I could write you up. Add a couple weeks, maybe months, for that little stunt."

Allen held steady. Made himself play it cool and strong. He stared off into a palm tree as he stood at military attention. "Ma'am, I hope not, ma'am. Sorry, ma'am."

ALLEN WAS QUIET BEHIND THE cart at chow. He slopped the noodles on to the trays, head down, and didn't respond to San Antonio who hissed at him about rec time.

"Get at you later," Allen said. "Stay with the plan. Gotta have that shiv."

"That's what I'm talkin'," said San Antonio. "Gonna bring it to rec for sure."

Allen nodded.

Back in his cell, he paced. He was in a sweat, fretting. He'd really fucked up trying to get the lighter. He'd planned on a major distraction with a fire in the trash can, but he didn't see how that would work now. That part had to be put on hold. He kicked his bunk, hurt his toe; looked at those goddam brown plastic sandals. He wanted to take one and rip it into shreds.

The plan was coming down to rushing master control. There was no other way.

At least they had the two shivs. They couldn't fuck that up, too. Maybe it was just as well it came to this. Keep it simple. Jump them. Element of surprise and all that. The more complicated the plan became, the more chance they were taking that something would go wrong. They couldn't afford that.

Number one: get the shiv.

Number two: get hold of Mo.

ALLEN HAD ONE MORE MOP DUTY that week, and it was a duty they all wanted. If he lost that privilege, he'd be sunk. He had to be careful to keep appearing as the poster boy for Mister Clean Junior, according to the deputies. Most of the time they just called him one clean asshole. They could say whatever they wanted to say. He never let the taunting get him down. He needed to keep his jobs, and it gave him a never-ending good feeling to know the deputies were being duped. A certain amount of ass kissing was required to stay on the floor, mopping and serving meals. They tried fiercely to get those jobs anyway. They all loved to mop. It was an easy way to get out of their cells, get around Alpha (pass a little contraband for favors), and play in the water. Allen was fortunate that he had made a name for himself as an efficient janitor of sorts. He was fast, knew how to mix the cleaning liquids without pissing off Haver, and the floors weren't sticky when Allen got through with them. One thing Miller hated was sticky floors. He'd been known to kick a bucket of filthy dregs across the day room.

Allen slid the mop and bucket into the laundry closet and closed the door. Slightly. He extracted the phone from under the washing machine. It still had juice, a bar or two. He quickly dialed Mo. He didn't answer.

Allen sat in the dark on the floor, clutching the phone.

Desperate.

"Mo. This Friday at four o'clock. We gonna bust out of here. Hell or whatever. You gotta be ready, man. Be at the end of the long road to Alpha, near route 19 under that billboard. Tarvis told me about it, some high weeds there and easy access to the highway. They be four of us. Get the clothes, cash, passports and meet us there. If you don't see us, we had to abort. Or we be dead. Gonna try you later, man."

He slid the phone back under the washer. He'd call one more time before Friday. It occurred to him, in a mad rush of emotion, that they were *on*. No turning back. He had to show the boys, tighten it up, and get everybody ready. Mentally, physically.

He shook so badly he thought he'd vomit.

Plenty of time for that.

He grabbed a bunch of rags and the long-handled floor buffer. Had to look busy. He had a job to do.

CHAPTER THIRTY-TWO

Come On, Baby, Light My Fire

IT WAS THREE IN THE MORNING, BUT DUVAL didn't know that. He was sound asleep, occasionally tossing on the narrow cot that Alpha Juvenile Correctional Center called a bed. It was a miserable piece of shit for a kid six feet, one eighty. His shoulders nearly covered the bunk side to side, and his feet usually dangled off the bottom edge. The "linens" were a joke; sheets were forbidden because they had been used so many times for attempted suicide. Scratchy military style blankets and lumpy pillows were issue.

But tonight, he slept soundly. He didn't hear the key in the lock.

He didn't see her standing over him.

She didn't move for several minutes. The ambient light from the moon glazed the stainless-steel fixtures, the long, lumpy outline on the cot. It was peaceful there, for once, the blanket pulled up under his chin and none of the daylight hate hardening his features. She touched his shoulder.

He bolted awake, a look of fear shot through his expression. He rose up on one elbow and looked up at her. He didn't say a word, so used to being struck mute in the presence of authority. But this was different. They weren't in a jail cell or police car. They were in his cell, the world asleep. Unaware.

Then he came to his senses, but barely. "What the fuck," he said. "Ma'am."

"Precisely."

He was nude. He wasn't supposed to sleep like that, but what were they going to do? Check him at midnight? Under the covers?

Well, apparently so. And here she was. Deputy Bettinger, checking up on him.

She pushed him lightly back on the cot. She was breathing hard.

He saw the opportunity. She wanted something from him. She was not the boss here. It was an odd place to be, on a level playing field with the deputy.

She quickly took off her blouse. Her breasts were huge and white, like melons. He almost laughed, but the erection he was dealing with was serious, and it appeared that she meant business. She whipped the blanket off the cot and threw it on the floor. Her fingers ran down his arm and over the rest of him, lightly at first and then insistent.

"Come on," she whispered.

They were on the concrete, and he was moving over her between those white fleshy thighs. Not thinking at all, just in the act, but then he thought of white caps, the ocean. That one time he raced over the waves, free, with abandon. But this was not freedom, and this was not abandon. This was plain crazy. What was he thinking? He wasn't thinking. He was moving, pumping. He wanted to split her in half.

The light from the window fell on the green serge blouse piled above her head, and he saw the cigarettes and lighter outlined in the pile of fabric, on the concrete, just beyond her blond raggedy head of hair, the wisps flung around like fresh cut wheat.

He kept at it. Her eyes were closed. Soft mewling sounds came out of her, like an animal suffocating.

He braced his elbows on either side of her head, and with one hand, he reached for the blouse. For the lighter. Slid it across the concrete. It skittered into a corner beyond the sink.

She didn't open her eyes as he bucketed on top of her.

They were both naked. It all happened so quickly, so urgently. A tangle of humans and blanket on the concrete floor, now spent.

He rolled off her, limp, on his side. He sat up, the realization of it all striking him. He scooted off toward the corner, suddenly aware of what they'd done. What *he'd* done because, if caught, it would be all on him. She must have seen the terror on his face.

"Why?" He whispered. "Ma'am,"

"Why not? I like bad boys."

He couldn't tell anyone. Who'd believe him?

But he had the lighter.

This, he told Allen over a miserable glob of oatmeal the next morning. "Man, I got the lighter. It's complicated. But I got it."

"We gonna burn," said Allen.

"Oh, yeah," said Duval.

CHAPTER THIRTY-THREE

Four to Go

HE'D CHOSEN FRIDAY, AND THEY STILL HAD a few days to go. Friday was a lax day, when all two- and three-day shifts changed at four o'clock. A time of new beginnings, and endings for those who were lucky enough not to have to work the weekend. There was even a sort of camaraderie among the deputies and boys who could stomach each other. It was the one day of the week evening chow was set out in the hallway. Master control at one end, the exit at the other, and the closet with the trash can full of paper in the middle.

Now Duval had the lighter. The trash can—as a blazing distraction—was back in the plan.

Allen wheeled the last of the breakfast goodies in the direction of the side door loading dock. "I'll take it the rest of the way," said Pilson who was watching the cart come toward him.

Real nice of you. You douche bag.

Allen glanced at the closet entrance in the hallway. He handed over the cart to Pilson and sidestepped to the door of the closet. Yanked it open. Trash can was still where he'd put it. Fully loaded with the papers and textbooks pages from Duval's mischievous classroom dive. Allen figured he'd find a way into that closet with the bottle of alcohol and douse it all real good Thursday. That wouldn't be difficult. After all, he was handy with that mop and clean up and getting in and out of places. Mister Clean Junior.

Friday was the perfect day.

Allen needed that shiv.

THE BASKETBALL COURT HAD BAKED all day in the Florida sun. It was hotter than a frying pan turned on full blast out there, and Allen didn't care. It was a constant condition he was almost used to. They either baked or froze. It was worse than being a lump of bread. At least bread was treated with some kind of love, pbj, and a squeeze or two.

His nose adjusted to the hot, humid air. Allen loved it; green air, not grey air. He shook his arms, ran in place. He was out of the cell, and the feeling was like a shot of something from the old life, but not quite. He wore loose shorts and a t-shirt for rec, and the tighty-whities were tight. He tucked the front of the shirt into his underwear just in case the shiv had to go there. He thought of everything. The shoe was also a consideration. He bent down and loosened the laces, the one time they were allowed laced up athletics. Allen had to do what was expedient.

His wing of the cell block was due out.

Where is fucking San Antonio?

Broken leg or death were the only excuses one had to get out of rec. But all in all, they didn't want out of it. Hot as it was, lame as it was, they were still *out*. San Antonio had to be there.

Allen ran around the court, accepting a pass, his gaze darting toward the door and at the other boys. If San Antonio didn't make it outside, Allen would have to think of another way to get that shiv. Probably on the meal cart. He was really sick of juggling all these details. He just wanted to get the hell out of there. But he wanted, no, *needed,* that shiv.

There he was. San Antonio straggled out with two other youth.

Allen ran past him. "Look alive, scumbag. You got it?"

San Antonio nodded and chased after Allen with the ball. He half turned. "Check the deputies. Not yet."

They did another loop around the court, and then the fake tussle occurred.

"Now." Allen had the ball. He faked a struggle with San Antonio who obliged nicely.

"Hey, you carryin' that ball? Gimme," said San Antonio. He palmed the shiv out of his underwear, on to the side of the ball, and into Allen's front. So quick, Allen hardly felt it, but he knew it was happening.

"Aw right, motherfucker," he said. Allen ran toward the fence, adjusting himself. San Antonio dribbled off with the ball. Haver and Pilson were still standing on the other side of the court, pointing, arguing, laughing. Completely clueless.

Allen didn't want to push it. He danced around the perimeter of the court. Figured he had another ten minutes before he got back to the cell and unloaded the shiv. He hoped it didn't castrate him before that.

But it was in there nice and upright against his hip. He elbowed it, took another loop around the court. San Antonio leaped into the air and put it in the basket.

Allen gave him a high five. "Goddam, you did it."

"Watch your goddam language, Allen," yelled Pilson. "Aw right, motherfuckers. Back to your cells."

Allen and San Antonio got in line, sweat pouring off them, grinning. "Friday," whispered Allen.

He was exhilarated. He looked for Duval, who nodded. "Friday," mouthed Allen. He caught Tarvis's eye. He was standing in the corner, running in place, his gaze fastened on Allen, then San Antonio. Finally, he nodded and dashed for the end of the line.

CHAPTER THIRTY-FOUR

Game Time

"J, SERIOUSLY, YA GONNA DO THIS, MAN?"

"Don't have time here to be jawin' 'bout it, Mo. We be out the door at four, or die," said Jesse Allen. He'd found a minute to get in the laundry closet and call cousin Mo. He was lucky as hell the phone still had a charge.

"Live free or die, that it, J? Wow, you is one crazy motherfucker."

"You'd be crazy, too. We see you Friday then."

"I be ready. Good luck, man."

IT WAS THURSDAY AND ALLEN HAD MEAL and mopping details. He was extra vigorous on the swiping, buffing, and serving end of it. Everything clean, in order. He hated to leave a mess behind, especially when he was going to make the biggest mess Alpha had ever seen. He chose his uniform carefully, all tucked in, smoothing the wrinkles on the sleeves and pant legs. He didn't want any gigs from the deputies. Not before he kissed them all good-bye. Appearances mattered. He knew that. That and lying his ass off.

He put the bottle of alcohol in the waist band under his shirt.

He buzzed Swanson in master control. "Sir, got cart duty, sir. And I have to bring that trash bag from laundry down the hall." He left the specifics unspecified.

Swanson buzzed him out of the cell block and Allen made a show of dragging a trash bag from the laundry closet out of the day room and down the hallway. He reached the closet, opened the door, and stowed the bag. Got the alcohol out of his waist band and dumped the contents into the trash barrel full of paper. He tossed the empty bottle in the corner. Into the dark.

"Never say I didn't give you anything, Duval."

They were ready.

He marched back to the cell block like he was on parade. But then he checked himself. *Better be low key and all. Before we get that fuckin' key.*

ALLEN COULD HARDLY HOLD IT IN, but he had to hold it in or blow the whole plan up.

San Antonio, Duval, and Tarvis were all in line for class in the computer lab. It was eleven o'clock. He managed to get behind Duval. "Trash can all ready to blow. Four o'clock you gonna head for that closet and set fire to it. You still got that lighter?"

Duval's face was stone. "Got it."

Allen, ever the eager beaver, took the stack of handouts from Miss McBride and went down the line to each boy, passing out the papers. "Instructions for accessing the lesson in Rosetta," he said. Nice and loud. They were studying Spanish. "Best you know how to speak Spanish," he murmured to Duval, who pushed his chair back and took the handout.

"Shut the fuck up," said Haver, his arms crossed, a hard look around the eyes.

"Sir, yes, sir," said Allen. He finished with the paperwork and took his seat at the computer. He caught Duval's expression and nodded. Duval turned to San Antonio, jabbed him in the ribs. "Four today."

"Fuck, I know." His eyes were directed at the screen, his hands shaking.

Tarvis laid four fingers on his keyboard.

Miss McBride stood behind a long table at the back of the lab, a textbook open at her middle. "Who would like to volunteer something we might say in normal conversation, translated to Spanish?"

Allen's hand shot up.

"Mr. Allen?"

"*Haga rápidamente,*" he said. "Do it quickly. You know, Miss McBride,

I'm serving the meals and such, and I have to do it quickly. A lot of stuff we have to do around here. Quickly."

"Good effort. Actually, you would say, *Debo hacerlo rápido,* if you are saying, I must do it quickly. Or in a command, *hazlo rápido.* Note the difference in the verb construction."

"Oh. Yes, ma'am, Miss McBride. Do it quickly. Hazlo rápido." His gaze skimmed Duval, Tarvis, and San Antonio, and he sat down.

"Perfect command, Mr. Allen. Thank you."

Allen sat up straight, the perfect student.

TARVIS'S STOMACH CLENCHED, and it wasn't the oatmeal or hunger pangs. They were going to do it. Today. *Four o'clock.* He'd either be free or dead by 4:30. The thought was somehow exhilarating, freeing. He had to hand it to Allen. It was a plan.

Do it quickly.

A pretty good plan, and the best ones were simple. This one based completely on surprise. Get the key and get out. He worried about that. There was more than one key on the ring, but all in all he was pretty good with that sort of thing. He'd even done a short gig in a hardware store, making keys, stocking shelves, sweeping. He wondered if he'd ever go back to that kind of life, or any life at all.

He was on board with Allen and the boys. He just didn't want anyone to get killed or hurt. Well, there was always that to think about. Except he wasn't going to think about it.

CAROLINE LOOKED AROUND THE computer lab. Allen was busy as ever, tight as a tension wire, buzzing around. The boy had initiative, she had to say that for him. But something was not right. He seemed to focus his attention on several boys. The whispering, the jabbing at each other. She supposed that was boys being boys, but she wanted to say something to Will.

Miller had disregarded all of her warnings and flag waving. "It's prison, Miss McBride. What do you expect?"

Yet, she didn't expect to feel this amount of anxiety. She'd been there almost five years, and something was different. Or maybe she was different. Five years in prison is a long time, and it can certainly change people. Will had pointed that out, so had Harv and Art.

She wasn't going to get out today. She was going to watch them. Something was in the air. She just didn't know exactly what.

She sighed. "*Vámonos.* Are you logged in? We're going to study the lesson on visiting a restaurant…" Collectively, they moped. The closest most of them would get to a restaurant was three years away.

ALLEN COULDN'T CONCENTRATE on the Spanish lesson though he considered it might be handy. His mind was on turquoise water, on a seaside shack serving cold Modelo and shrimp tacos. Girls in skimpy bathing suits. Sun on his legs and back and face until he burned and burned.

He thought of Duval. He turned to him, seated at a computer down the line. Duval felt Allen's stare and he returned it. His fist landed on the keyboard, a thumbs up in assent. Allen wanted surprise but he didn't want drama. And he didn't want to startle those around them. They weren't charging the hill or storming the beach. He wanted the thing done before deputy staff knew what hit them. That is why the four of them had coordinated their escape in time with the clock, their movements down to the second. The clock hung over the door to master control. It was an old-time analog with moving hands, odd for a new million-dollar building, but such as it was. It told time, and when the short hand struck four and the long hand swept past that number, they would strike. Precisely. They needed to keep their eyes on Allen. He planned to drop that ladle like a gong. Drop everything and run. Allen and company to master control, and Duval to the closet.

Thing was Allen had been watching and crunching info for weeks. The deputies were like clockwork; whoever was on duty at the desk signed out and walked out right on time.

They would be waiting.

ALLEN PLACED THE MEAL CART closer to the door to master control than usual. Swanson didn't seem to notice the close proximity, at least, he didn't say anything. Haver was at the desk. Allen could see him at the board, his back to the door. Deputy duty was light today. Pilson had already taken the other two wings of the cell block back to their bunks, and he'd disappeared. He was known to retreat to the can with *Playboy*. Another piece of gossip Allen had picked up.

Where was Miller and the rest of staff? Diddling with their weekend plans. No one had seen Miller all day. Allen thought he'd seen Miss McBride walking around in her classroom, Mr. Art was on vacation, and Mr. Will was somewhere, always bent over his piles and piles of paperwork. No one else was around.

Yes, it's Friday. TGIF.

Allen worked in slow motion. He arranged the ladles, he removed covers from the rice and gravy. *Oh yum, boiled grease and wormy pasta for dinner. They can have them.* Suddenly, the years of smells, the food he'd eaten, flooded through his head like an avalanche of shit. He couldn't wait to get out of there, but he had to wait. For exactly the right moment. His eyes shifted to the clock, six more minutes to go. He couldn't ruin it now. They were so close. He didn't want to get riled, drop anything, cause any commotion in the run-up. Draw any attention. Just do his duty and get the fuck out of there.

Duval, San Antonio, and Tarvis sidled up together at the back of the line. Allen could see the terror in their eyes, their faces frozen in fear, and hate, and near frenzy. He couldn't say a word. He couldn't even look at them. He could only think. He picked up a ladle and stirred the slop in the metal bucket. *Hold tight, boys. Just a little more and we be gone.*

They were all in place.

Allen looked above the door; he checked the back of the line again. He nodded, so discreetly, only the three in the back noticed. The long hand swept four o'clock, and right on time, Haver came through the door of master control.

Allen dropped the ladle, caught the door with his foot as it opened, and shoved the cart into the door jamb. The cart wobbled and clanked but Allen held it steady. San Antonio was right behind him. He threw Haver to the ground, his face a mask of surprise and outrage. So completely baffled, the deputy froze to the spot, propped on his elbows. But not for long. San Antonio grabbed the mace from under the counter in master control and directed it at Haver. He fell back, gagging and coughing.

Tarvis yanked the key ring off the hook on the wall. They had the cuffs and a stick. They all raced back out into the hall.

"What the fu...." Someone dropped a tray. The rest stood watching with their mouths open, feet planted. They shrunk against the wall. Two boys started off down the hall after Tarvis, Allen, and San Antonio, and stopped, looking left and right.

Allen screamed, "Duval, you motherfucker!"

Duval was nowhere in sight. Then he dashed out of a door in the hallway, and around him smoke billowed in a grey cloud. Duval danced wildly in the hallway. Allen, for one second, thought of a mad puppet, Duval's arms flapping up and down, his legs kicking in the dim light. He yelled something unintelligible, some crazy joy. "EEEEEEHAAW!"

"Motherfucker, no time to dance," Allen shouted. "Let's bolt!"

But Duval ignored him. He'd gotten hold of the shiv and was running toward Haver. Back to the area around master control. The point of the fake knife aimed for the deputy's fat middle. Haver was still on his back, scuttling off on the floor toward a corner, and hacking from the mace. He had the radio in his hand. Duval kicked at the radio. Hard. He was missing a sandal but the force of his size eleven foot caught Haver on the wrist. The deputy howled and scraped at his face.

Tarvis doubled back down the hallway. "We don't have time for that shit, Duval. Besides he ain't worth it. Go!" Tarvis stepped in front of Duval and knocked the shiv out of his hand. "Run, motherfucker. I'm right behind you."

Haver was still scrambling around the floor. The mace had done the trick. The deputy looked like he was melting, molten-hot rage mixed with sweat and terror.

Duval's eyes were wild. He was grinning. He and Tarvis turned and ran.

"WHAAA?" Duval's hollering echoed down the hallway, a mix of fright and glee.

THE BOYS OF ALPHA BLOCK

Haver backed against the wall, moaning, then yelling. "Pilson! Where the fuck are you?" The boys at the meal cart were coughing, doubled over, hugging the wall.

Tarvis and Duval sprinted to the end of the hallway. San Antonio and Allen were already at the door, "Hurry it up," said Allen. Tarvis fumbled with the key ring. They had one door and the gate to go.

Frantically, Tarvis tried the keys in the lock. Smoke filled the hallway, a perfect screen. A couple of inmates had followed them, but now collapsed and didn't move. Duval was laughing. "Get the fuck back there, man. Party at Alpha!" They could hear the screaming. The cart crashing against a wall, and then again, with the slime of dinner, grease and fluffs of soft mush splashing everywhere. Pots exploding on the concrete. Slop under the boots and sandals and all over the uniforms. The slipping and the shouting.

"Get the fuckin' fire 'stinguisher!" A male voice yelled.

"Not today," someone yelled.

Tarvis found the master key that worked the locks. They pushed against the door and it opened. The hallway door slammed behind them. They were out on the sally port and Tarvis still clutched the key. He wrestled with the lock of the gate, the sweat making his fingers slip against the metal.

Allen looked up at the razor wire. "If this key don't work, we be fuckin' flyin' over that wire, man." But it did.

Oh, thank you Mo. Ya called it. Key and all...

They were all oddly silent. Running. The four of them. Only the sound of their sandals hitting the asphalt as they raced across the parking lot for the road down to the highway. They rounded the bend like four horses in the stretch, huffing. All eyes on the end of the road. The smell of freedom rushed at them, the humid Florida air was heaven. Allen didn't know if he was running or floating or flying. It was so new. He was born again. He looked back quickly. No one followed them. The prison compound squatted still and dead.

Mo was there under the billboard. The back door of the car shot open and the four jumped in, cramming themselves into the back, staying down on the floor.

Allen bounded into the front seat. "Man, hit it." Mo peeled out onto the highway, and they were gone.

No one said a word for a full ten minutes.

Then San Antonio reached over the seat and hit Allen on the shoulder. "What'd that take? Sixty seconds?"

"No, 'bout six months," said Allen. "Element of surprise, man, it worked." He turned around. High fives all over the place.

"Didn't get to throw Haver into the spaghetti," said Duval. His head poked up from behind the front seat. He looked glum, sweaty and wild. "Didn't get to jam that shiv into his fat gut."

Allen gritted his teeth, remembering the bruises and his hate for the deputy. He looked out the car window, and the emotion seeped away. "Haver's there, we're here," he said. He grinned at the three squooshed into the back.

"I'd give anything to see his face about now," said San Antonio.

"Well, fuck, let's go back then," said Allen. He punched Mo, lightly, in the ribs.

They all laughed so hard, the car seemed to buck and wobble all over the road. "Easy now, Mo. Keep it steady."

Mo was quiet. He steered, a smile on his lips. Five sets of eyes stared ahead at the asphalt as the car sped away from the prison. Mo cut the speed.

"Hey, we gotta book it, Mo. No drivin' like a Granny," said Duval.

"That's all we need, to get picked up. Just shut yo trap and enjoy the ride."

Allen didn't stop smiling. "Hope no one saw you sittin' there in the weeds."

"No-sir-eee, my man. I angled her just so. Ain't you noticed? This ain't my regular cherry red and silver ride? This here's a loaner; no traceable plates, real non-de-script."

The car had a '50s feel, scratchy plush seats, old tobacco smell to it. Peeling paint, a color blue so faded it was distant memory. "Think it's a Ford?" Allen didn't care; he was glad it had four wheels.

"Yeah, thank 'ol Henry while you're at it."

Mo gunned it off the main highway and took a back road to zigzag west. "Man, why you goin' west? Ain't we goin' south? To Mexico?"

"Got to do it this way, Jesse Allen, my free man. Keep to them back roads. But first things first, boys. Suit up, clothes are in the bag in the way back. We be stylin'."

"DON'T THINK SO," SAID TARVIS. He hadn't said a word since their escape, looking out the window at lush hot Florida. A hard stretch of land. *My land.* A terrible longing, and loneliness, etched around his eyes.

"Stop the car, Mo," he said.

"No, man. What you talkin'? We got miles and miles to go."

"Not me. Just slow it down. I'm jumpin' out."

Allen and Mo turned their heads to the back, San Antonio and Duval set eyes on Tarvis.

"It'd be easier on ya, anyway. Three instead of four," said Tarvis.

"Guy means business," said Mo. Then he whispered to Allen. "Don't want him here if he don't want to be here, ya feel me?"

Mo pulled over to the side of the road. The embankment had been mowed, but beyond, a thick tangle of palm and kudzu clogged the view.

Tarvis reached up, touched Mo on the shoulder. "Thanks. I'm a ghost."

"Best be." Mo didn't look at him. He stared straight ahead at the road.

Tarvis nodded at each boy. That was it. In seconds he was out of the car.

Mo spun off down the highway.

ALLEN LUNGED TOWARD MO, now feverish and hoarse. "Think that was a good idea? Just letting him go?"

"Too late, and no time to think 'bout it. It be done. And what's the diff? He got no idea where we headed."

Allen settled back. "True. But he do know the car."

"What, a faded blue piece of shit? Like Florida ain't full up of that?" Mo's wrist rested on the top of the steering wheel, not a care in the world. "Like I was about to say, we gotta go west before we go south. Got a nice big bucket waitin' for you."

CHAPTER THIRTY-FIVE

Put the Box Away, Boys

TARVIS STOOD ON THE SIDE OF THE ROAD and stared after them, and, for an instant, regretted the move. He remembered the day he went to Alpha. The heat, the wretchedness. He felt bad now, but for different reasons. Against all his better judgement, whatever that was, he'd been on that crazy-ass team. *Hasta la vista, boys.* Now he was alone, a fugitive on the run, and if he got caught, he'd be in deep, deep shit.

But then he threw himself onto the shoulder of newly mowed stubble, lay on his stomach, his face in the grass smelling the earth. It was green, it was fresh. He was free.

Who's to say what made me decide? One insane moment. No time to think, just time to react.

Seems to be the story of my life.

Tarvis would forever wonder why he chose the path that he did. He was only sure of one thing. He'd heard his Uncle Tendris, long dead but alive in spirit. For Tarvis, his uncle's words reverberated in his soul like the strings of his Martin. "Music will save you, Tarvis. Don't you forget it."

How could he forget it? Music was as much a part of him as his brain, his arms down to his fingers and tapping feet. He had to get back to it.

He figured out which way was north, and he began to walk. He cut across a swampy field and found a back road. And walked. He'd grown up in central Florida. He knew the hard stretch he'd chosen. Hours he walked. Hot and hungry, but free, and determined to get where he was going. He found a remote gas station slash convenience store way out in the sticks, cases of Nehi and water stored along the back next to the restrooms. He crept around the squat little building and peeked inside. When the clerk stepped away, Tarvis slid in and out, his arms full of chips and beef jerky. Grabbed a few bottles outside. And kept going.

He was close to the Gulf now, north of Tampa. He could almost smell the salt blowing over the hammocks to the mainland. Scrubby islands that acted as barrier but weren't really any barrier to the power of wind and water. He walked, and he knew he was closer to home. He'd find a shack. He'd find Miralisa. And he'd get to Millie. She'd have that guitar stashed somewhere. He needed it. That's all he needed right now.

THE BOYS MADE PROGRESS. Mo knew the back roads, and they all knew they were being followed, that an alert had gone out to all the counties. They heard the helicopters buzzing overhead. The sheriff and company couldn't know what they were looking for, but they were looking all the same. Mo peered up above. "Motherfuckers. What they gonna do? Stop ev-ry motha' fuckin' car in Florida?"

He stuck to the speed limit, the boys hunkered down when he cruised through a small town at the speed limit, his baseball cap jammed down over his eyebrows. "Hey, Jesse, lettin' ya know. Plenty of water and sandwiches in the back."

"Beer? Where's the damn beer, Mo?" San Antonio stuck his head up from the back seat, the cooler flipped open. It was cramped back there, but they didn't care. Except there was no beer.

"We got plenty time for that later." Mo turned off the road down a lane between hedges and palms. "Not too much later."

Mo pulled off the road into a patch of sea grape and mangrove. Beyond the thick screen of growth, a dock jutted out onto the dark water. "Hansluette Bay, my friends," said Mo, his arms draped over the steering wheel. "Your ship sails after sundown."

A white thirty-footer with a small cabin and fishing lookout on top bobbed at the end of the dock. Mo turned off the car. "We wait. Nate's on board, got a load of nets and gear in case anyone asking what we're up to. But I think we be aw-right."

Boat'll take all of us. Next stop, the Yucatan." Mo slumped down in the front seat, pulled his cap over his eyes, and in about one minute he was snoring.

They relieved themselves, they stretched. They napped.

It was quiet up there. No helicopters. Jesse Allen crept down to the water's edge, dug his toes in the sand, waded up to his knees. San Antonio stood next to him. "Bro. Anything ever feel so good?"

"Nah." Allen stared out at the horizon, at the light ripple of waves under the setting sun. *How could it all go down so well?*

THEY BOARDED THE CHARTER. Nate, the captain, raced south through the choppy Gulf. He didn't talk or look left or right. He pushed the boat faster, and faster, his braid flapping back and forth across his ripped t-shirt. He yanked the red-white-and-blue bandana down over his forehead. He gripped the wheel and pushed it hard. He was bound to get as far away as possible even though they weren't safe in international waters. They had hours to go to reach the Yucatan, some 400 nautical miles away, then the boys were on their own.

They stared up into the sky. The chopper—a piece of shit that looked like an orange on a stick—circled overhead. Then a cutter pulled up starboard, a short distance out. The speaker blared.

The four threw themselves below and huddled next to the bunks. Allen took a swig from the bottle of rum he'd been clutching. "Guess this is close as we get." He passed the bottle around.

TARVIS SET THE RIBS IN THE SMOKER and picked up his guitar. Miralisa sat under the buttonwood, her skirt like a flare of petals around her. She had teeth so white, lips so red. Tarvis went over and kissed those lips. He sat down next to her and started in.

I will not throw my love away
If I did,

*I would have to leave you
And I don't want to…*

His voice had gotten an edge to it, ragged and bluesy. His arms were strong as he settled the Martin against his bare chest. His fingers sure, his eyes not leaving Miralisa.

He'd finally found her again, and she'd agreed to come with him for a time. Stay at the old cabin near the Withlacoochee River. They swam out to the hammocks, fished in the river, made fires and love all night. Tarvis didn't want the world to move. They'd been there a week after he got the job building Backer Trace's shed, fixing his roof, cutting down some dead pines. He'd made good money. Backer had known Tendris. Owed him. They were a family up there in the northwest Florida woods. Nobody got much news, and if they did, they didn't care. Tarvis felt good, cut off from the world and all he remembered of it.

Miralisa reached out. Her fingers ran down his arm. She smiled and got up to check the ribs.

"Like 'em smokin' hot. Like you," he said.

She laughed.

A crackle on the forest floor made Tarvis jump. He was a bit jumpy still. It had only been a month or so since they'd run down that road out of Alpha. He'd heard the boys had gotten caught. They were back in the system. Something clawed at Tarvis's soul over the whole thing. But he couldn't do anything about it. At least for now. He'd just lay low. Someday he'd find Mo and Allen and the boys and, what? Thank them?

Truth was, Duval had tried to kill Haver, the sorry motherfucker. Tarvis blew out a sigh of relief. At least they'd dodged murder.

He heard it again. Then the unmistakable radio voice, a click. More crackling on the forest floor.

Tarvis crouched, stared off into the thicket of trees. He looked over at Miralisa, her polished shoulders in the white lacey blouse, the long shining hair falling over her arm as she reached for a bowl of berries and melon. It was the last sweet thing he would see for a long time. He mouthed, good-bye. She sat frozen, like a small deer, her eyes off in the distance behind him.

Swanson and Brown walked out of the woods. They wore denim and t-shirts, gear slung about the waist.

"Tarvis," Deputy Brown said.

The boy stood up slowly, and straight, the guitar still clutched in his fingers. "Sir, Tarvis Philip James. Sir."

CHAPTER THIRTY-SIX

A Resolution

CAROLINE SAT ACROSS FROM TARVIS in the visitors' station of the county jail. A deputy stood at a slant-topped high desk against the wall. He cast an eagle eye at them. She folded her hands on the table. Tarvis plunked his clenched fists down across from her. "Watch them hands over there," the deputy yelled. Tarvis didn't look at him. He didn't move, his face a mask of resignation.

"How are you, Tarvis?" Caroline inclined her head, her expression earnest. He didn't seem the worse for wear. A lot of tension around the eyes, but he looked healthy, strong. She'd only had the boy in class a short time, but she had gotten to know him better since the breakout when it had flown through the prison rumor mill that Tarvis had had some mitigating influence on the whole charade. He'd saved Haver from Duval who had been intent on stabbing the deputy with the shiv.

Tarvis smiled. "How'm I supposed to be, Miss Caroline? Fu…Sorry. Pretty much screwed. Sorry 'bout that, too."

"You made out a bit better than the rest," she said. "I hear they picked up the shivs in the clean-up and they've got the others on weapons charges, besides macing the deputy. On top of the escape and time owing."

"Yeah, I'm so lucky." His eyes roamed the cold white room. Vending machines stood in an alcove, tables and chairs were lined up for visitors. A couple of ratty sofas were tucked against the wall under a line of windows. Tarvis and Caroline had the place to themselves.

"Do you want some chips, or a candy bar?" She pointed to the alcove.

"Nah, you have to buy a card at the desk and it's a hassle. Miralisa was here, machine ate five bucks, and it's the last she saw of that."

"Any other family come to see you?"

"My Aunt Millie, but she cry all the time she here. I told her, it's okay. I see her when I get out. Whenever that be." Tarvis wrung his hands and quickly glanced at the deputy who noisily chomped on a bag of tortilla chips, his head in a magazine.

"I hear you were caught in the woods," said Caroline. "I've been talking with Deputy Brown."

"Yeah, he's one decent dude. Swanson was with him when they come for me. I think I gave myself away back there at Alpha—I told Swanson about the blues and playin' the guitar up in them Northwest woods and such. Get this, Swanson wanted me to play him a tune." Tarvis shook his head and grinned. "Didn't work out so well. I wasn't feelin' too musical. Though I did sing the blues."

"How long now?"

"Three for time not served, plus some for the escape. Don't know yet. Haven't been sentenced. They gonna be a bit lighter 'cause Haver say I saved him."

"You made a good choice."

"Yeah, didn't I though."

CAROLINE PULLED THE CADILLAC into the parking lot of Alpha Juvenile Correctional Center and got out. The place was deserted. Weeds grew up along the chain link, some of it as high as the razor wire. Someday soon the place would be buried in growth, and good riddance. Birds wheeled in the blue sky heading out to the Gulf, the air was thick with humidity. She wanted to scream. No one would hear her. The place was closed.

What of the boys? Where are they all now? Will they be all right?

Her fingers clung to the chain link, and she shook it. She never wanted to go in there again.

Not long after the prison break, all hell broke loose in the juvenile justice system. The boys were interviewed one by one, and this time officials listened. Witnesses came forward about the ongoing abuse. The deputy staff closed ranks, but it didn't serve them; most of them were busted in rank, including Sergeant Miller who was now a desk jockey downtown and hating it. Nurse Rainer, Reverend Temley, and Harv Sanders supported closing the facility. Will Bonner had the last word. Some progress had been made with the boys. But not enough. The abuse outweighed the good, and the place was closed down for good. The remaining boys went into the county jail system to serve out their sentences, most of them curtailed significantly.

Caroline had mixed feelings; of unfinished business, of sadness at the waste of lives, but there were the bright spots. She planned on teaching at the Bradley Detention Center where Harvey was going to be the new director. Art would be there, too. There was work undone, work to do.

And Will. He was foremost in her mind.

She looked at her fingers entwined in the metal wire. Cage closed. The diamond caught the sun. It was suffocating out there in the blazing heat and humidity, but that was fine. She could hope, and suddenly she was happy thinking of the work ahead, of new beginnings for all of them. Especially for her and Will.

Acknowledgements

Thank you to my wonderful readers and editors who, initially, helped me whip *The Boys of Alpha Block* into shape: Judith Horner, K.M. Rockwood, Arthur Vidro, Paula Jenkins, and Darlene Dziomba. Without their eyes on the details, their questions and suggestions, the book never would have made it to The End of those early drafts.

Special love and thanks go to the teachers I worked with in the Manatee Country Juvenile Justice System: the late, great Art Monson, retired Navy captain; my talented, laughing lunch buddies, Toni D'Andrea and Cathy Stover, and our fearless leader, Harry Reif. There was never a group of teachers so dedicated, no-nonsense, empathetic—and funny—as this group. It was the best job I ever had.

Thank you to Miles Henry Sullivan for the words to "Love Away." If you could hear him play this on his Martin, you'd think Robert Johnson had landed on those fingers and soul.

Thank you to my editors at TouchPoint Press, for your faith and support: Jennifer Haskin, Ashley Carlson, and Sheri Williams.

And, especially, thank you to the boys I taught for five years, the hundreds of them. I never met a student I didn't like, who didn't have possibilities, who didn't teach me to stretch and view things just a bit differently and out of the ordinary and thank God for that.

About the Author

Nancy Nau Sullivan is a former newspaper journalist and English teacher. She taught at a boys' prison outside of Tampa, Florida, for five years, and later in Argentina and in the Peace Corps in Mexico. She has a master's degree in journalism from Marquette University and is the author of a memoir, *The Last Cadillac*, and the Blanche Murninghan mystery series. Nancy lives in Northwest Indiana. Find her at www.nancynausullivan.com.

Made in the USA
Monee, IL
10 June 2021